The Bear Wagon

Jason Vail

THE BEAR WAGON

Copyright 2017, by Jason Vail

A Hawk Publishing book.

Cover design, maps by Ashley Barber

ISBN-13: 978-1976297304
ISBN-10: 1976297303

Hawk Publishing
Tallahassee, FL 32312

The Bear Wagon

The Bear Wagon

The Bear Wagon

May 1263
to
July 1263

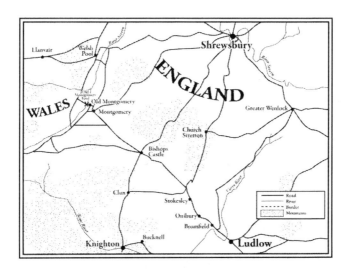

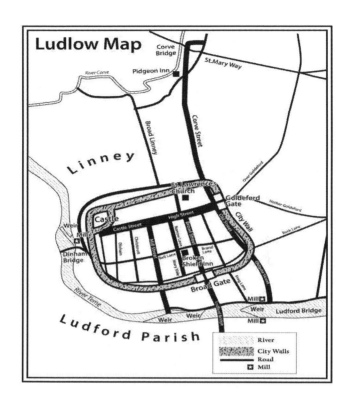

Ludlow Map

Corve Bridge
River Corve
Pidgeon Inn
St.Mary Way
Broad Linney
Corve Street
Linney
Over Goldeford
St.Lawrence's Church
Goldeford Gate
Nether Goldeford
Castle
City Wall
Weir
Castle Street
High Street
Rock Lane
Mill
Dinham
Bull Lane
Brand Lane
Dinham Bridge
Chestnut
Mill Street
Broken Shield Inn
River Terne
Mary View
Broad Gate
Mill
Weir
Weir
Weir
Mill
Ludford Bridge
Ludford Parish

	River
	City Walls
	Road
	Mill

9

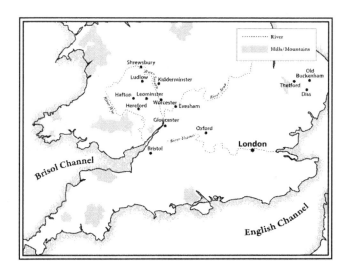

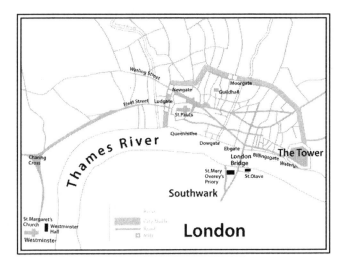

Prologue

"It's time. Let's get moving." One of the raiders shook William Attebrook's shoulder and moved to the next man, where he repeated the order.

William sat up and rubbed his face, surprised that he had got any sleep at all, clad as he was in mail with the forest floor for a bed; the roots of the trees stuck into a man like knives.

He stood up, rolled his cloak and groped through the dark to find his horse, which was tied up in the horse line, detectable by the stink of horse shit.

He tied the cloak to the saddle and buckled on his sword belt, his anxiety rising. He had never been in a battle, had never really expected to be in one. Although war was supposed to be the business of his class, very few actually engaged in any fighting. England had been safe enough until recently, except for the Welsh, who thundered out of their hills now and then to raid and pillage as they had done during the winter. Fortunately, no Welsh raider had come near William's home manor in a long time, not even during the recent troubles. But he was about to have battle now.

The impulse to turn about and ride away was intense, but he could not. It would ruin his reputation among these men, some of whom were knights, and, if not formally knights, they were land-holding gentry like him; many were his neighbors, drawn into the war they were about to start between King Henry and his brother-in-law, Simon de Montfort.

The men mounted their horses and rode south along a small brook lined with trees, following their guide. They moved slowly over the open ground because the horses carrying the scaling ladders could not maneuver well in the wood itself.

The brook crossed a road where the stream could be heard gurgling at the ford, then wound west. They crossed another rivulet, and came to a third, which they followed southward. The breeze brought the aroma of smoke from

11

Kilpeck village which was perhaps only a quarter mile away. They were getting close.

The guide stopped at last, and dismounted. "It's just through there."

He pointed toward the line of trees along the brook to the left. How he could tell was a mystery to William. It all looked the same to him.

The leader whispered, "Dismount. We'll carry the ladders from here. Quiet! No talking!"

The party crept through the wood and leapt the stream, the stink of leaf mulch in their noses. A small herd of pigs started at their approach and fled across the field on the other side of the rivulet. Everyone froze, listening for alarm calls from the castle that lay ahead somewhere in the gloom. But no voices pierced the night, and after a few moments, with pounding hearts, they climbed the gentle slope to the castle.

It was so dark due to the overcast that the castle did not appear until they were almost on it.

William had never been here, but two of the men who were familiar with the place had made a little model in the dirt as the leader had told them the plan of attack. It was unremarkable, as castles went, a motte-and-bailey affair, the motte, which confronted them, itself about thirty feet tall, capped with a circular stone tower that they could now make out as a grey smudge. On the other side lay the bailey, a crescent-shaped enclosure about a hundred yards across. The bailey was surrounded by an earthen embankment on which stood a wooden palisade.

Even such simple castles were difficult to take. William had heard stories about the campaigns in Ireland when the English had invaded a century ago, and about how twenty English and Frenchman at just such a castle near Waterford had withstood the assaults of hundreds of savage Irishmen — far more of a threat than this party presented, which numbered forty-three.

The smallness of the attacking party meant that the two main ways of taking a castle — by storm or siege — were out of the question. That left a ruse, which usually involved a party disguised as merchants getting into and capturing the gatehouse to allow the remainder to enter, or a surprise night attack. A ruse had been rejected because no one had thought it practical. The countryside surrounding the castle was open and there was no way to conceal the attackers as they approached. Any group of more than ten men who came on in daylight would be met with suspicion. That left a night attack.

The plan was simple, like any good one. A party of six slipped across the ditch at the base of the motte, dragging their ladder. They climbed the steep side, planted the ladder in the earth, held there by one of the party, while the others climbed to the top of the wall. Their job was to seize the tower or at least the access ramp from the bailey, for it was the place of refuge that the defenders would seek when the bailey was overrun. Towers on mottes were especially hard targets, and those in the bailey needed to be cut off from its protection if they were to succeed. But during the night it was held by only four men, for towers were cold uncomfortable places and everyone else slept below in the hall and barracks.

At the same time the others, including William, went left and raised their ladders against the palisade by one of the horns of the crescent. They were into the bailey within moments without the alarm being sounded.

William and the others jogged around various buildings — a smithy, chicken coops, a well house, a barn and stable — toward the hall which loomed beside the main gate, two square towers of stone.

He spotted a figure emerging from what had to be a privy, for the fellow was pulling up his drawers. The figure froze at the sight of everyone, then unfroze and dashed toward the hall as William gave chase.

"Strangers!" the figure shouted, "Strangers in the castle!"

Soldiers in the gate tower — the watch roused at last from careless slumber — spotted the invaders at the same moment and the alarm bell began to peel, falling silent as a squad of men attacked the gate and drove the few defenders inside.

The fellow from the privy reached the hall doors, eluding William's grasp. William and two others threw their shoulders at the door, but the thump of the bar and the failure of the door to yield ended their efforts.

The possibility of a barred door had not been overlooked. Two wood axes had been brought along, and the two sergeants detailed to carry them set to work hacking at the front door.

Within the hall there were sounds of pandemonium muffled by the closed door and shutters: shouts of men blundering about in the dark to find their weapons, the shrieks of women, the cries of children.

Then the sounds grew louder as someone cracked one of the shutters. William saw a flicker of movement out of the corner of an eye just as an arrow shot from a longbow slammed into his upper chest with stunning force. He staggered back at the impact, the wind knocked out of him, astonished that he had not been killed, for although the bodkin point had penetrated his mail it had not pierced the thick gambeson beneath it. He yanked out the arrow and swung his shield up as another arrow flew into the night, passing by his head with a *zzzhhh!*

The open shutters on that window and another presented an opportunity not merely for defenders to shoot out, but for the attackers to force an entry into the hall. One of the attackers pressed an open shutter wider with his spear while another man bent to allow a fellow knight to stand on his back to leap inside.

But the knight who was about to leap hesitated.

"What's wrong?" asked William, who had shaken off the effects of the arrow, and come to the open window. As afraid as he was of the prospect of leaping into the darkened hall, he felt compelled to press forward at the front of the attack.

"The hall's caught fire," the knight said.

And it was true. Someone must have stumbled across the hearth during the panic and scattered the coals, for the rushes on the floor had ignited. The flames were spreading rapidly across the floor, reaching the timbers of the far wall as William watched. He could see several women trying without success to contain the blaze with blankets.

Already the hall was filling with a haze of choking smoke.

There was no point now in trying to force an entrance. The attackers stood back as the blaze spread and the light within grew brighter. In moments people began spilling out of windows and the front door opened, emitting a crowd of scrambling women and children, which the attackers allowed to slip through their ranks, on the lookout for armed men who might be concealed in the rush. But the few men among the panicked throng appeared to be unarmed servants. Although they were unarmed, they were gathered and made to sit on the ground with the women and children, under watch.

Finally, when the fire reached the roof and the heat from the blaze had driven those outside halfway across the bailey, the constable and his companions emerged from the hall. They threw down their swords and advanced toward the attackers with raised hands.

"Do you yield?" the leader of the attackers cried.

"We yield, you sons-of-bitches," the constable said. "You'll pay for this. The King will see to it."

"I think not," the leader said. "It is a new day. And we will have our rights at last."

The news of the fall of Kilpeck Castle spread across western England as if on the wings of crows. It was not the only stronghold to be attacked by Montfort's supporters in the coming days; there were six or seven others. But the tales of the attack on Kilpeck were the most lurid. It was said that the attackers had deliberately set fire to the hall and burned to death everyone inside. It was too good a story not to be believed.

The Bear Wagon

The Bishop of Hereford, an ardent supporter of the King, heard about the atrocity the day after it happened — Kilpeck was only nine miles from Hereford — and assigned a deacon to find out the names of those responsible. As in all things, he was motivated as much by self-interest as by loyalty: Kilpeck was held by England's justicar, Robert Walerand, and it did not hurt one's prospects to be in his favor as well as the King's.

This did not take long. After the mysterious death of the King's chief intelligencer in western England, a certain draper based in Ludlow, the Bishop had taken it on himself to establish his own spying network. The deacon, who managed this network, made inquiries and within a few days he had the names of the most prominent men involved in the attack.

The deacon committed the list of names to a letter. Copies were made of the letter. The original went to the King. The copies went to Walerand and other supporters of the King so that they could put a watch on those indicted, and take whatever measures they deemed necessary, both for their own safety and the protection of their property, and to exact retribution when the time came to do so.

Chapter 1

"Harry! They're gone! It's safe!" Jennie Wistwode rapped on the front door— *they* being her parents, the owners of the Broken Shield Inn across the street. "You can come out now!"

"You have to open the door," came the muffled reply. "I can't reach the latch."

"They haven't fixed that yet?" Jennie asked with disapproval as she opened the door for Harry who was sitting on the floor by the threshold because he had no legs to speak of, having lost what he had been born with just above the knees. "You've been living there a month. How long does it take to fix a door latch?"

"There was a stick by the door I've been using to lift the latch, but someone seems to have removed it," Harry said as he swung himself over the threshold. "That woman, no doubt."

That woman was Frances Bartelot, the former tenant of the house. She had lost the tenancy the previous month through an unfortunate series of events, but was allowed to remain as a guest on the new tenant's sufferance. She was an uncommonly severe woman, quick to find fault with the smallest thing, fussing over this and that, and things being out of place. You couldn't put a cup down but she would remove it before you were finished. She found fault with Harry's very existence, not to mention his presence in what had been her home, and he was a rather large thing despite being legless. It was the humiliation of having to share the house, Harry supposed. Even though he now had a craft as a woodcarver, she still thought of him as Harry the beggar. In her defense, everybody in Ludlow still thought of him that way. People often came by the shop to gawk at him through the shop window and make rude remarks, the gist of which was that he did not belong there and that he had taken airs far above his proper station in life.

Harry reached the handcart that Jennie had brought to the door. He glanced up and down Bell Lane. No one was in sight. He scanned the inn across the street. Even though the shutters were open, no one was at the windows.

"Hurry up," Jennie said. Neither of them wanted to be seen together. If her parents found out, the repercussions could be enormous, for they were forbidden to see each other.

"I'm hurrying as fast as my little legs can manage."

Harry grasped the cart's rail in preparation for heaving himself up. Jennie took him around the waist to help.

"Jennie, my dear," Harry said, "you would be more useful if you held the cart on the other side. It has a tendency to flip over. I can manage here."

"Right."

With Jennie anchoring the opposite side, Harry pulled himself into the cart with an ease that would have surprised any onlooker, as the loss of his legs had been compensated by the development of very strong arms and shoulders.

He settled onto a pair of woolen blankets that Jennie had provided, which made a comfortable bed. A large wicker basket occupied the remainder of the cart. Harry flipped the lid to look inside. Jennie swatted his hand away.

"Let it be a surprise," she said.

"Very well," Harry said. He grasped the rails on either side as Jennie took up the lead rails. "Off we go, then!"

He said this in a lofty tone, as if he was a lord ordering a servant.

"Watch yourself," Jennie said over her shoulder as the cart lurched forward.

Harry regarded the back of Jennie's head with affection as they traveled down Bell Lane, crossed Raven Lane and then Mill Street. Although she wore the obligatory wimple over her light brown hair, that fell down her back in a thick braid, as she was yet unmarried, Harry took delight in the sight, which was almost as exciting in its way as a view of her calves. He had been able to steal such views now and then owing to his low vantage point. She was a rather broad girl, taking after her parents, and had the same blunt features, but for all that she was attractive, with a smile that could brighten a conversation like a candle in a dark room.

As they neared the end of Bell Lane, the going got steeper and Jennie began to puff at the exertion, but she did not flag and in short order they came to the gate and passed through, the way now downhill toward the river.

Harry would have liked to have gone out onto the bridge to take the view; it had been a long time since he had been able to enjoy it. But Jennie turned up Linney Lane, which struck Dinham Street just before the bridge, a rickety wooden thing badly in need of repair, and headed toward their chosen destination, the mill lying upstream.

There was a small meadow on the other side of the mill race between the bridge and the mill. It was used to house the miller's small band of sheep. But today the sheep had given way to a dozen young couples armed with blankets and wicker baskets like Jennie and Harry. The miller and his family were at a table by the door to the mill. The parties exchanged waves as Jennie pulled the cart across the bridge and into the meadow. Heads turned to watch their progress. The sight of Harry being pulled about in a cart was not exactly new, but this was the first time it had been seen in these parts.

Jennie halted at a spot by the fence which afforded a good view of the river. She fetched the basket while Harry deposited himself on the grass, and then brought down the blankets, which she spread out for them.

"There," she said with satisfaction. "Better than your old digs."

"Anything is better than my old digs." Harry's prior appointments had been a stall in the Wistwode stable which he had shared with bales of hay.

"You weren't heard to complain when you were in them," Jennie said.

"Your mother would have thrown me out if she's heard even the breath of a complaint. She didn't like me there in the first place."

Jennie chuckled. "A waste of space, she called it. Father's the one with the soft spot for you. God knows why."

"That woman could squeeze a penny from a length of straw."

"Which is why we are well off and you are not."

"Not for want of trying."

"I'll give you that. Although traffic in saints' heads can only take you so far." One of Harry's chief sources of profit at the moment were carvings of the heads of saints, especially that of a young woman who had died mysteriously in Saint Laurence's churchyard and had been proclaimed a saint by all who had seen her, although the church had not yet agreed. "You need to branch out."

"I'm trying. It takes time. You can't just snap your fingers and conjure business. You could help more, you know — talk me up around town."

"I've been doing that, you ungrateful wretch."

"Well, then, what's in the basket?" Harry asked, changing the subject.

They watched the river while they ate. The flow had diminished from the floods of spring and there was hardly any water over the weir upstream, a trickle at best so that boys could be seen on the weir playing in the wet. The weir directed the flow through the millrace which was out of sight around the corner of the mill building itself. But ducks could be seen feeding in the wash by a spoil island made of gravel across from where the millrace emptied back into the river.

"What's that?" Harry murmured.

"What's what?" Jennie asked.

"I don't know. Something." That something was an unnatural quiet, for the creaking of the wheel, which never stopped even when the mill wasn't in use, had ceased.

The miller noticed it, too, for he rose from his table and went inside.

But he was gone only moments before the wheel began creaking again.

Harry was returning to his ale and ham before a sight on the river caught his eye. The ale cup stopped in midair.

"What is it now?" Jennie asked.

"Jennie," Harry said, pointing at an object in the water.

"Good God!" Jennie cried when she saw the thing.

It was a body, that of a girl face down in the wash just emerging from the millrace, her hair bobbing in a graceful fan about her head. There was something odd about how she floated, for her hands were united at the small of her back. Several ducks paddled close and nibbled at the girl's shoulder and feet, which were bare.

Jennie leaped to her feet. She slipped down the steep bank and waded into the river, which was only knee deep here, scattering the ducks which fled in a flurry of spray. She grasped one of the corpse's shoulders and tugged it to the bank.

Many of the picnickers in the meadow, alerted by the commotion, gathered at the bank to see this marvel more closely, obscuring Harry's view.

"She's dead!" Jennie could be heard to cry.

"Of course, she is," Harry murmured. Even though he had some experience in the finding of dead bodies in unanticipated places, he was shocked at having his pleasant afternoon disturbed in this way. Death was an ever-present fact of life but it was still chilling when it struck you in the face.

Some of the onlookers began to clamber over the fence for a closer look.

"You stay here!" Harry barked. "We need to fetch the coroner. Until he's had a look at things, disturb nothing." He spoke with such authority that those already down the bank returned to the top.

"I know where he is," Jennie said, having reached the top of the bank. She glanced at Harry. "You best make yourself scarce. My father will be with him. You know that." Her father, Gilbert Wistwode, was the coroner's clerk in addition to being an innkeeper.

The Bear Wagon

"How am I supposed to do that? I'll not get far in my condition," Harry said as Jennie hurried toward Linney Lane, but not loud enough for her to hear.

Chapter 2

"Ha!" Gilbert said with triumph as his bowling stone came to rest half a foot from the cone on the Pigeon Inn's pitch. "See what you can do with that!"

"You think you're a bowler, do you?" Stephen said with more confidence than he felt. "I'll show you."

He put his left boot back on his maimed foot, which had been aching as it was prone to do from time to time.

He stepped up and sent his bowling stone rolling down the pitch. It had been his intention to knock Gilbert's ball away from the wooden cone, the point of bowls being to have your stone the closest to that cone. But his shot went wide.

"You missed again," Gilbert said. He sipped from his tankard.

"It's a learning process," Stephen said, sinking to a place beside Gilbert. He recovered his own tankard from the tabletop.

"It's a good thing for you we aren't playing for money."

"In which case you'd be paid with promises." Although Stephen now got a full coroner's stipend, the expenses of keeping a house and his horses had eaten all of it up so that this morning there were only two farthings in his purse. It would be a lean month.

Gilbert was reaching for the round stone between his feet when his daughter Jennie rushed through the gate on Broad Linney Street, spotted them through the crowd, and hurried over. Her mouth was a grim line.

"Oh, dear," Gilbert muttered, forgetting about the bowling stone. "I wonder if I'm in trouble."

Jennie's appearance certainly suggested that Edith Wistwode, Gilbert's wife and her mother, had sent her with a summons for him to report about some fault, which must be quite large to provoke such an expression.

But Stephen noticed that Jennie's skirt and shoes were sopping wet and caked with dirt from the street. This was not normal and heads were turning to follow her progress because of it.

"What is it, Jennie?" Stephen asked, dread rising in his heart.

"You need to come quickly, sir," Jennie panted. "There's been a death."

"Where is she?" Stephen asked Jennie as they passed through the gate and crossed the bridge over the millrace to the meadow.

Jennie pointed toward where the millrace emptied back into the river. He saw a curious thing over her shoulder: the inn's handcart in the miller's shed tucked behind a horse cart as if someone had tried to place it out of sight. He could think of only one reason why Jennie and the handcart would be here. But he said nothing and strode to the bank where Jennie had indicated he would find the body. He had half hoped it wouldn't be there, that the nightmare about to begin was something he could avoid.

He and Gilbert slid down the steep bank to the brief gravel beach where the dead girl lay, her legs in the water.

"Good heavens!" Gilbert murmured as they knelt beside the body. "The poor girl!"

"Indeed," Stephen said. "No mistaking murder for a drowning this time." For the girl's hands were tied behind her back at the wrists. The leather thong employed for this purpose had been drawn so tightly that it dug into the skin and her hands were blue, whereas the rest of her that they could see was a mottled yellowish waxy color on the backs of her legs although the forward side was purplish. "You take that arm. I'll get this one."

They hauled the girl up the bank with the help of a couple of spectators, and laid the girl on her back in the grass.

"I'm getting tired of this business," Stephen said as he caught his breath.

"It's a living," Gilbert sighed.

"That's the irony, isn't it?"

"What?"

"Never mind. You there, take her into the miller's. We'll examine her inside."

This did not sit well with the miller's wife, but Stephen was in no mood for a debate and his expression showed it.

Stephen had the dining table dragged to a window overlooking the river and weir. The spectators drafted to carry the body placed it on the table. The miller's wife watched with horror at what was being done on the table where her family took its meals, before she fled the room.

"You can all go now," Stephen said to those who had jammed into the room. Although they backed out, the fact that the door and windows on the meadow side were open ensured that those able to crowd close would be able to see what happened next.

Stephen shut the windows and the door to loud expressions of discontent. It darkened the room and might make it difficult to see important things, but he couldn't bear all those staring eyes.

He glanced at Gilbert, expecting him to do the distasteful work that lay ahead. But Gilbert was looking out the window at the river.

Stephen almost ordered Gilbert to get busy. But he thought better of it. He turned the body on its side and cut the thong with his dagger, then lay the girl on her back, aware of the fragrance of decay in this confined space in a way he had not in the open air. Her hair, a white-blonde undarkened by death or her time in the water, straggled about her head, dripping water on the table and floor.

"How long do you think she's been dead?" Stephen asked.

"A couple of days, at most, is my guess from the bloat and the smell," Gilbert replied, not turning from the window. "The dead do not usually float in these waters before that amount of time has passed. Must we do this? Isn't it obvious how she died?"

Stephen stared at the girl's face, her lips a bluish O drawing back in a grimace from her teeth, her eyes open and flat and foggy, her features distorted such that it was doubtful that anyone who did not know her well could recognize her. "I agree. But I think it must still be done."

Gilbert turned from the window. "Very well."

Stephen held up a hand. "I'll do it. It's my turn, anyway."

He grasped the collar of the girl's dress and cut it away down her chest, wishing for a pair of gloves and a sharper blade, until it lay apart like a man's unbuttoned coat. He had thought he might then be able to slide her arms out of the sleeves, but this proved to be impossible due to the bloating. So he had to cut the sleeves as well.

Stephen then bent close, looking for any wounds that might indicate some other manner of death than drowning, paying particular attention to her head and neck. But he saw nothing other than cuts on her cheeks. He wondered how they might have got there, since they looked fresh and had not had a chance to clot.

"Help me turn her over, will you?" Stephen asked Gilbert.

It was then they had their greatest shock. Her back and buttocks were crisscrossed with lash marks as if someone had whipped the girl savagely with a wand. Like the scratches on the girl's face, some of these wounds looked fresh.

"What do you make of that?" Stephen asked.

"I . . . I cannot say."

"How old do you think she is?"

"Fifteen? Sixteen at most?"

"Hardly more than a child."

"Yes, who would handle such a young woman so?" Gilbert sighed. "She was pretty, not beautiful, but certainly she must have been pleasing to the eye, a delight to her parents . . ." He glanced toward the door, thinking of Jennie.

"Perhaps it was her parents who did this."

Gilbert looked shocked at this suggestion. "No parent could be that savage." But there was a note of doubt in his voice, for they both knew that some parents could be cruel.

Stephen crossed to the door and opened it a crack. "You all got a look at her. Does anyone know who she is?" he asked the people assembled outside.

Heads shook all around. He shut the door.

"We'll have to see she's buried right away," Stephen said returning to the table. Several flies were orbiting around the corpse. He swatted at them. The flies swirled away, unconcerned at the threat, and returned immediately. "She'll be black and full of rot by morning in this heat. We may never find out who she is."

"And then we'll never find out how and why she died," Gilbert said sadly.

He crossed the girl's arms on her stomach as much as the swelling in her limbs would allow and was about the bind them in place with the remains of her clothing when he stopped and bent over her hands.

"Look here," Gilbert said, pointing at one of her fingers.

There was a small gold ring on the little finger of the girl's left hand. The swollen and wrinkled flesh had nearly concealed it.

"I see," Stephen said, embarrassed that he had missed it when he cut the bonds.

"There is a design on it. Perhaps someone will recognize it." Gilbert put his fingers on the ring as if to pull it off. "The finger is too swollen. It won't yield."

Stephen exhaled. "There's only one thing to do."

He took the hand and cut off the finger. It wasn't the first time he'd seen this done to a corpse, although he had never stooped to it himself. Gilbert shuddered and swallowed. Stephen put the severed finger on the girl's stomach. The gold ring lay in his palm.

"Have the miller's wife find someone to make a shroud for the girl," Stephen said. "I'm sure the parish will pay for it.

And have them save the dress. We may need that besides the ring."

Chapter 3

"Well, Harry," Stephen said, "I see you got some sun today."

"Yes, well, it was a brilliant day, best in weeks," Harry said as he lifted himself onto the bench opposite Stephen in the Broken Shield's hall. "Who wouldn't want to enjoy it?"

"Where did you go? The back garden?"

"That's it," Harry replied, although the back garden referred to was on the north side of the house they both occupied now, and it got sun in summer only at one corner for an hour or so. "And how was your bowls? Lose much money?"

"My game was interrupted," Stephen said. He fingered the little ring taken from the dead girl's finger.

"Was it really? I'm sorry. What happened?"

"I think you know. I saw the handcart. There's no reason for it to be at the Dinham mill unless it took you there. The question on everyone's lips is, who pulled the cart?"

"Nobody I know."

"Ah, a stranger. And whom did you meet? You had to have been there a long time to get that sunburned."

"I am not sunburned. I am ruddy. It is my natural complexion."

"The only time I have seen you ruddy is when you're drunk."

Harry glanced at Edith Wistwode, who was pouring ale for a customer across the room. "You won't say anything, will you?"

"My lips are sealed."

"Until you want something. Then it will be, Harry, do this or I'll blab to Edith. What you got there?"

Stephen handed over the ring.

"So that's what it looks like," Harry said, turning the ring over. It looked smaller than it was in his big hands. "I wondered."

"You were there?"

"Under the stairs."

"Only you could have hidden there." Stephen remembered the place. There had been a small stair of three steps leading out of one side of the chamber. He had not given it a thought at the time.

"Me and a pair of rats. What's all this mean?" Harry held out the ring. A small golden disk was attached to the band. In the middle was an odd design, a goat's head and forelegs attached to a fish's tail. Above the figure were the letters "LEG II" and below "AUG."

"I'm not sure."

Harry handed the ring back. "Must be a pagan thing. Gilbert didn't know?"

"He thinks it might be Roman, but that's it."

Harry grunted with satisfaction. "All that education he's got — did him no good here." Harry did not approve of education. It gave one airs and did not leave one any more sensible than before.

Jennie emerged from the rear of the hall where the buttery and kitchen were located, carrying a tray of cold sliced beef and bread. She took a few steps toward Stephen's table, which had the best spot by the fireplace, but veered away at the sight of Harry to another table where a trio of cloth merchants were hunched over their cups. Harry pretended not to notice. Since Stephen and Harry had moved into a house across the street, they had continued to take meals at the inn because Stephen could not afford a housekeeper with all his other expenses. Edith disapproved of the attentions that Harry and Jennie had been paying to each other so when they came together for meals they had to be waited on by another of the servants.

"She looks a bit sunburned, too," Stephen said.

"How can you tell in this light? Anyway, it's no secret that she was at the mill. She fetched you."

"You know, Harry, you two are going to have to be more discrete. By this time, half the town knows you were trysting with Jennie at the mill. It won't be long before Edith finds out. Then she'll do something extreme, like marry off Jennie to a passing peddler just to keep her safe from you."

Harry pursed his lips, alarmed at this prospect. He was not normally a thoughtless person, but love made people stupid.

"She wouldn't dare," Harry said.

"She is a mother. Of course she would dare."

"Jennie wouldn't put up with it."

"You wait. She might protest, but she'll do what she's told in the end."

"What am I going to do?"

"It was doomed from the start. You know that."

"But I'm a settled man now! Edith will come round in time, don't you think?"

"I don't think it's your present or former profession that bothers Edith, although they may have something to do with it."

"My situation," Harry said. He patted his thigh.

"Yes," Stephen said. "That."

"No one likes a cripple."

"I've come round to thinking that it depends."

"On what?"

"If you were rich it wouldn't matter if you were ugly as a gnome and without arms as well."

"But there's no likelihood of that unless I turn to robbery or join the government — although government work isn't making you rich, so I suppose it must be robbery. It's getting dark. I should go find my first victim."

"Well, I think I know of something that might help with your finances."

"Like what?"

"Gilbert mentioned that he had heard at market that the Bromfield Priory are looking for a skilled woodcarver to do some work in their church. You might go there and apply."

"How am I to get there? It's five miles off! It's not like I can just pop down the road."

The Bear Wagon

"I suppose I shall have to take you. The trip might be worth my while. One of the brothers there may be able to tell me about this ring."

They were not able to leave until Tuesday, despite the urgency of the errand. When Stephen went down to the castle's pasture early Monday, he discovered that his mare had gone lame from a stone to the hoof and besides she was in heat. Mares in heat can often be ridden, but that depends on the mare. This one did not like being brushed, let alone bearing a rider. This meant Stephen had no horse for Harry, unless he was to carry him behind on the stallion, and that would have been too much of an embarrassment in broad daylight. As he had used up his stipend in salaries, rent and farrier's fees, he had no money for a cart or a horse. So he put the randy mare in a paddock with the stallion hoping that something would come of it.

The delay afforded Stephen an opportunity to attend the burial of the drowned girl, had he been inclined to do so. But he had stood at the lips of so many graves the last few months that he had had more than he could bear of death and its sad aftermath. Gilbert went alone and reported back that no one else had been there but the priest from Galdeford parish, where the poor girl had been laid to rest without a coffin in the pauper's field which lay on Upper Galdeford Road.

At supper that evening, Stephen ambushed Edith Wistwode on her way to the kitchen and asked if she would lend the inn's hay cart to get Harry to Bromfield. Rumors of the tryst at the mill had reached her ears. She was in a bad mood and scowled as she passed Stephen's table. She glanced from Harry at the table by the fireplace to Jennie sweeping up the shards of a shattered pitcher by the bar, nodded curtly, and then hurried off to the kitchen at the rear of the inn. Stephen was surprised it was so easy and she asked no fee for the service. But getting rid of Harry for a few days, or even a week or more if she was lucky, probably was profit enough.

Tuesday morning saw further delay in that Harry got a job late Monday that took him through the following morning to complete, not exactly wood carving but repairing a favorite broken chair that needed a few pieces made to replace the failed ones and then gluing them together.

Thus, they were not ready to go until mid-afternoon.

Stephen fetched the stallion from the pasture and led him into the inn's yard, where Harry was waiting within the cart. It had first been proposed that the groom Mark would drive the cart, but Mark had balked at the suggestion of being marooned for two hours or more in a cart with Harry. Since Harry had some experience cart driving, it had been decided that he could be trusted to drive himself.

Stephen was just resting his saddle on the stallion when he heard Gilbert say from the inn, "There he is."

At first Stephen paid no attention, not caring who "he" was or considering that he might be the "he" in question, until footsteps signaled someone's approach and a familiar voice said, "Stephen, there you are!"

Stephen turned in surprise as he recognized the voice, one he had not heard in years, and if he were to tell the truth one he had hoped not to hear again for many years more.

"Well, William," Stephen said to his elder brother, "what are you doing here?"

"I've come for you," William Attebrook said, his face as grim as Stephen had ever seen it.

"What have I done now?"

"It's not what you have done," said the woman behind William, his wife Elysande, a beautiful and as remote and cold a woman as ever walked the face of the earth. "It's what has been done to us, to our family."

"I don't understand."

"Ida!" William burst out. "My little Ida is missing! Someone has stolen her!"

Chapter 4

"You must find her for us," Elysande said.

This did not come out of her mouth as a request, but as a command. One of the things Stephen had never liked about Elysande was her presumption that she could order him about like some servant. The fact that she came from a better family than their branch of the Attebrooks did not give her that license.

"Please, Stephen," William said with some effort. "I know we have had our differences. But we need your help."

Stephen nearly snorted at this gesture of humility. William and Elysande were alike in that bending the knee to anyone took considerable effort. "I have the scars and broken bones you gave me as a result of those differences."

"You're family. It's time you acted like it."

"And did your duty," Elysande said.

"Ah," Stephen said. "That's more like the William and Elysande I remember, a pair of bullies. Have you been to the sheriff?"

"We doubt that will be much use," Elysande said. "Arundel has no regard for us after what you've done."

"You've heard about that at Hafton?" Stephen asked. Last autumn he had made an enemy of Percival FitzAllan, the earl of Arundel and now sheriff, by helping some lords allied with the rebel Simon de Montfort attack and raze the castle of one of Arundel's retainers. An attack on a retainer was an attack on the principal and demanded action. FitzAllan had no proof of Stephen's involvement, but proof was not required to spark his rage and desire for vengeance. "But we're friends now after I made him look good to the King over that business with the bad money."

"We've heard he still hates you," William said.

"I suppose he probably does. He savors his hates like a good wine."

Stephen's gaze wandered past William and Elysande to Harry in the cart. Harry was quiet, watching this exchange. Harry caught Stephen's eye. Harry's eyebrows rose and his mouth formed a question: What are you doing?

Stephen took a deep breath. He had let his anger over past grievances get the better of his judgment. Ida should not have to pay for William's sins against him. He recalled the last time he had seen her. She had been four years old when Father had sent him off to London to be an apprentice to Ademar de Valence, a royal justice, and to train for a career in the law in preference to the priesthood for which all had agreed he was not well suited: golden hair in thick ringlets framing a soft and sweet face, pink-cheeked and blue-eyed, with petals for lips and a child's delicate teeth. She had hugged him before he mounted his horse and cried, the only member of the family to give any indication that he might be missed. She would be sixteen now and a woman. He could not imagine what she must look like, but she had to be a beautiful girl.

"What happened?" Stephen asked.

"We don't know," Elysande said. "She is fostering with the Ivery family. They hold the manor at Stoke Prior. She decided to come home for some reason."

"Was she escorted?" Stephen asked. He did not know where Stoke Prior lay exactly other than somewhere south and east of Leominster; it was a good ten miles. No young woman would make such a journey by herself.

"Of course she went escorted!" Elysande snapped. "Her maid and four men from the village!"

"Go on," Stephen said.

"They got as far as the road south of Mortimer's Cross." Elysande's voice broke.

"And then?" Stephen prompted after a pause when she did not continue.

"Then her party was attacked on the road," William answered. "All were killed except her."

"How do you know she wasn't?" Stephen asked.

"We did not find her body with the others."

Stephen said nothing. This did not mean that Ida was not dead. She could have been taken away, cruelly used and then killed. But he said nothing of this possibility.

"When did this happen?" Stephen asked.

"Yesterday morning," William said.

"Have you been to the place?"

William nodded.

"Where are the dead now?" Stephen asked.

"We had them taken home," William said.

"We must return to the place straightaway," Stephen said.

"Are you sure I must accompany you?" Elysande asked.

"I wouldn't expect you to trouble yourself," Stephen said. He fished for the drowned girl's ring in his belt pouch and gave it to Harry. "Harry, you'll have to get to Bromfield by yourself. Ask the brothers if they can tell you anything about this."

"Right," Harry said. Glancing at William and Elysande, he added, "*Sir.* Be my pleasure."

Harry gathered up the slack in the reins to gain contact with the horses' mouths, then released them slightly, and clicked his tongue to urge the pair forward. "See you when you get back — sir!"

The cart drew out of the yard. Gilbert watched from the doorway and Edith peeked from a window and jerked out of sight when she saw Stephen notice.

Stephen had never seen Harry drive before and he watched the turn into Bell Lane with some trepidation, fearing an accident or the wagon overturning. But all went well and Harry disappeared up the lane.

"Who was that ghastly creature?" Elysande asked.

"A friend," Stephen said. "William, we must get going right away. We cannot afford to waste a moment."

Chapter 5

"What are we going to do now?" Dickie drained his ale cup. "He's leaving!" He had thrown up the cup quickly and the ale had splashed over his pug nose. Drops fell from the blunt tip. He wiped the drops away with the back of his hand. He was a hardened soldier, but that nose, a missing front tooth and an infectious grin made him look much younger, and had caused many an opponent to underestimate him, for he was a remorseless killer.

"Keep yer voice down. That's not necessarily a bad thing," Everard said. He rubbed his chin, which was quite large and jutting, square as the blade of a spade beneath a nose that had been flatted during a beating by his father before he was big enough to fight back. The chin needed a shave, he thought, as he worried that the fat woman who ran the inn would mark the attention they were paying to the people in the yard and, perhaps, say something to them that might give him away. He watched out the window as a little fat man crossed the yard to the target and spoke earnestly to him for a few moments. The target nodded in agreement, and the fat man hurried to the stable. Meanwhile, the man the target had called William looked on this development with impatience. The woman Elysande turned away with crossed arms and studied the pigeons on the rooftop across the street. Everard found it hard to keep his eyes off the woman.

Everard forced his attention to the target, this Stephen Attebrook. He was a tall fellow, black-haired and leanly built, but reputedly strong and quick. He looked like a fighter. The client had warned him of this, but Everard was not concerned. He had fought more than thirty judicial duels as a hired champion in his lifetime and at least as many single combats arising from challenges, perceived slights, grudges, cross words or merely for the thrill of it, and he had yet to meet the man who was his equal.

"What do you mean, it's not a bad thing?" Dickie asked. "He'll get away. And it looks like he's got company." From what they had overheard, Attebrook and this William intended to travel south together, and William was accompanied by two servants who would go with them.

"He'll be in the open on the road, won't he?" Everard said. "It's not like we've had much luck so far." They had been in Ludlow for three days and had not had a chance to catch Attebrook alone. Everard had thought to find him after dark in the street — a young fellow like him, unmarried, surely had to visit a tavern or whorehouse to relieve his desires. But Attebrook had not ventured from his house across the street after sunset. Everard was willing to be patient; it was a hunt, after all, and a hunter needed patience. But the men chaffed at the waiting and the watching.

"He'll be on the road surrounded by people," Dickie said.

"An opportunity will present itself," Everard said, downing the last of his ale. "Tell the others to get the horses tacked up and get packed. Move!"

"Right," Dickie said. "What about you?"

"I'll meet you on Broad Street. Now go!"

Dickie rose and left the inn.

In the yard, the little fat man, whom Attebrook had addressed as Gilbert, emerged from the stable with a saddled mule. Gilbert used a bench by the stable door to climb into the saddle. He plopped down like a grain sack. The mule protested this treatment by lurching to the right, nearly pitching Gilbert to the ground. His satisfied expression at having reached the saddle evaporated, replaced by alarm as he grabbed the mane to keep from falling.

"Well done," Stephen said. "You're doing so much better."

"Thank you," Gilbert said. "Although there's nothing like a good fall from a mule to make one's day."

"Are you sure we must have him?" William asked. "He'll slow us up."

"I'm not allowed to leave home without him," Stephen said. "Besides, now and then he says something useful."

"Now and then!" Gilbert muttered.

"Huh," William replied.

Attebrook mounted his stallion, and the man William mounted his own horse. These three and the two servants leading packhorses drew out of the yard. Elysande strode to the inn.

Everard left three farthings on the table; two for the ale and one as a tip to that attractive girl he'd heard addressed as Jennie. Then he went out to Bell Lane.

The traveling party was turning right toward Broad Gate. Everard jogged to the corner and watched them descend the hill toward the gate. He hoped the boys would hurry. It could take a long time to tack a horse. And the target was getting farther away by the moment. But at least he knew where they were going.

Chapter 6

It was twelve miles to Mortimer's Cross, or Croft's Cross as it was sometimes called since ownership of the land was disputed between the Mortimers of Wigmore and the Crofts of Croft's Castle in a lawsuit that had dragged on for so many years that most people had forgotten who started it. It took just over two hours for Stephen and William to get there.

The village did not lay on the direct route between Hafton and Leominster, so it might seem odd to someone who did not know the lay of the land why a traveler going from one of those points to the other would go out of his way through Mortimer's Cross. But there was a simple explanation for this. Anyone between Leominster and Hafton had to pass through a hamlet called Shobdon, which lay to the east.

Years ago when Stephen and William were children it had been possible to take a lane northeast of Shobdon across to the main road connecting Ludlow and Leominster, thus avoiding Mortimer's Cross altogether. But the lord of Ledicot, whose lands the lane passed through, had hit on the idea of charging a toll for the use of the lane because so many people from the west traveled on it, to the detriment of the road's condition. It was a stiff toll. Those who suffered to pay it still took the lane, but those who did not went through Mortimer's Cross. It added a good hour to the journey.

The imposition of this toll had occasioned much controversy in this part of Herefordshire. Most people opposed it, because of the inconvenience, but the people of Mortimer's Cross favored the toll. Perhaps that had to do with the fact that until the toll, the place had consisted of three or four houses huddled about a road crossing. Now there were more houses and several fine barns where people paid to spend the night, and an alehouse where weary travelers could rest their tired feet even if the ale wasn't much good.

William led them through Mortimer's Cross to a fork in the road about two hundred yards south of the village. The left fork led to Leominster after many meanderings and was known locally as the Leominster Road. The right fork after many meanderings led to Hereford and was known, not surprisingly, as the Hereford Road. They took the left fork. Trees and thick shrubs lined the road so that Stephen could barely see into the fields that lay to the left and right.

William continued down this way for another hundred yards or so. He stopped at a thick copse of oak and elm. There was a lane of sorts to the left through the shrubs that allowed carts into the field. There was a similar break, though more overgrown, across the road to the right.

"It happened here," William said. "This is where we found the dead, most of them."

"Most of them?"

"Adele, the maid, managed to stagger on to the village before she died. We finally found one of the men over there." William gestured toward the River Lugg, visible to the east by the trees lining the bank.

Stephen slid off his horse. He knelt, hitching his sword aside, and examined the ground. There were signs of many horses on the road and of a wagon having passed by, distinguishable from the track of a cart by the evidence of two sets of wheels made as the vehicle turned. These marks were hardly visible, only fragments here and there trampled by many feet. Stephen doubted the track had any significance, but his eyes followed the turn of the wagon out of habit since it was something that did not seem quite right. The track emerged from the break to the west. *That* was odd. Most farmers could not afford wagons. They were large and heavy and most required four horses to pull them. Farms favored cheaper two-wheeled carts that were much lighter and often got by with a single horse.

"What happened to the horses?" Stephen asked as his eyes followed the track and he wondered about it.

"The horses?" William asked, confused by the question.

"The horses Ida and the others were riding."

"They were taken as well. I had assumed that was the point of the attack."

"They just happened to take Ida along for sport."

"Yes," William said grimly.

"You've not told Elysande of this suspicion."

"I did not want to increase her grief. She has enough as it is."

"So you don't think Ida's alive."

"I am preparing myself for the possibility of her death. It seems the most likely thing."

"Yes," Stephen said striding toward the break to the western field.

He pushed through the shrubs to the field. A few steps away, there were signs of a campsite: a fire that had dirt placed on what had been left of it, the reek of shit in the air, depressed places in the grass where people had slept — and a dead dog.

William followed Stephen through the break.

"You haven't seen this before?" Stephen knelt beside the dog. The body was flaccid, the rigidity that followed death having worn off, and had not yet begun to bloat or smell: more than a day dead but not much longer than that. There was blood on the dog's jowls, neck and forelegs. Stephen lifted the jaw. Someone had stabbed the dog in the neck.

"The maid was attacked by dogs," William said after a long silence. "They bit her all over her body, even her head and neck. It was terrible. Pieces were torn from her." He shuddered at the memory.

"Did she say anything about the attack before she died?"

"Not that we were told. Other than to ask that someone be sent to Hafton for help. That's how they knew to fetch us."

"What about the others?"

"They were bitten as well, although from what I saw of their wounds an axe killed them."

Stephen rose and returned to the break in the foliage. He knelt there and searched among the grass. There at the margin where the grass and the track merged, he spotted two dog prints. They were quite large. Going back to the dead dog, he measured its forepaws with his fingers. He checked this measurement against the prints in the grass. They were bigger than his measurement.

"They had more than one dog," Stephen said more to himself than to William. "Probably a pack of them if all the dead were savaged."

"Why didn't they just ride away from them?"

"From the dogs? Perhaps they were surprised, pulled from their horses and couldn't."

"The bastards!"

"A unique way of robbery, I'll say that for them, if it's true."

Stephen looked around for more evidence of dog, and noticed a large pile of it at the base of a pine tree: too great a pile to be made by a single dog or man. He strode over to get a better look at this oddity, despite the stench and the unappealing nature of the task. It looked as though someone had dumped out a bucket of shit, for there were splashes of the foul stuff up the trunk of the tree and some distance from the pile. He could not imagine why this would be so. Suppressing a gag, he backed away and counted the impressions in the grass where someone had slept: eight of them. Eight men could have filled it nicely, but he had never known an Englishman to shit in a bucket when a bush was available.

"We need to go back to the village," Stephen said, making for the road.

"What for?"

"To find out who works this field."

When they got back to the village, Gilbert was taking his ease with a tankard of ale in the alehouse yard at one table, while William's two servants, who had followed with two packhorses, occupied another table. The contented expression on Gilbert's face was overtaken by disgruntlement and he was about to make some comment critical about having been left to fend for himself on the road. But the criticism died on his lips.

"You found the place?" Gilbert asked instead.

Stephen nodded.

"Anything?"

Stephen filled him in on what he had seen.

"A terrible way to die," Gilbert said. "Chewed by dogs." He spotted the alewife. "Mistress! Can you come here for a moment?"

The alewife came over with a pitcher in one hand and a pair of cups in the other. "A drink, gentlemen, while you're standing there?"

William accepted a cup and tossed it back. The alewife poured another. He drank deeply again and turned toward the road.

"Mistress," Gilbert asked as she finished refilling William's cup, "did a wagon pass through here a couple of days ago? Round about the time of those murders?"

"There would have been a pack of dogs with it, and about eight men," Stephen added.

The alewife's lips pursed in disapproval. "I remember them. As unsavory bunch as I ever seen. Hard men. I feared even letting them in the yard. But they caused no trouble, not even the dogs. Obedient dogs, those — remained in the road while the boys drank their fill."

"It never occurred to you that they were the killers?" William spat from the fence.

"We aren't stupid, sir," the alewife said. "Of course, it occurred to us."

"Why then didn't you go after them?"

"With what? We've no horses. They was long gone before that poor woman showed up at my yard. It was hard enough to send a boy to bring you. He had to run the whole way. And we've no swords or any weapons to speak of, and they was all armed."

"With axes?" Stephen asked.

"And swords and bucklers as well," the alewife said. "A few of them, as I recollect."

"How far can they get with a wagon?" William asked. He tossed his empty cup to the alewife, who made no effort to catch it and it fell to the ground. As it was a leather cup there was no chance of it breaking.

"They've probably got two days on us," Gilbert said. "Thirty miles or more."

"I did not ask for your opinion," William snapped.

"He offers his opinion when he feels like it," Stephen said.

"You put up with this impertinence from all your servants?" William sneered.

"He's not my servant. He is his own man. Besides, he sometimes has useful things to say."

"I daresay!" Gilbert said. "I'm kept you out of trouble more than once."

"I'll give you the one." Stephen turned back to the alewife. "Did they say where they were bound, by any chance?"

"Not that I heard." She gestured toward a table under an oak at the far side of the yard. "They kept to themselves. We didn't have conversation other that a few pleasantries. I'm surprised they managed even that."

Stephen gazed down the road toward the place where the attack had occurred. "They could have gone anywhere, then."

"The road has many forks," Gilbert murmured coming to his side.

"Yes, at some point we will pick the wrong one, and that will be it."

"There is one other thing," Stephen said to the alewife. "Tell me about the wagon."

"What about it? It was a wagon. I did not pay much attention."

"Wagons are not just wagons. They come in all sorts. What do you remember about it?"

The Bear Wagon

The alewife's brow furrowed. "Well, it reminded me of the kind that the bear baiters use. You know the sort: large, sturdy, squarish, barred windows."

"That would explain the dogs," Gilbert said. Bear baiters always had a pack of dogs with them. The primary amusement of bear baiting was having dogs attack the bear. Sometimes the baiter employed his dogs. Mostly, though, people in the crowd put forward their own and there was betting on the outcome, which was invariably the death of a dog. The point of betting was to see whether a dog would survive and for how long.

"So," Stephen said, "a bear baiter's wagon. Did it have a color?"

"Of course, it had a color," the midwife said.

"What was it, then?"

"Well, the paint had mostly worn off, as I recollect. It had been red once, I reckon, red with a green stripe across it at the roof."

"A red wagon losing its paint," William fumed. "That's very helpful. How many of those are there in England, do you think?"

"Did the bear make any noise?" Gilbert asked.

"Noise?" the alewife responded.

"You know, the usual bear noises: huffing about, grunting, growling, banging the sides."

"I don't think so. Quiet as a mouse. I didn't hear nothing, anyway. Some whimpering, perhaps, but I'm not sure. Do bears whimper?"

"Unhappy bears might," Gilbert said. "I'd be unhappy to be locked up in a wagon."

The alewife frowned. "A couple of the village boys tried to get close for a look, but one of the gang ran them off."

"Is that all you can tell us?" Stephen asked.

"I can't say as I paid that much attention. We get a lot of folks come through here, especially in summer. Odd as you can imagine. They weren't any more out of the ordinary than anybody else."

William stalked to the fence and stared across the road at the fields and forest beyond. His mouth was a thin line and he looked almost in tears, and he shook as if trying to hold them back.

Stephen went to his side as the alewife hurried off to see to a party of travelers who had just come through the gate.

"It's not much to go on," Stephen said to William, "but it's something."

"I'll never see her again," William said. "She is our only child, you know. Her sister died an infant after you left, and Elysande and I had no others. So sunny and sweet. So innocent. A delicate flower." He sighed, gaining control of himself, embarrassed that Stephen should see him like this.

"You're giving up?" Stephen asked. "Gilbert and I will need money for expenses if we're to go on. And one of the packhorses."

"I'm not giving up until I've tracked those bastards down and killed every one of them."

The days are long in summer, and there were still four hours left before nightfall, so the little party set out southward on the road to Leominster, hoping to close the gap as much as they could before the end of the day.

Stephen ignored William's complaints about the pace, which he kept to a walk to spare the horses, which had been pressed hard to get this far. He watched the roadside for some sign of the wagon and the dogs. Here and there he spotted dog prints, fading in the dirt, and an occasional pile of shit that had to be dog since most people did not do their business on the verge but had the decency to retreat behind the foliage. But of course whether these were presents from the dogs he sought was anyone's guess. It was not unthinkable that the dogs might have belonged to other travelers. He also hoped for some sign of what happened to Ida, but that was hoping too much, and he knew it.

The Bear Wagon

Two miles from Mortimer's Cross they came to a hamlet of a half dozen houses around a small stone church called Cyningaslæn, or King's Grant, for those who thought in French. Stephen called to a woman laying washing across her fence to dry if she had seen a bear baiter's wagon come through the day before.

"Did I ever!" the woman called back. "Their damned dogs took after my sow and killed four piglets! The bastards kept three and let me have the corpse of the other, and wouldn't pay for any! Said I could enjoy mine for dinner! That they'd done me a service serving it up! What do you want with them?"

"It's a personal matter."

"Personal, is it? I can't imagine what business you'd have with that riff-raff, sir. A bad bunch. Looked like out-of-work soldiers, armed to the teeth. You know how much trouble they are. That's why my boys didn't take out after them."

"Better to lose a couple of piglets than a son."

"That was my thinking, although I don't like to have to swallow the insult."

"I don't suppose she minded swallowing the piglet though, in the end," Gilbert muttered, rising up in the saddle to ease his bruised behind. "Looks like she's got a few to spare." A mob of piglets could be seen in the garden around a fat sow lying in the dirt. "Perhaps we should buy one. I wouldn't mind roast piglet for supper tonight rather than hard biscuit."

"Did they take the road to Leominster?" Stephen asked the woman.

She nodded. "It's the only road here. Don't go nowhere else."

"What time did they pass by?"

"Just before dinner."

"Noonish, then," Stephen remarked to Gilbert.

"We're only a day and a half behind. What do you make of that? Twenty miles?"

"I suspect we'll catch them in Leominster. They're bound to have put on a show there. They're certain to need the money."

"They weren't all riding horses, were they?" William asked as he came up, having gone ahead again.

"They were, sir," the woman said. "I thought that a bit odd, given their shabby appearance. Give 'em one for me when you catch 'em!"

"We will!" Stephen said.

"You should have brought more men, though."

Leominster was a small market town lying between Hereford and Ludlow. Like most towns in the Welsh March, it had a wall, which consisted of a ten-foot ditch and a fifteen-foot embankment topped by a palisade. The traveling party rode through the Bargate suburbs in the approaches to Bar Gate. This was the road everyone coming from Mortimer's Cross took to reach the town. There seemed no reason to think that the bear wagon had not done so as well.

At Bar Gate, the entrance was blocked by a cart piled with hay as high as the roof of the passageway. They stopped behind the cart. One of the wards, noticing them, came around the cart, and said, "That'll be a pence each for you to enter, and the same for the horses."

"We're tracking a party of about eight men," Stephen said. "Former soldiers by the look of them in the company of a bear baiter."

"Bear baiter? I ain't seen no bear baiters lately."

"It's a red wagon, or was before most of the paint wore off. There was a green stripe around the top."

"I don't recall seeing any such wagon." The ward's mount twisted in a humorless smile. "Though I might recall, if I had a little help."

"What sort of help?" Stephen asked, although he had a good idea.

The Bear Wagon

The ward extended a hand and rubbed his fingers with his thumb. "A little offering, so's we can get some ale. Guarding is thirsty work."

Stephen was about to motion to William to pay the man. But William slid from his horse, grasped the ward by the throat and thrust him against the wall. The ward made choking noises and his eyes bulged. The farm boys with the cart watched these unexpected and amusing proceedings with goggling eyes and open mouths.

"They stole my daughter," William snarled. "I have neither the time nor the inclination for your games."

"He could talk better if you stopped choking him," Stephen said.

William glared at Stephen but dropped his hold to the ward's collar.

"There would also have been a pack of dogs with them," Stephen said. "Hard to miss."

"Why," the ward asked, alarm on his face, for William was a big man and strong, more than his match even on a good day, "would fellows with a wagon do something like that? Are you sure you've got the right ones?"

"I've no doubt," William said, giving the ward a shake.

The other ward saw what was happening and put his hand on his sword. Stephen shook a finger at him and the second ward halted where he was and did not draw. Then he ran into the town.

"The bailiffs will be arriving shortly," Gilbert said.

"Perhaps it was the Welsh!" stuttered the ward in William's grasp.

"It wasn't the fucking Welsh," William said. "They were as English as you."

"Well," the warden said between gasps, "my mum's Flemish."

"Fuck your mother," William snapped.

"This isn't working," Gilbert said.

"When I want your opinion, I'll ask for it," William snapped. He shook the ward. Being so much larger, this gave the impression of a mastiff shaking a terrier. "You know something. Otherwise you wouldn't have demanded a bribe."

Up to now, William had not indicated that anything more than a beating was in the offing. Yet the ward, though smaller and lighter, did not seem that intimidated by the prospect, probably because he was well familiar with its effects and had weathered more than his share without any lasting injury.

But then William drew his dagger and the stakes went up.

Stephen was about to dismount to intervene if necessary when a dozen bailiffs appeared at a dead run.

"Oh, my, that was quick," Gilbert said, turning his mule in preparation for a dash from danger. The appearance of bailiffs was a matter of concern, but it was made worse by the fact they all carried halberds, a dreadful weapon capable killing even an armored man. Gilbert had not seen what halberds could do himself, but he had listened to Stephen's stories by the fire with his son, Gillie.

"You, there!" one of the bailiffs shouted at William. "Lay off!"

"Do you know who I am?" William thundered without slackening his hold on the gate ward who had begun to squirm at the possibility of rescue. "I am William Attebrook of Hafton!"

The chief deputy scowled. "I don't care if you are the Earl of Arundel himself! You have broken the King's peace! You are under arrest!"

"He is not as impressed as he should be," Gilbert said to Stephen. "Or isn't your brother important?"

"Well, it is rather a small manor," Stephen said. "Our cousin the earl is the one with clout in this part of the county."

William, for his part, was not willing to be easily arrested. He cast aside the captive ward, who fell onto his back. "Stephen! Assist me!"

"They have halberds, William," Stephen said. "I suggest that you come away as fast as possible, and while you still have all your arms and legs."

William might have got away even then, but no one had taken hold of his horse and it had wandered to the hay wagon, where it had found a free supper. When William reached to grasp its reins, it shied away to the other side of the cart. This gave the bailiffs time to surge forward. Three of them got between William and Stephen while the others piled onto William. He struggled, but, outnumbered, four of them bore him to the ground, where one produced a thong which was used to bind William's wrists behind his back.

"Damn you, Stephen," William snarled as the bailiffs pulled him to his feet. "Damn you to hell forever."

"That did not work out well," Gilbert remarked after William had disappeared through the gate, surrounded by bailiffs, leaving the abused ward at his post and who smirked at them from the door to the right gate tower.

"There's never been any love lost between us," Stephen said glumly. "So I doubt this will make much of a difference."

Instead of riding away, however, Stephen dismounted and approached the ward. The ward shrank inside the doorway in case Stephen offered further violence. But Stephen dropped two pence borrowed for the journey in the dirt.

The ward glanced at the pennies. After a moment, he bent to pick them up. Stephen put his foot on them.

"You saw something," Stephen said. "What?"

"I did see such a wagon, sir," the ward said. "Yesterday. In the street there. It stopped at the Blue Pony. All those dogs! Such a racket! The fellows went inside for a drink. Then those with horses rode away toward the north." He gestured to the cart track rimming the town ditch.

"What about the wagon?"

"It went that way." The ward pointed toward the track leading south along the ditch.

"The dogs, too?"

The ward nodded. "Except for two, which went with the riders."

"You didn't hear them say where they were going, did you?"

"Unfortunately not, sir."

Stephen eyed the ward closely for signs he might be holding out for another penny. But he decided the man was telling all he knew. Stephen removed his foot from the pennies.

"Thank you," he said.

"My pleasure, sir. If only your friend had not been so impulsive."

"If only," Stephen said.

Everard and Dick watched the commotion at the gate from down the street.

"What was that about?" Dick wondered.

"Damned if I know," Everard said. "Come on. We've got to keep him in sight. He could go anywhere in this rat warren."

As they trotted toward the gate and the cart track that led southward around the town, Dick asked, "Should we do it now?"

"No," Everard said. "Not yet. Not in broad daylight. Not in town." It was not uncommon for there to be tracks following the town ditch. The tracks always skirted back gardens since towns didn't allow people to build their houses smack against the ditch, and housewives often could be found outside tending those gardens who could be depended on to raise the hue and cry at the slightest thing. Dick was a good fighter and a killer without conscience, but he had the brains of a fish. He never gave a thought about what to do after. And the getting away part was as crucial as the deed itself, if you didn't want to decorate a tree. So far in their rather long career at this sort of work no one had connected them with any of it. And that's the way he wanted to keep it.

"But this may be our only chance."

"No, there will be others. Be patient."

Chapter 7

Harry stopped the cart at the gate to Bromfield Priory. It was a timber and wattle building made in imitation of a fortress' gate tower. But everybody who lived in England regardless of his station had an appreciation for towers and it was obvious the gate was decorative rather than functional.

A porter emerged from a doorway within the gate and came to the side of the cart. The porter was a strong man, to judge by the massive shoulders beneath his red woolen shirt.

"Well," the porter asked, "what's your business?"

"I've come to see the prior," Harry said.

"Want him to pray you a new set of legs, eh?" The porter chuckled.

"That's been tried. Doesn't work."

"How'd you lose 'em?"

"Fell under a cart."

"That's too bad. Knew a fellow once who lost his legs — both sliced clean off!" The porter made a slicing movement with his right hand. "Idiot raised his shield. Not as lucky as you. He lived only a couple of days after."

"What about you?" Harry noticed that the hand was missing two fingers.

The porter grinned. "Parried poorly. Stuck my hand out too far."

"Ah," Harry replied in a noncommittal tone since it was unclear to him how such a thing could happen.

Sensing the uncertainty, the porter said, "You're not a fencer, I take it."

"No, I've a friend who is. You were a soldier, then?"

"I was, and a good one. But those days are long past."

"My friend has the same problem. Lost part of his foot. Now the only work he can get is as coroner."

"Really? That friend wouldn't be Stephen Attebrook, would it?"

"It would."

"A friend of Attebrook may not be welcome here. There's some bad blood between him and the prior."

"I'll just pretend I don't know him."

"You could do that."

"We're only acquaintances anyway. Why should it matter?"

"I suppose it shouldn't. Come on, I'll take you to him." The porter grasped the horse's bridle. "We don't ordinarily allow horses in the cloister, but owing to your circumstances I think an exception can be made."

The porter led the horse and cart across the yard to the cloister gate and then through into the cloister itself, which was bounded on the north by a stone church, straight ahead the chapter house and dormitory, and to the right the hall and kitchen. Harry had not spent much time in such places; in fact, the only time he had been in a priory was when his legs were cut off by a priory barber-surgeon, and he had not then been in any condition to pay attention to the surroundings.

The porter left Harry at the door to the chapter house and went inside. Harry stewed in the cart. He began to think that he had made a big mistake. What was Stephen thinking, sending him here to beg for work from someone who disliked him? And Stephen intended to make the introduction? Stephen often had odd, hare-brained ideas, but this was one of the worst, especially since Harry was the one who would suffer for it.

Two monks emerged not long after. Both were about Harry's age, which as far as he could reckon was between twenty-eight and thirty; his mother had been confused about the year — it had been either the seventeenth or eighteenth year of Henry III's reign, or something like that — and had lost count. This wasn't surprising. She had had eight children and Harry had been lost in the middle and left pretty much to fend for himself as soon as he could walk.

One of the monks had the self-assured air of a leader. He had a long face which was fortunate because he had a long nose as well so it did not stand out as much as it might have otherwise. The nose was craggy with a twist in it. His grey eyes were lively, his brows heavy and thick, his hair, what there was of it was brown. It was cut close to his skull which was shaved above the ears. His woolen habit could not hide his broad shoulders. The right arm was concealed by his sleeve but his other hand hung down, the fingers thick and strong.

He said, "Oswald says you wanted to see me. He indicated you might have some trouble coming to me, so here I am."

"You're the prior, sir?" Harry asked, trying to sound as respectful as he could, but feeling it was not a convincing effort. He had little practice at this and he felt uncomfortable about the need to suck up to the prior to get the work and worried about what had to be certain rejection because of this bad blood Oswald the porter had spoken about.

"I am Bertran. And you are?"

"My name is Henry, but everybody calls me Harry."

"Harry . . ." Bertran rolled the name around in his mouth, looking thoughtful, his eyes on Harry's stumps. "You wouldn't be Harry the beggar? The one at Broad Gate?"

Harry nodded. "I used to be. Now I'm Harry the woodcarver." He added, "I've heard you have the need of one."

"Of one what? A beggar?"

"No, sir. A woodcarver."

There was a pause and the horse took advantage of it to drop great clods of horse manure right by Bertran's feet. Bertran did not seem affected by this, but the other monk looked at the deposit with horror because of the ruin it visited on the cloister's raked drive.

"Yes," Bertran said, drawing out the word. "I had heard that. We were down to the market and people were talking about you."

"I hope they were saying good things," Harry said, doubting this was the case.

"Mostly people were scandalized," Bertran said, confirming Harry's doubts. "They cannot believe you've risen so above your station as now to call yourself a craftsman."

"Just trying to make a living, sir. It isn't easy being in business. Sometimes I think begging's a more lucrative profession."

"It's hardly a profession," the other monk snapped from behind Bertran.

"People do what they must to survive, Brother Edwin," Bertran said. "Still, one wonders what credentials you have as a woodcarver. It does not seem you have been one long."

"I've always been a carver, sir. I carved all sorts of stuff in my idle hours. Just I didn't try to sell anything I made — until recently, that is. After that girl died in the churchyard at Saint Laurence's, I made a few likenesses of her. People liked them and bought them."

Bertran nodded. "I've seen one of those likenesses. She must have been a beautiful girl, if your carving was any indication."

"She was. Very beautiful."

"Have you references?"

"I have one, but you'll not like to hear it."

"Oh?"

"My friend Stephen Attebrook said I should come here to ask for work."

Bertran's eyes narrowed and whatever friendliness that had been in them vanished. "Attebrook is your friend?"

"I like to think he is." Harry went on, even though it didn't matter since he had lost any chance of obtaining the priory job. "I carved a bench for him. He was happy with it. He meant to come here with me and tell you how good it was and how much he liked it."

"That is hard to believe," Bertran said. "He would not dare to show his face here now that I am prior."

Bertran turned toward the doorway.

The Bear Wagon

"Off with you!" the monk Edwin snapped at Harry. "Out of the cloister before you foul it any more with your presence!"

Edwin's sharpness made Bertran pause. He came back to the cart. "I am forgetting my manners," Bertran said. "You may stay for supper and for the night, if you wish. Edwin, have a couple of the boys help Harry to the dormitory. I doubt he can negotiate the stairs. Oswald, take care of the horse and cart, and see that this mess is cleaned up before Brother Edwin's head bursts."

Chapter 8

Stephen turned in the saddle to see William's two servants as he led the party onto the track around the town's south wall. They were both brawny men with square faces and square hands. "Gibb, ride back to Hafton and let Lady Elysande know what happened. She'll want to collect William's bail, I expect."

Gibb looked uncomfortable.

"I don't know as she will," Gibb said at last. "She and our lord have hardly been on speaking terms for years."

"She'd let him rot in gaol?" Stephen asked.

"She'd think it would do him some good," Gibb said, not meeting Stephen's eyes.

"Huh," Stephen grunted with a slight smile. "She'd be wrong there. Nothing will change him."

They came to the Ryeland Street Gate on the south of town. Like all the roads leading away from the town proper, it was lined with houses and shops for a good quarter of a mile.

"They could have gone that way," Gilbert said.

"I don't think so," Stephen said.

"Guessing again."

"Maybe. But it doesn't lead to any places a bear baiter would go. Just small villages."

"Perhaps they are not ordinary bear baiters."

"What are you saying?"

"You'd think a bear baiter would stop here. It's a substantial town, and a source of ready money. Yet it seems they did not."

Stephen was disturbed by this suggestion, but reckoned Gilbert's thought no more of a guess than his own.

"We'll ride on to South Street Gate and see what the warden has to say," Stephen said.

But the gate wardens had not seen a bear wagon. South Street led to Hereford. Had Stephen been a bear baiter, he would have gone to Hereford. So they wasted a good hour asking the shopkeepers along South Street if they had seen a bear baiter's wagon recently. But they learned nothing.

With no evidence that the bear wagon had gone down the Hereford Road, they continued on the track to the Etnam Street Gate, which gave access to the town from the east.

They reached the road and turned on it, on the lookout for people to question. Yet although the windows to the shops were open, there did not seem to be anyone in them.

"It's an invitation for theft," Gilbert said.

"There!" Stephen pointed to where the road curved right. A crowd was gathered at the bend. "Something's going on."

The existence of a crowd seemed like good fortune, since it meant they had only to ask their questions once.

The crowd was so large that it spilled across the street, blocking passage to anyone who might want to travel along it.

"What's going on?" Stephen asked a woman holding a baby at the rear of the gathering.

"A boy fell down the well," the woman replied. "They're trying to get him out now."

"He lives?"

"No. He drowned, the poor fellow."

Leominster was the southern-most reach of Stephen's jurisdiction as coroner. Until he rose to the position, the coroner's duties had been performed by another part-time deputy, but Stephen had discharged him since his stipend did not cover the man's wages. So now, this sad business was his. He slid from the stallion and pushed through the crowd, hoping that it would not take long. "Make way, make way!"

"Who are you?" asked a man wearing a blue floppy hat and an apron covered in flour who did not seem interested in giving way.

"I am Stephen Attebrook, and I am the king's coroner here now."

"Huh," the baker grunted. "You're the man who deprived Jimmy of his livelihood, are you?"

"I am the man who deprived James of his livelihood, *sir.*"

"Sir," the baker said with the least amount of respect he could get away with. He turned about and shouted to everyone else, "Make way for his lordship, the coroner!"

A sea of faces turned in Stephen's direction and a lane opened up to the well. Two men who had been bending over the well stepped back from it.

"What have we got here?" Stephen asked the two men when he reached them.

One of the men gestured at the well. "A young lad fell in, sir."

Stephen looked into the pit. About fifteen feet down, a pale scrawny arm and a leg were visible in the dim light against black water. A rope dangled over the edge and hung into the well. There was a loop at the end as if they had been trying to snag an arm in order to haul the body out.

"What was his name?" Stephen asked.

"Obadiah," answered a woman at the edge of the crowd. She had tear tracks down her dusty cheeks. "His name is . . . was Obadiah." She seemed surprised that he would ask.

"Your son?" Stephen asked.

The woman nodded.

"I'm sorry," Stephen said even though that trite phrase was inadequate to address anyone's grief, let alone a mother's. No amount of sympathy could soften the pain of such a loss. He knew very well about such pain. It had been more than a year since his woman Taresa had died of fever, and the hollow in his heart had still not closed up.

Stephen drew up the rope. "This isn't working," he said to the two men who had been fishing for the corpse. "Someone will have to go down the well."

The fellows shifted from one foot to another.

"Not me," one of them said.

"Nor me," said the other. "I ain't going down there for all the money in the world. There's a devil at the bottom of that pit."

The first man nodded. "This is the third death in that well in the last year."

"It's cursed," the second man said. "It sucks people in."

"And you're still using it?" Stephen asked.

"Well, it is a long walk to the river, and you know how foul river water is," the first man said. "Not fit to drink."

"Will anyone volunteer?" Stephen called out to the crowd.

There was a rustling of voices in response, but no one stepped forward. More than a few people crossed themselves and uttered muffled prayers.

"Gilbert?" Stephen asked.

Gilbert patted his ample stomach. "I'm not sure I'll fit. It is a rather narrow well."

"It isn't that narrow," Stephen grumbled.

Stephen looked around for the two servants, Gibb and Herb, but they were nowhere in sight. Nor did they answer when he called their names.

Gilbert gazed into the pit. "It would be a shame to leave it as the poor boy's grave. You're thin and fit. You could do it."

"I suppose I'll have to," Stephen said.

He resized the loop at the end of the rope so that it would fit around his body under the arms. He removed his sword belt and handed it to Gilbert. Then he held out the other end of the rope to the two men who had been fishing for the dead boy. "Take a good hold and play it out as I go down, in case I slip."

"Right, sir," they said.

Stephen swung his legs into the pit, not convinced the two fellows would belay him if he slipped on the stones lining the pit walls. But he could depend on them to hold him up so he wouldn't drown if he hit the water.

He sat on the well wall for a few moments, gathering his courage, for now that he was about to embark on this task it seemed more dangerous and creepy than it had when he was on flat ground. Meanwhile, the crowd pressed close, everyone anxious to watch the doings in the pit, and probably hoping that he fell and died along with the boy. That would be something to keep the gossips going for months.

With all those expectant faces looming, there was no putting it off any longer. Stephen wedged one foot against the planks on one side and the other foot on the other. He slipped, drawing an excited gasp from the onlookers, owing to the fact that he had no toes on his left foot. The last time he had done anything remotely like this had been when he was whole in Spain. There had been a wager made about whether he could climb up a rock cleft while fully armed. But he lodged his heel and the side of the damaged foot into a crevasse, thus disappointing the spectators. And using hands and feet together, he inched down the stone tube, thinking himself to be rather like a spider.

The well was deeper than it looked from the top, and Stephen was gasping with the exertion when he reached the water. It was dark and dank and sinister way down here, and stank of mold. It was easy to imagine ghostly hands reaching out of the black water to drag him under — or the boy's corpse suddenly coming to life to do that very thing. No wonder no one had volunteered.

Stephen freed the rope from around his shoulders and struggled to loop it about the boy. The body was still rigid in death and the arms did not move so it took more time and effort than he expected, and was difficult from his precarious position straddling on the walls of the well.

"Hoist away!" Stephen cried up the tunnel to those waiting above.

Many hands on the rope hauled away and the body drew upward. Water cascading from the corpse's sodden wool shirt showered on Stephen's head as the body ascended. He climbed back up rather than wait for those above to send down the rope, eager to be out of the pit as soon as he could.

When he reached the top, hands grasped his arms to help him out, which he was grateful for, since he had nearly reached the limits of his strength.

The boy had been laid out on the ground. Gilbert was kneeling beside him. Stephen joined him. The lad looked to be no more than seven or eight with arms and legs as thin as willow branches.

Gilbert brushed the boy's long auburn hair from about his face and neck. "This was not a drowning." Gilbert pointed to bruises on the skinny neck. There was a large purplish mark on either side of the throat and more at the back of the neck.

Stephen put his hands on the boy's throat. His thumbs covered the two marks on either side of the neck and his fingers matched those on the rear.

"Someone throttled him," Stephen said. "And look at this." On one arm and both legs there were bite marks.

"Could have been a dog," Gilbert murmured.

Obadiah's mother, hearing these words, broke into a prolonged howl. Several of the neighborhood women hugged her and were about to lead her away.

But Stephen stopped them with a raised hand. He stood up. "When did you last see him?"

"Last evening," the mother said between sobs. "I sent him out for tallow for the lamp. We'd run out, and it was dark. We always sit up and tell stories to the children around the lamp until we put them to bed. And he never came back!"

"Where do you live?" Stephen asked.

"Have a care, sir!" said one of the neighborhood women at the mother's side. "Can't you see she is distraught!"

"She can be distraught later," Stephen said. "I said, where do you live?"

The neighborhood woman pointed around the bend. "They live down Worcester Street about a quarter mile."

"And where did you send him for the tallow?" Stephen demanded.

The mother pointed toward Etnam Street Gate.

"So he passed by here," Gilbert said. "Sometime shortly after sundown."

"There was a wagon that came through here yesterday," Stephen said to the crowd. "There was a pack of dogs with it. Does anybody remember seeing it?"

"They stayed in my yard, there," said a burly man with a soiled apron, blackened hands and the aroma of smoke about his person.

Stephen glance up and across the street to the place indicated: a blacksmith's with a large open space beside the shed covering the forge, and a rack for restraining horses so they could be shod.

"When did they leave?" Stephen asked the blacksmith.

"Before dawn. They were gone when I awoke."

"How many men were there?"

"Two is all I saw. And the dogs of course."

"Did you hear anything last evening?"

"I heard the dogs yapping a bit, and those fellows talking." The blacksmith shook his head. "It seemed nothing to remark about."

"Did they mention where they were headed?"

"No, they knew where they were going."

"How can you be sure?"

"They didn't ask for directions. Most people coming through want to know the way to Bromyard."

Stephen nodded. Bromyard was the first town that lay on the Worcester Road. People usually found their way by asking directions to the next town that lay along the route to their destination since it was easy to take a wrong turn.

"Do you think they're heading east?" Gilbert asked.

"It would seem so," Stephen said, staring down the Worcester Road.

Chapter 9

It was a good thing the local jury had already been assembled, except for one man, a lace maker who hurried out from the town as the crowd began to break up and return to their shops and homes. So getting a verdict of murder did not take too long. Nonetheless, Stephen chaffed at the delay. While England was a small country, it was easily large enough to vanish without a trace if you wanted to, or lose any pursuit by a simple change of direction.

"What are you going to do about William?" Gilbert asked as they mounted up.

"Leave him."

"Not very brotherly of you. Gaols can be so unpleasant."

"We haven't the time to waste if we're to catch them."

"Well, yes, time is important. Although the fellows and I," Gilbert said indicating Gibb and Herb, who were emerging from a tavern down the road where they had repaired for ale, which was how they had avoided a trip down the well, "could go on to Bromyard and find out where they went before the trail grows too cold, while you deal with the problem of William. It shouldn't take long."

"And how am I supposed to do get him out? We haven't the money to spare for bail."

"Use your wits. You've given evidence of owning a small portion, unless you left them at Ludlow. It's only twelve miles to Bromyard from here. We should make it by nightfall if we hurry."

"Only twelve miles! That's a lot to ask of the horses," Stephen grumbled, searching for excuses to reject this plan.

"Is it?"

"What do you know about horses?"

"I know on which end you feed them and which end the shit comes out of. Isn't that enough?"

"You know it isn't."

"Gibb and Herb will advise me, then."

"About time to look for a place to settle, isn't it, sir?" Gibb asked, for Stephen and Gilbert had reached the two servants at the tavern's gate. "This place has beds in the loft."

"Gilbert thinks we should press on for Bromyard," Stephen said.

Gibb's face fell. "It will be dark in a few hours. I don't think we can find our way in the dark."

"I can," Herb said, with a hiccup.

"Shut up," Gibb said. "You couldn't find your way out of turnip bag."

"I can find my way better than you," Herb said. "I've been to Bromyard more than once. Had a girl there in my youth when I worked my dad's pack train. Pretty thing."

"The prettiest thing that would be interested in you is a toad."

"Careful," Herb said. "It sounds like you're talking about my wife."

"Well, then," Gilbert said. "That's settled. Off we go." He reined the mule about with some difficulty since the animal had taken a culinary interest in a pot of flowers. He waved, his back to the three. "Don't take too long, Stephen! Oh, and Herb! Leave Sir William's horse with his lordship!"

"Lordship? What lordship?" Herb looked around, bewildered, for there were no lords anywhere near.

"He means me," Stephen grated.

"Oh, right, sir. Certainly. What do you need Lord William's horse for?"

"Never mind." Stephen held out a hand.

Herb passed the reins to Stephen and followed Gilbert with Gibb as his side, who threw a parting glance filled with regret at the tavern.

Eyes on the Etnam Street Gate, Stephen considered what to do, his mood sour. He was prepared to go to the ends of the earth to avenge Ida and find her body so she could be properly buried and not left in a field to be picked at by birds and ravaged by wandering pigs. But he wasn't prepared to risk his life, and reputation, or what little there was of his fortune for his brother. He should just turn about and follow Gilbert and to hell with William. Yet something rooted him to the spot in the middle of the street. He could move neither forward nor away. He could not put his finger on what held him there, and he struggled to understand it. It felt like obligation, but how could that be?

Alex, the blacksmith, noticed Stephen lingering in the road, and came back to him.

"Is there a problem, sir?" he asked.

"There is always a problem," Stephen grumbled at the interruption of his thoughts. "No matter what you do, there is always a problem."

"Do you think the killers really were those fellows with the wagon?"

"I am sure of it. The boy isn't their first victim." When Alex did not comment, Stephen went on, "They kidnapped and probably killed my niece."

"And you're after them. That's why you're here," Alex said with sudden understanding. "I wish there was something I could do to help. Obadiah was my cousin, the poor lad."

Stephen's eyes fell from Etnam Street Gate to Alex. "There is something you can do."

Stephen tied the horses to an apple tree in the priory orchard, which lay to the east of town between the embankment and the River Lugg. The three-quarter moon was a pale smudge behind the overcast, and in the resulting dark, the trees were faint silhouettes and the embankment and palisade a looming presence that was sensed rather than seen.

He groped his way toward the embankment, hands before his face holding up the iron pry bar Alex had given him to deflect the low-hanging branches of the apple trees. It smelled fresh here, of grass and flowers, the welcome odors of summer. Then the breeze shifted and brought the stench of the town: wood smoke and privy, for the most part, with a delicate undercurrent of horse manure.

For a moment he thought he heard something moving through the grass behind him. He paused to listen. The sound did not repeat itself, and he dismissed it as an animal or the wind.

Stephen located the ditch when he put out a foot expecting hard ground and it touched air. This nearly caused a fall, but he recovered without having to suffer an embarrassing tumble to the bottom. Town ditches were supposed to be kept clear, but were often used to dispose of unwanted rubbish, and Stephen did not want to show up for his appointment covered in offal.

He followed the ditch north until he came to a wooden footbridge and a breach in the embankment. He crossed the bridge to a sally port the monks used to reach their orchard outside town.

A head appeared on the wall above, a dark oval against a lighter sky.

"Is that you, sir?" Alex asked.

"It is," Stephen whispered. It was unlikely that there was a watch nearby and the monks of the priory slept in a dormitory far across another orchard inside the wall. But he felt compelled to keep his voice down nonetheless, even if Alex did not.

"I won't be but a moment," Alex said.

There was a long pause and then thumping as Alex removed the bar to the gate, and the gate swung open.

"There you go, sir," Alex said, holding open the gate door. "Best of luck. Careful of the watch. There's a couple of boys about. But you should see their lanterns well enough to avoid them."

"Thank you, Alex."

Stephen rested the pry bar on a shoulder and climbed the wooden steps set to the grassy embankment while Alex shut the gate and settled to the ground just inside to await Stephen's return.

The Bear Wagon

It had been a long time since Stephen had visited Leominster and he had trouble remembering the layout of the streets. Off the main ones the lanes twisted and turned, making for a warren that could confuse even people who lived here. But he knew where the main ones were and where the gaol was. The easiest way to get there was down Etnam Street to South Street and up to the Corn Market. So he walked south along the palisade toward Etnam Street Gate.

Presently he bumped into the priory's wall, which ran up the embankment to the wall walk at the top, where there was a gate. Stephen passed through the gate and paused for a moment for a look around. Then he descended to the path that ran along the foot of the embankment to avoid having to use the stairs at the gate tower, where there was likely to be at least a pair of wardens.

Heedful of the wards in the gate tower, he crept by it when he got there, although his stealth was not enough to avoid startling a cat, which howled and scrambled off across the yard to the right, alarming a dog in the next garden which had slept through Stephen's passage but now barked frantically. Stephen cringed and knelt by the fence, hoping to be invisible against it in case a ward in the tower happened to look for the source of the disturbance. Nothing stirred in the tower, although Stephen wished someone would throttle the dog.

He padded round the corner onto Etnam Street. It was a broad street, the houses lying shoulder to shoulder into the distance. There would be nowhere to hide if the watch made its appearance. Heart in his mouth at that possibility, Stephen jogged toward the end where Etnam ran into South Street and ended.

About halfway, he stumbled on a pile of unseen rubbish that someone had dumped in the street. He avoided plowing into the ground with his face only by an instinctive shoulder roll remembered from his wrestling days. But his pry bar went clattering into the dark.

Stephen scrambled around, searching for the bar. As he found it, he heard chuckling from a first-floor window on the other side of the street.

"What are you up to in such a hurry?" a voice asked.

"If I don't hurry, she won't be there," Stephen said, looking up for the source of the voice as he climbed to his feet, fearful that the voice would call for the watch.

"Ah," the voice replied, "well, give the girl my regards, whoever she is."

"Thanks, I will."

"Mind the watch. They went by a while ago. No telling where they are now."

Stephen reached South Street without further mishaps or conversations and turned toward the Corn Market, which lay not far ahead on, appropriately, Corn Street, which met South Street just beyond a broad avenue coming in from the west. Corn Street, little wider than an alley, emptied into the marketplace that was neither wide nor broad as marketplaces go, but it did well for a town Leominster's size.

As Stephen reached the market, the clouds parted and moonlight illuminated the expanse, the houses forming its walls, and the guildhall to the left. There was a set of stocks before the guildhall. Alex had said William was on display in the stocks for the edification and enjoyment of anyone who happened by. It wasn't often that a local lord, even a minor one of no account like William, could be set out for whatever humiliation townspeople thought was appropriate. But it seemed that William had been taken in for the night. This was bad for Stephen since it meant he had to break into the guildhall now, but good for William. Stephen had spent a night in the stocks once himself and knew it was not an experience one could relish.

The guildhall was typical of guildhalls. Its first floor jutted out for some distance, supported by timber pillars to form a porch. People used the porch to shelter from the rain and on market days it was the most favored spot for vendors because of this fact, commanding the highest tolls.

The Bear Wagon

The merchants and craftsmen of Leominster apparently thought well of themselves because they had supplied the hall with a grand door consisting of two carved door panels rather than the merely serviceable one. Stephen lifted the latch. It was locked.

He tried one of the ground floor window shutters. It was not latched, but when it opened, it revealed that the window was blocked by three wooden bars, each as thick as his wrist. No doubt they were there to deter people such as himself, for guildhalls often held the valuables of the various guilds that met there.

Stephen stood there, perplexed about what to do now. He could probably snap the bars with the pry bar, but that might produce a lot of noise. He had an acquaintance who was a master burglar and he asked himself what that fellow would do. But that burglar's habit was to climb to the roof and, using ropes, get into an upper story window, which usually wasn't barred. That approach was beyond Stephen's abilities. There had to be another way.

Then he remembered that the ordinary burglar employed a simple, direct approach. Stephen knelt below the window he had opened and probed the plaster-covered wicker between the timbers supporting the structure. The wicker was dry and hard, but he knew that it was but a veneer to keep out the weather, and that it would yield to a blow and that beneath it there was a lattice of wooden wands filling the space between the timbers.

He looked around to make sure there was no one watching from any of the windows overlooking the marketplace and raised the pry bar. His heart pounded. He would not have wanted to call it fear, but that's what it felt like.

At that instant, he heard voices coming from a small lane that emptied into the marketplace on the left. Yellow light showed faintly at the mouth of the lane, growing brighter with every moment — the watch!

Stephen closed the shutters and dashed toward an alley coming into the market from the east as quickly as his bad foot permitted. He crouched in the shadow afforded by a cobbler's shop at the lip of the alley and watched two men carrying a lantern emerge from the other lane. His plan was to wait until they passed, and then return to his work. But the watchmen sat down on the platform supporting the stocks. One of them swung a cloth bag onto his lap and fumbled in it, producing an object he handed to the other watchman. The fellow receiving the object took a bite out of it and handed to the other, who did the same. One of them said something that Stephen could not make out. The other watchman laughed. It looked like the two intended to remain there for some time.

Stephen chaffed with impatience, but told himself to wait them out. But half an hour went by and they did not move. One of them lay back and put his hat over his face against the intermittent moonlight. Watchmen were not supposed to sleep on duty, but everyone suspected that they did so. Here was the proof. There was no telling now how long they'd be; half the night most likely.

Out of mounting desperation, Stephen was considering knocking the two watchmen on the head with the pry bar when a slight breeze at his back brought the scent of apple trees. This led to the realization that there was an orchard at the end of the alley. Of course! The priory's orchard! This in turn led to the thought that perhaps the guildhall had a back garden that abutted the orchard.

He padded down the alley. His heart lightened to see there was an orchard here that stretched into the dimness of the night.

Wattle fences separated the gardens of the houses surrounding the marketplace from the orchard. Stephen crept along the fences until he saw that his deduction was almost true: the guildhall's garden did not border the orchard, but it could be reached by crossing a garden that did. Wait until he told Gilbert of this brilliant deduction. He would simmer in Gilbert's admiration.

He hopped the fence, crossed the yard, careful not to crush any of the vegetables in the garden plot that stood in the way; hopped another fence, and there he was. Success never felt so good.

Tables and benches were scattered about the garden around a bowling pitch and he fell over an unseen bench as the moon slid behind some clouds.

Stephen picked himself up, glad he had not broken his neck, and listened for signs that he had been detected. There were none: the whisper of the wind, a dog barking in the distance, the rustling of some small creature in the grass.

There was a set of double doors here like those in front, and as elaborately carved. He tried them, a formality. The latch jiggered but the door did not budge.

Stephen set to work on the wall beside the door. He battered the clay and the wicker with an end of the pry bar. Breaching the wicker made some racket but no one seemed to notice. He had heard of burglars doing this while there were people sleeping inside a house, but he could not imagine how they had got away with it. The wicker was dry and frail and within moments he had made a hole big enough for him to slip into the hall.

When he poked his head through the hole, however, he discovered his progress impeded by a pile of sacks on a palette. It was a struggle to push the sacks out of the way before he could get through.

Although it was pitch dark, Stephen sensed he was in a pantry. He fumbled about until he found the door, which opened to a passageway connecting the hall in the front of the building with the back doors.

Stephen had been assured by Alex that there was a room at the rear of the hall used to house miscreants. Alex had not been clear on exactly where it lay, since he had never been inside the guildhall, there being no guild for blacksmiths in the town.

"William!" Stephen hissed. "Can you hear me?"

There was no response, and he hissed again.

After the third time, William's muffled voice came from somewhere to the right. "Stephen? Is that you?"

"Where are you?"

"In the fucking gaol, stupid."

"But where is the fucking gaol?"

"Over here, you idiot."

"But where is here? Just count to ten or something. If you remember how."

"And why should I do that?"

"So I can find you by the sound."

William began to count, and rather loudly too. The noise alarmed Stephen and he said, "Keep your damned voice down, for Christ's sweet sake. Do you want to awaken the neighbors?"

"You said to count. I'm counting."

Nonetheless, the volume diminished. Stephen followed the sound through a cracked door and across a chamber.

"You can stop now," he said when he reached a closed and padlocked door. "I know you're about to run out of numbers anyway."

Stephen applied the pry bar to the latch. The nails securing the latch to the door came free with a groan.

In some gaols, prisoners were further secured by a neck collar and chained to a wall. Stephen was relieved to find this was not the case, for William emerged from the room as soon as the latch came free.

"Come on," Stephen said.

He had been seething to get out as soon as he entered the hall, so he did not swerve into the pantry. He headed directly to the rear doors to the garden. The door was barred rather than locked. Stephen pulled up the bar, set it against a wall so as not to make noise by throwing it down, and stepped into the garden.

. . . and came face-to-face with a stocky man slapping a cudgel with a palm. A similar fellow straightened up from examining the hole Stephen had made in the wall.

"What have we here?" asked the first ward.

"If you know what's good for you, you'll get out of the way," Stephen said.

"Fancy words," the warden said.

He sneered and raised his cudgel.

Stephen kicked him in the groin, then punched him in the face. The ward fell over backward.

Stephen swung the pry bar from his left at the other ward who raised his own cudgel to deflect it. Before the weapons met, he changed the strike's direction so that it came upward from the right. The tip of the pry bar caught the ward on the chin and he went down without a sound.

"Not bad," William said from the doorway.

"Better than you could do." Stephen handed William his utility knife. "Cut some strips from their shirts. Tie and gag them. We can't have them raising the alarm when they wake up."

"It's a miracle they haven't raised the hue and cry already," William said, bending to the task.

"They probably wanted to be sure first. People get upset when they're awakened for nothing. But then why should that occur to you? You never care a whit about other people's feelings."

"What's that supposed to mean?"

"Exactly as it sounds. Hurry up there."

"I'm hurrying, damn you."

"I just pulled your ass out of gaol. You could be thankful."

"If you had stopped them from arresting me, that wouldn't have been necessary."

"I thought a day in the stocks would do you good."

"You're enjoying this."

"Well, perhaps not this part."

"I thought so." William stood up. "There. Where to now?"

"This way."

Stephen headed for the fence.

The overcast had broken and there was enough light from a three-quarter moon to see a way through the orchard. The tower of the priory church, visible over the treetops, told them where to go. It seemed only moments before they reached the embankment and followed the wall to the sally port, but Stephen was out of breath from the dash and his bad foot hurt.

"All's right with the world, sir?" Alex asked, rising from a shadow.

"Who's that?" William growled.

"A friend," Stephen said.

"I didn't think you had any friends in Leominster."

"I'm an affable fellow, unlike you. I have friends everywhere. Thank you, Alex. We best be away. We ran into the watch and had to tie them up. Since it was William here who did the deed, they should be free by now and raising the alarm."

"No one was hurt, I hope," Alex said. "All those boys are friends of mine, minus a cousin or two."

"Knocks on the head and probably wounded pride. But that's it. I was careful not to kill anyone."

"That's considerate of you, sir. I'd hate to be going to more funerals."

They went through the sally port and crossed the footbridge to the orchard beyond the ditch.

Stephen was grateful for the moon since it made finding the horses much easier. They were still there, only a few trees away. Now all they had to do was get on the road to Bromyard and put this place behind them. There would be a cost to what he had just done, but the time for payment would not come until later. He would worry about what to do about that then.

Stephen handed the pry bar to Alex. "Thanks for your help. You best get back before you're missed."

"Glad to be of service. Hope you catch them bastards, sir. Give 'em hell for me and poor Obadiah."

"Obadiah?" William asked. "Who's Obadiah?"

"I'll tell you about it later," Stephen said.

Alex had taken three steps toward the Bromyard Road when a voice snarled "Now!" and six shadows rose from the grass only a few feet away. Moonlight glinted on the swords in their hands. Alex ran off at the sight of them like a jackrabbit startled by hounds, but he was ignored as the six advanced on Stephen and William, who was just settling into his saddle.

Stephen stood frozen, surprised and momentarily uncertain what to make of this sudden development. The last thing he expected was to be assaulted by men with swords in an orchard in the dead of night where no one had any business being. He felt weak, as he always did just before a fight.

For butchery was what they intended and careful butchery at that. They did not come straight at Stephen and William. They fanned out in a semi-circle to surround the two, with the biggest and most threatening of the bunch coming straight for Stephen: the others were to hem him in so that he could not get away and to cut him down from behind if the opportunity arose. But it was the big one, slipping toward him with graceful confidence, feet swishing in the grass, who was the greatest threat.

Before the circle closed, William drove his mount through the gap. None of the assailants tried to stop him.

Stephen had left his sword hanging from the pommel of the saddle. He seized the sword, feeling as though his legs would give way. But once he had his hand on the grip, his mind cleared and his fear evaporated. He entered the empty place where thoughts were fleeting and usually impediments to action. There was only striking and parrying and stepping as the need required, as if his body acted on its own, devoid of any direction from him.

He turned to the man approaching from his right. Taking a big step, Stephen thrust at the man's face. The attacker parried with his long edge, rendering the thrust a failure. It would have been good had it landed, but almost before the ting of the blades' collision, Stephen whipped his sword around to cut from his left, and the assailant's head fell into the grass just as another head had done not long ago in another fight.

Without a pause, Stephen let the momentum of the downward cut carry him around. Sensing rather than seeing a cut at his head from another attacker now at his back, he crouched and cut backhanded at this fellow's leg. Stephen's sword passed through the leg as if it had not been there: he felt not even a jar as the edge severed muscle, tendon and bone.

Had his consciousness been working, he might have thought that was two down; only four to go. But he made no such calculation. He only saw the fellow beyond the man who had lost his head advancing at him as he knew the others were rushing at him now from behind.

He ran at the man in front of him, raising his sword above his shoulder for a wrath cut as if he meant to make a wild, panicked attack. The fellow proved himself to be something of a swordsman, for as Stephen cut downward, he both parried with his long edge and pivoted out of the way. Stephen had seen this move before; he had actually used it himself a few times. And he knew that after the parry would come a thrust, a mere holding out of the blade so that he impaled himself on the point.

This was a technique that Spanish swordsmen valued. Stephen and his friend Rodrigo had spent many hours in the yard working to perfect it because of its elegance, for it was not something a person did naturally. They had also developed a way to defeat it; or rather, Rodrigo had done so one scorching afternoon while the sun was high and they were drenched with sweat.

And for the first time Stephen put Rodrigo's idea into practice. He checked his cut, which he had intended to do anyway. But rather than making a thrust of his own, a thrust that would have missed because of the attacker's pivot, he parried the enemy's blade with his left hand, punched him in the eye with the cross of his sword and then cut him to the head as he fell.

To Stephen's surprise, the survivors checked up at the death of the third man. He had expected them to press forward. After all, three-to-one odds was death in the end for an unarmored victim.

But the big man glanced behind at a figure approaching in the dark.

It was William. He had not deserted Stephen after all.

William had his sword before him and a saddle blanket wrapped around his left forearm as a shield of sorts. A thick saddle blanket could absorb a sword cut although the wielder would have a terrible bruise. But he'd still have the arm.

"Let's go," the big man said.

"What about —?" one of the others asked.

"Let 'em lie."

The three attackers backed away then ran into the dark. Within moments there came the thud of horses' hooves on the turf as they rode away.

"I thought you'd run away," Stephen said.

"It was a clever ruse," William said. "To distract them. Otherwise, you'd never have managed that. We're even, then?"

"I suppose we are."

"Good. No thank you is required, by the way."

William turned about and headed in search of his horse.

Chapter 10

Bromfield Priory had no separate accommodations for visitors. They were given space at one end of the monk's dormitory, so two priory servants had to be summoned to carry Harry up the stairs to the long hall where the monks themselves slept.

"We had a cottage," one of the servants gasped in explanation between huffs and puffs as they struggled up the narrow stairway, "but it burnt down last November."

"With all the visitors we get to the Lady, you'd think they'd replace it," said the other servant. "But the prior keeps complaining that we don't have the money."

"You don't have to do this," Harry protested at this treatment. "I can sleep in the cart. I've a tarp and a blanket. That's all I need."

"No trouble," puffed the first servant. "Although I'll say, you are a bit of a load. It's like you're made of lead or something."

"Hard as stone, this fellow," grunted the other one as they reached the first floor and the dormitory at long last.

"You can put me down," Harry said. "I can get along on flat ground as well as anyone."

"I doubt that," said the first servant. But the two men lowered Harry to the floor with obvious relief.

"I'll just put your things away for you," the second man said, for he carried Harry's satchel as well. "You'll be over here behind the curtain."

The curtain spoken of was a series of blankets draped over a rope stretching from one wall to another to the right. Harry followed the satchel bearer through a gap in the blankets. Six beds sat close together in this portion of the dormitory.

The satchel carrier put the bag on the nearest bed. "No talking after lights out. You're not allowed to disturb the brothers."

"I'll do my best," Harry said. "But I find conversations with myself fascinating, as you would too if you cared to linger. I hope they don't mind my snoring, as well."

"If we get any complaints we'll be back to toss you out."

"That is such a relief. I would hate to be a burden."

"You're already one, son. I'd have said a small one before we lugged you up the stairs."

They left, and Harry turned his attention to the bed. He had never slept in a bed before. All his life it had been a pallet of straw on the ground or a pile of hay and a blanket. The prospect of an actual bed made him giddy. He prodded the mattress, which was suspended from the bedframe by a lattice of ropes: it was filled with straw. Well, not that much luxury.

Harry pulled himself up, removed the padded leather gloves that protected his hands from the rough ground and leaned back on his satchel, which had to make do as a pillow since the bed did not come with one. There was no one about to needle for amusement and nothing to do but wait for supper time. He hated being bored. At least when he had been a beggar at Broad Gate there had been Gip the witless gate ward to pester or the passersby who refused charity. But here there was nothing but the cooing of pigeons on the window sill and before long they went away. He twiddled his thumbs for a while, his thoughts jumping randomly from one thing to another.

The two servants would have thought he was joking when he said he enjoyed conversations with himself, but that had been the truth. He had spent many happy hours debating himself on this point of theology or that, discussing the politics of the day or ruminating on the faults of people he knew; sometimes he did this silently but other times aloud, playing each part to the full as much as his lack of legs allowed. But nothing arose from the depths of his consciousness as a suitable topic.

Eventually, he dug into the satchel for one of his knives and a block of wood he was fashioning into the likeness of the girl who had drowned at the weir. As he had only his memory to rely on, he wasn't sure if it would turn out to look like her. But he wanted to give it a try. A suggestion of the face already showed in the block. Another hour or two and he might have it.

A bell rang from somewhere in the cloister. As it was the time decent people sat down for supper, Harry surmised it was the call to the evening meal. He expected the two servants to return for him, but no one appeared.

After some time, he deduced that he would not be fetched after all. There was nothing for it but to head to the dining hall unassisted.

Harry sat at the top of the stairs, a bit anxious at having to descend them. He had never negotiated such a long flight before. He took a deep breath and lowered himself to the top step. He continued this way, arms growing wearier, until he reached the halfway point when a misjudgment sent him tumbling to the bottom. He lay there waiting for the pain to subside, glad he had not cracked his head.

He was only feet from the dining hall when Bertran appeared in the doorway. Bertran knelt beside him.

"I'm sorry," Bertran said. "I gave orders that you be fetched for supper. But I'm having a bit of trouble being obeyed, it seems."

"Not to worry. I enjoyed my tumble down the stairs. Nothing like a good fall to get the blood flowing."

Harry noticed Bertran's right arm protruding from the sleeve of his robe; or what should have been his right arm. It was cut off about halfway between the wrist and elbow.

Bertran saw that he had been found out. He raised the damaged arm slightly. "Your friend did this to me."

"You didn't parry well?" Harry asked, guessing that Stephen had lopped off the arm with a sword.

"Have you heard the story?"

"Story? Stephen never mentioned you."

Bertran's mouth turned down. "Parrying had nothing to do with it. Wait here."

Bertran retreated to the dining hall and came out with a wooden platter holding a half loaf of bread, a cup of ale, a small half round of cheese and a cube of ham. He put the platter on Harry's lap and sat on the ground beside him.

"That's very unprior-like," Harry said through a mouthful of bread. "A proper prior lords it over people."

"I have only been prior since last autumn. I'm still learning my way."

"Well, don't let them see you like that. They'll be even less inclined to obey you. Why won't they obey you?"

"They resent my election. I was forced on them by the bishop."

"I thought being a monk was all about obedience."

"It is, sort of." Bertran glanced toward the dining hall. "Edwin's scheming for a way to unseat me. He has all the others behind him, but one."

"And he seemed such a pleasant fellow, too. At least he's out in the open about his distaste. Not trying to stab you in the back."

"He is a man without subtlety. He has many gifts, but that's not one of them."

"That's a polite way of saying he's thick as a plank of wood."

Bertran grinned. "I'm told that diplomacy lies at the soul of leadership."

Harry scoffed. "What idiot told you that? Leadership is about instilling fear. Have a few lashed. The rest will fall into line."

"I doubt that. Here, you see? You are the friend of my enemy, yet I serve you with courtesy."

"It's because you want something. Although I am grateful for supper. What do you want?"

Bertran stood up. "Come with me. I promise our conversation will not be idle from now on."

Harry polished off the ale, wiped his chin, pulled his leather gloves back on and hurried after Bertran as fast as a legless man is able to do so.

The prior reached a door in the east range near the church long before Harry and waited for him. He held the door open while Harry plumped inside. The door opened into a corridor where another door gave access to a dim chamber to the right. Bertran went through it. When Harry made it through that door, he realized he was in the south transept of the church. They crossed the nave to the north transept.

There on the floor was a carving of a woman taller than Harry. It had broken into four pieces. The paint was old and flaking off: black for the hair, blue for the cloak and white for the undergarment. And red, faded to pink, for the woman's lips.

The prior pointed to an iron form attached to the stone wall. "We came in one morning for Mass and found it on the floor. Apparently, it had fallen. Edwin declared that it was a sign of disapproval from the Lady Mary to my selection as prior."

Harry prodded the carving. "I'll give you that the wood is old and dry, but this damage couldn't have happened from a fall."

"Well, I thought not, but I am not an expert on wood. And I didn't want to point fingers at anyone."

"Sure you would. You just don't have enough of them."

"Pointing fingers would not solve my problem."

"No, you'll need a miracle for that."

"Well, I'd like a miracle, but I'll settle for a new statue."

"The sooner the better, I suppose."

"Yes."

"And you'd hire me, the friend of your enemy to do it?"

Bertran removed a small carving from his pouch. "Did you make this?"

It was one of Harry's likenesses of the dead girl from Saint Laurence's Church. "I did."

"It was left here by a visitor as an offering. I had no idea what it was or of whom it was. It is beautiful work."

"Of course, you did. Everybody in Ludlow knows that's my work. But you already knew I was Stephen's friend, so you did not come to me."

Bertran sighed, indicating his confession.

"But you're desperate now," Harry said.

Bertran gestured toward an object lost in the dimness against a wall. "We hired a carver from Shrewsbury, but as you can see, his work was not satisfactory."

Harry swung toward the object. It was a partly completed carving of the saint, or at least an attempt at one. But the eyes had not come out even and the nose was hooked and crudely fashioned, and the face bloated and overbroad. It gave off a sinister air rather than one inviting a feeling of awe and admiration. A statue like that would invite mockery and derision if put on display, and drive worshippers away.

"I cannot understand how he could produce such a monstrosity," Bertran said. "His work was good, what I saw of it, and he came with the best references."

"Too much drink, probably," Harry speculated. "So why the urgency?"

"The bishop is coming in four days to hear the brothers' complaints about my leadership," Bertran said.

"And you think a new statue of the Lady will put his mind at rest?"

"I had hoped it might make a difference."

"Then you are a fool. You best spend your time preparing your accounts and your arguments."

"Still, I would like another."

"Have you thought of glue? It's a wonder substance for broken things."

"The damage will show. It must be a new statue. Can you do it?"

"Child's play," Harry said.

"I think it is more than that, but I take your answer as a yes."

"There is the issue of payment. A small matter for the likes of you, but a big matter for my short self."

"I'll give you one pound if you make another —" Bertran waved at the unhappy carving "— by the time the bishop arrives."

Harry could barely breathe at this proposal. One pound was an impossible sum of money. He could buy twenty sheep with that amount if he had a mind to. He dared to hope that much wealth might even be enough to overcome Edith's opposition to a marriage to Jennie. "I'll not be responsible for painting her. Someone else will have to do that."

"Done."

Chapter 11

It rained during the night after Stephen and William left Leominster, which made sleep nearly impossible when they stopped to rest the horses several hours before dawn.

By dawn the rain passed, leaving them chilled and damp and shrouded by a fog so thick that when standing on one side of the road it was impossible to see the other.

Thus, they mistook a lane for the road when it swerved as English roads were prone to do without any obvious reason, and went down it for half an hour before they realized their mistake as it dwindled to a footpath, and had to double back. So it was a couple hours after sunrise before they bumped into Bromyard at last.

The fog had lifted only a little so that the air felt leaden and the houses lying more than a few feet from the roadway were only vague shapes when they were visible at all. They saw a few people here and there going about their business and heard muffled voices, but apart from this infrequent activity it seemed like Stephen and William were the only people in the whole world. Had a church bell not peeled ahead, they might well have missed Bromyard altogether.

The only sign they had of the town's main street, which was one of their objectives, was a yawning gap to the right. The sound of a woman arguing with a pottery maker over the price of a pitcher provided further proof they were in the right place.

They passed the potter's shop where the woman and the potter paused in their dispute to watch them draw by and resumed when they had gone a safe distance, the appearance of armed men always being a matter for suspicion and worry, and Stephen and William were especially grim.

They had not spoken to each other since the events outside Leominster, which was just as well as far as Stephen was concerned. The fog did nothing for his mood.

The main street descended while curving to the left and dead-ending at another road. There was a field across the road, and within it outlines of the town's market cross, a round wooden structure open to the air that resembled a tent. A figure emerged from the shelter of the market cross and jogged toward them.

It was Herb.

"My lord, I —" Herb started to say but stopped and gulped at the expression on William's face.

"We could have used you back there," William growled.

Stephen raised a hand. "I sent him off with Gilbert — to track the wagon."

William grunted. "Where is it, then?"

"I don't know, my lord," Herb said.

"Pppphhh," William spat.

"Any sign of it?" Stephen asked.

"There might be, sir."

"Where?"

Herb pointed toward the south. "That way."

Herb fetched his horse and led them down the road into the fog. There were a few houses here, most behind wicker fences with large front gardens, but they gave way to countryside after about a hundred yards.

Gilbert was standing in the roadway at a point where a lane curved off toward the west.

"Ah," Gilbert said as Stephen and William halted, "you made it. I was beginning to worry."

"What have you got?" Stephen asked.

"We canvassed the shops on the high street," Gilbert said. "Most people remember the wagon coming through town. It did not stop at any of the taverns —"

"I wouldn't have expected that," William snorted. "Eleven miles is only a half day's travel."

"Well, begging your pardon, sir," Gilbert said. "I'd have put it at perhaps three quarters of a day. And fellows like that tend to cherish their refreshment."

"I'm not interested in your opinion."

"Of course, you aren't, sir. But Stephen might be. Aren't you, Stephen?"

"I haven't heard one yet, but in principle, yes."

"Right, of course. Here you go, then, I think the wagon stayed the night there." Gilbert pointed toward the field at his back.

"This is doing us no good," William said. "They're getting away."

"Let's have a look anyway." Stephen slid from the stallion and followed Gilbert through a gap where the fence had been torn down. Deep ruts from wagon or cart wheels were visible in the gap, along with the hoof marks of many horses. There were quite a few dog prints in the mud as well.

Gibb was squatting by the remains of a fire which he had been poking with a stick. He discarded the stick and stood up while Stephen squatted by the fire. It was clear from raindrop pockmarks on the ashes that it had been put out by last night's rain. He pressed a finger into the ashes. At bottom they were still warm. All about on the ground was further evidence of wagon, cart, horses and dogs.

"Good to see you are well, sir," Gibb said. "Is his lordship …?"

"Well, if you don't count a day's discomfort and injured pride," Stephen said as he rose.

"Is he … out of sorts?"

"Yes, and he's already snapped at Herb and Gilbert. You might want to make yourself small."

This did not prove to be possible, as William strode through the gap in the fence to join them. But despite a sour glance at Gibb, he did not say anything to the servant.

"A wagon and a cart, I'd say," Stephen said to William. "Looks like they stopped here for the night."

"And were joined by those fellows on horses who rode away at Leominster," Gilbert dared to add.

"What of it?" William said.

"What of it?" Stephen asked. "It looks like the boys who stole your horses rode off for a little robbery somewhere, while the wagon waited for them here."

"I'd tend to agree, given what we know about their character," Gilbert said.

"Not a hasty conclusion, then?" Stephen grinned.

"Hasty, but not without reason this time."

"You say that only because I've confirmed your guess."

"It wasn't a guess, any more than yours was. I do hope no one was killed."

"I wouldn't put money on that," Stephen said.

"Nor I, sir," Gibb said.

"Shut up," William said. "Servants are not entitled to an opinion."

"Sorry, my lord."

"So," Stephen said. "We know they came here and stayed the night. Which means that wagon left only this morning, probably headed for Worcester because that's where this road goes. They're only a couple of hours ahead of us. And wagons are slow. We should catch them today at last."

The road to Worcester crossed the River Frome a short distance from the campsite. There was only a ford at the bottom of riverbanks that rose at least ten feet above water that was ankle-deep. The river bottom was mud and rocks and so did not reveal the sign of anyone's passage, but the road on the other side was littered with tracks not only of wagon wheels, dogs and horses, but men, for it looked as though the wagon had needed a helping push to rise from the river. These tracks were fresh and well defined, unobscured by traffic to the town. This reinforced Stephen's conviction that it would not be long before they caught up with the killers.

Stephen went into a trot which he kept up for a mile before lapsing to a walk so as not to tire the horses. They would never catch up if he pressed the horses too hard.

The fog began to lift, revealing a countryside of gentle hills on either side of the road, with fields stretching to hilltops capped with trees.

Stephen fell back to one of the packhorses, where he retrieved his gambeson and mail shirt, which he put on, and then his arming cap, helmet and shield. William did the same with only a bark or two to Gibb who was leading the packhorse.

By the time Stephen was settled into his war gear they had covered a half mile, so he broke into a trot again. This was the way of a soldier's cavalry march, alternating walks and trots, not the headlong canter.

Presently, they passed someone's fish pond on the left of the road and came around a gentle bend — and there to Stephen's astonishment was the bear wagon, just as it had been described: faded red paint on the body of it and green trimming. It was up against a hedge at the side of the road.

Stephen swung his shield off his back, spurred the stallion and drew his sword. William did the same.

But there were no enemies to strike down. In fact, there were several corpses lying in the road and the grass along it. The wagon itself had been abandoned. No horses stood at the traces and the rear door was open.

"What the devil?" William said, looking around in bewilderment at all the dead.

Stephen dismounted, counting the bodies: at least eight men and two women that he could see. He knelt by one of them, a prosperous merchant of some sort by the quality of his clothes. He had been killed with a single blow to the crown of his head that penetrated his skull to the eyebrows. Stephen went round the others. They had all died the same way, cut down by axes and swords. One man had his arm cut off just above the wrist as well, the sort of wound you saw on an inexperienced man who raised the arm in a futile effort to parry a cut from above.

"Another robbery," Gilbert said as he joined Stephen and William.

"He has a remarkable ability for stating the obvious," William growled.

"He only offers the observation because it might have eluded you," Stephen said.

"Why do they kill them?" Gilbert asked in shock at the scene, dismounting. "Why don't they just take people's money and be done with it?"

"Because they enjoy the killing," Stephen said.

Gilbert shuddered. "I refuse to believe there are such men."

"Then you would be blind," William said, "in addition to your other faults."

"What do you know of such things?" Gilbert said. "You've never been out in the world. You've spent your life in the comfort of your manor."

William advanced on Gilbert, seizing him by the collar and raising his sword. "I've had enough of your impudence! None of your ilk speaks to me that way!"

A few swift strides and Stephen caught William's sword arm.

"You forget," Stephen said to Gilbert. "He's lost his daughter to them."

Gilbert stepped back as William's grip relaxed. "I did forget. I'm sorry. I truly am."

"There is no pain so sharp," Stephen said, releasing William's arm.

"What do you know of it?" William asked. "You've not lost a child."

"I lost a wife," Stephen said, although he had not formally married Taresa before she died, a thing he regretted. "That is close enough."

"Wives," William spat, "they can be replaced."

"Elysande would be troubled to hear you say that."

"She cares no more for me than I for her."

"That is sad," Gilbert murmured.

Just then Herb dashed up and gasped, "My lord! Sir! There's one alive!"

"Where?" Stephen asked.

Herb pointed to a spot beyond the hedge where he had repaired to relieve himself.

Stephen broke through the hedge. On the other side, a young man lay on his side, hands clutching his stomach.

Frightened grey eyes locked with Stephen's. "Please help me," the young man whispered.

"We will do what we can," Stephen said. He pulled the young man's hands aside and lifted the hem of his shirt. There was a slit in his belly as long as a sword blade was wide. It wasn't bleeding much, but stab wounds usually didn't on the outside.

"What happened?" Stephen asked.

The story came out in disjointed fits, but pieced together is was a sad tale. The young man, whose name was Mabb, and his wife were part of a traveling party from Worcester on their way to Leominster and thence to Shelburgh in the west. He was a journeyman carpenter looking for work. They had come up to the bear wagon and the horsemen with it and exchanged hellos and the horsemen had attacked the traveling party. It had only taken a few moments.

"My wife," Mabb gasped. "One of them grabbed her by the hair and tried to ride away with her. I managed to pull him from his horse but one of the others stabbed me."

"Can you remember what any of them looked like?" Stephen asked when the story was finished.

Mabb shook his head. "It's all a blur. There is one, though. I think he was the leader. Tall, big, high forehead as if losing his hair. The others called him Huck." He grasped Stephen's forearm. "Did you find my wife? Did you find Eloise? Is she dead, too?"

"What did she look like?" Gilbert asked from the gap in the hedge.

"She is so beautiful," Mabb whispered. "So sweet. I do not deserve her."

"She is not blonde by any chance?" Gilbert asked.

"What does that have to do with anything?" William said.

"It may be important," Gilbert said, undeterred by William's hostile tone.

Mabb nodded. "She was very fair."

"I think she lives, Mabb," Gilbert said. "There is no body matching your description among the dead. Only two older women."

"Praise God!" Mabb said.

"There is something you need to see," Gilbert said to Stephen.

Gilbert led Stephen to the bear wagon. The stench coming from within the wagon was awful: a toxic cloud of shit and piss as bad as any gaol. The stink was at its worst around a bucket in the near corner.

Stephen could see why the wagon had been abandoned. The right front wheel had struck a deep pothole and the axle had snapped.

"No bear was kept in here," Gilbert said.

"From the smell I would tend to agree," Stephen said.

"And there is this." Gilbert reached inside the doorway and brought out a red ribbon, which he handed to Stephen. It was badly soiled so that he dared only hold an end. But he could tell it was silk embroidered with silver thread.

William, who had followed, snatched the ribbon from Stephen's hand with a cry.

"What is it?" Stephen asked.

William trembled. "It belongs to Ida! I gave it to her at Christmas! She always wore it!"

"She was in this wagon," Gilbert said. "And now she is not. What color was her hair?"

"Blonde. Why?" William asked.

Gilbert gazed down the road toward Worcester. "Then, if you will allow my opinion, I think she still lives. She was taken away, along with Mabb's wife."

"There were other girls in the wagon, too," Stephen said, apprehension dawning at last.

"Yes," Gilbert said. "These fellows, led by this Huck, have been driving about the countryside with this bear wagon stealing girls, fair-haired haired girls. But to what purpose?"

"To sell them," Stephen said. He did not go on, but the others knew what he meant.

"Dear God!" William cried. "Not my Ida! We'll never catch them now."

"The good news is, she still lives," Stephen said.

By this time Gibb and Herb had carried Mabb out to the road. Stephen knelt by Mabb again.

"Mabb," Stephen asked, "you didn't happen to overhear where they were going, did you?"

Mabb's brow furrowed. "I did hear someone say it was still a long way to London."

"A long way to London," Stephen murmured to himself. He stood up.

"What will become of me, sir?" Mabb cried. "You won't just leave me here!"

"No," Stephen said. "One of our boys will stay behind to help you."

He crossed to one of the packhorses where he dug out a wineskin from William's belongings. He tossed the skin to Gibb. "It's not for you. Wash the wound in this and bandage it. Make sure he keeps it clean. And get him back to the priory at Bromyard right away. The rest of us — we're going to London."

Chapter 12

Harry's cart was brought around at dawn to carry him, his toolbox and the ugly, half-completed statue of Saint Mary to a small hut by the river where a bridge crossed to the mill on the south side.

A woman with a baby in her arms came to the door at Oswald's call.

"I've brought you another guest, Ellie," Oswald said.

"Do we have to feed him, too?" Ellie said, shifting the baby to her other hip.

"Nah," Oswald replied. "This one's on the prior."

"Well, that's a relief. He looks like he could eat a horse for supper despite his lack of pins." Ellie peeped over the side of the cart at Harry's stumps. "You a woodworker, too?" she asked Harry with a sniff.

Harry nodded.

"I hope you're better than the last one. I see you have his piece of crap there. I don't know why you're bothering to save that thing."

"I wasn't planning on saving it," Harry said. "I intend to start over."

Ellie jerked her head toward the house. "You can put up in the bier. Don't disturb the lambs. We have a few sick ones in there."

"The lambs …" Harry murmured.

"Yeah," Ellie said, "we run a guest house for sheep here."

"I see. That's all right," Harry said as he lowered his tool box using a strand of rope since Oswald did not seem interesting in helping and Ellie made no move to assist. "I'm fond of sheep. All that wool."

Ellie laughed. "You wouldn't be so fond of them if the ram had a run at you. The bastard knocked me down the other day."

"I'll try to stay out of his way. I know what a problem an upset ram can be."

He made slow progress toward the threshold, even though it was only a few feet away, owing to the fact that he had to drag the toolbox behind him.

Ellie watched with interest, as did two boys who appeared at a window. The boys laughed and pointed.

"Look at him go, Ma!" the older boy cackled. "Look at him go!"

Two large dogs emerged from the house as Harry reached the threshold. They sniffed his face. He held very still for this, a little concerned that they might not like him. But thankfully, the dogs did not find him objectionable.

Ellie had mercy on Harry as he started to struggle through the doorway. "Al," she said to the older boy, "you and your brother lug that toolbox to the shed. And don't drop it, nor break nothing. He's here on a job for the prior."

"If you're good, I'll let you see me stumps," Harry said as they dragged the box away.

Harry tossed his satchel through the doorway to the bier and went out the back door after the two boys. The shed was a lean-to, just a thatched roof attached to the back of the house, although wattle walls rising to a man's height gave it the appearance of a room. Perhaps at one time it had been used for storing tools, the usual occupation of such sheds. But now there was only a work table with clamps and a bench, and wood shavings strewn about the ground. Clearly, the other woodworker had used the space. Oswald came around the corner with an unmarred block of wood which he put in the block and secured it upright with the clamps.

Harry lifted himself to the bench and then to the table top to the amazement of everyone there. It was a good thing it was a sturdy table, too, and didn't wobble.

"Let's have that toolbox up here as well," Harry said to the boys.

Harry took the uncompleted figure of the drowned girl from his pouch and set it on the table. Then he removed a mallet and chisel from the tool box.

The others peered at him. This made him uncomfortable. He wasn't used to an audience. Normally, no one had paid his whittling and carving any mind, except for Jennie, and she didn't count.

"Can we watch?" Al asked.

Harry bit back a sharp reply, for he wanted everyone to go away.

"I suppose," he said. "For a while."

With a glance at the figure of the girl from the weir, he lifted the mallet and chisel to the block.

Chapter 13

Stephen and the others pushed hard in hopes of overtaking the gang during the fifteen miles to Worcester, but they reached the town shortly after noon without seeing any sign of their quarry. They crossed the Severn bridge about the time that decent, ordinary people were rising from dinner and returning to work. This meant the streets were filling again, making movement slow down Broad Street to High Street, where they turned south toward the cathedral close.

High Street dead-ended at the close. They took the street to the left, which led, after another sharp turn to the right and some meandering, to the Sidbury Street Gate and the road to London.

Just short of the fork with the road to Tewksbury, Stephen glanced back at Gilbert and Herb to make sure they had not fallen too far behind. Gilbert was drooped over the cantle of his saddle, looking miserable. But the most significant thing was the state of their horses. They plodded along, just when Stephen was thinking of asking for another trot, heads low, looking as exhausted as the two men who rode them.

"We need to stop!" Stephen called to William.

"What for?" William answered, not turning back and the reply nearly lost to Stephen's ears.

"To rest the horses!"

This time William swiveled in the saddle to get a look at Stephen and the others. His lips were a scornful line. But he slid from his mount and loosened the girth. He led the horse across the street to the yard of an inn at the crossroads.

A pair of grooms came running to take care of the horses.

"Just feed and water them," William growled. "Don't bother to untack, though you can remove the bridles. We won't be here long. And oats — give them oats, not hay."

"Of course, sir," one of the grooms said, staring at the sight of the two armored men. "Is there trouble, sir?"

"It's none of your business," William snapped. He sank to a bench by one of the tables in the yard. "Have some ale fetched, and bread and beef as well."

"Right away, sir," the groom said. He shouted the order through an open window as he and the other groom led the horses to the stable behind the building.

Stephen set down his shield and took a place on the same bench, but some distance from William, while Gilbert and Herb settled on the bench opposite them. Gilbert rested his head in his hands, unable even to expend the energy to assess the inn, as he was in the habit of doing with others in the same business as the Wistwode family.

Herb leaned back against the table. "I don't think my arse's ever been so sore."

"It'll be sorer before we're done," William said.

"I know that, sir," Herb said hastily.

"Who were those men back there?" William asked Stephen.

Gilbert peered at Stephen through his fingers. "What men? Where?"

"Well, I can't be sure," Stephen said. "But there's a fellow who bears me a grudge. He's sent men to kill me before. I suspect he's hired another batch."

"FitzSimmons!" Gilbert exclaimed. "He had another go?"

"Yes," Stephen said. "Seems like it."

"When?" Gilbert asked. "Where?"

"Back at Leominster," Stephen said, and he told Gilbert the story.

"Dear God, that was close," Gilbert said when Stephen finished. "Worse than the last time."

"Yes," Stephen said.

"Do you think we've seen the last of them?" Gilbert asked.

"We left three in the grass," Stephen said. "I doubt they'll be bold enough to try again."

Everard keenly felt the fact that the attempt on Attebrook had not gone as planned. The idea had been for the others to distract Attebrook while he came in and cut Attebrook down. He didn't shy from single combat, but why take chances when you didn't have to? He had been promised a lot of money for this job, and he meant to get it done with the least amount of effort and risk to himself as possible.

Neither Dickie nor Tom, the last of the men, said anything as they trotted along the Worcester Road, keeping Attebrook and his two companions in sight in the distance. They knew the power of Everard's temper and feared it.

They reached Worcester without Everard having arrived at a suitable scheme about what to do next, passed over the Severn bridge and entered the town. The congestion on the street required they close up on the target. Everard worried about this since a single backward glance might give the alert they were being followed. But neither Attebrook nor the two men with him looked about.

He spotted three crossbows hanging from ropes in a shop window. They were not heavy war bows, but the lighter version used for hunting. Such bows might not deliver a bolt with enough force to penetrate mail, but they could knock down a deer at fifty yards or more. There wasn't any meaningful difference between men and deer. The prospect of shooting Attebrook from such a distance to collect his fee was attractive.

He reined up at the shop.

"What're you doing?" Dickie asked. "They're getting away!"

"You keep them in sight," Everard said. "I'll catch up."

"But I know this country," Dickie said. "The road divides outside town. They could be headed anywhere."

"Leave Tom at the turn off."

Dickie nodded and continued toward the town gate.

Purchase of a crossbow and a quiver of bolts did not take long. But the brevity of negotiations meant that Everard paid more than he might have otherwise. However, he was in a hurry, so he threw coins at the proprietor of the shop, and as the fellow scrambled in the dirt to recover them before passers-by got there first, he tucked the crossbow under an arm and cantered toward the town gate.

Dickie and Tom were waiting in the road when Everard emerged from the town.

"What are you doing here?" Everard snapped. "I told you to follow them."

"They're right up there," Dickie said, pointing at nowhere in particular. "At that inn. In the yard. Having dinner."

"I wouldn't mind some dinner," Tom muttered. "It's been a long time since breakfast and I didn't get that either."

"Shut the fuck up," Everard said. "We've got work to do."

"I hope it don't turn out like last night," Dickie said.

Everard went down the road until an inn on the left came into view at a crossroads. He saw Attebrook at a table with his back to him. This was not the best place, since houses lined the road as tightly as they did in any town, but there were bound to be gaps and alleys that would allow flight into the countryside behind them. Then he noticed that Attebrook was wearing a mail shirt. Nobody rode about with a mail shirt on or ate dinner in one. He must be taking precautions after the events of last night.

"Well," Dickie asked coming to Everard's side. "Aren't you going to use that toy?"

"Could you make a head shot at this distance?" Everard asked.

"I might could," Dickie said, appraising the distance. "Why, you don't think you can?"

"It ain't certain enough," Everard said. "If I miss, it'll just let him know we're still here. He suspects, but doesn't know."

"Get closer, then."

"If I do that, we're likely to be spotted. Then we lose our advantage."

"So what are we going to do? I'm sick of riding around the countryside."

"We're getting a fortune for this. You've got no room to complain. Attebrook'll let his guard down after a day or two. Then we'll have him. It will be roast beef and wine for us for months."

"I do like the sound of that."

Stephen questioned the servants at the inn about whether they had seen a party of rough men on horseback with a number of young girls in their custody. Inn servants often paid attention to who passed by on the road, and it wasn't unknown for them to hawk the advantages of their employer to travelers on the road. However, no one had seen anything of the kind. This left him to guess which way they went.

There were several roads from Worcester to London. For instance, some people preferred to go toward Stratford; others liked the road to Evesham; and some people found the road to Tewkesbury more pleasing. The odds of picking the one the kidnappers had taken were small, so there was no point in trying to overtake them on the road now.

Stephen decided on the road to Evesham as he was finishing the last of his beef and bread, since it was the one with which he was most familiar.

The grooms brought the horses around from the stable, and the party mounted up and rode into the street. Stephen made a point of not looking back toward Worcester. But once they had set out at a brisk trot, he asked Gilbert, "Did you see them? Are they still there?"

Gilbert, who already looked miserable even though they had hardly gone a hundred yards, nodded. "It looks like the same bunch who were behind us coming into Worcester."

"That's them, then. They haven't given up after all."

"I'm afraid so."

"That means they'll probably try again."

"I'd say there's no 'probably' to it."

"At least there's only three of them now."

"Only three?"

"Yes," Stephen grinned. "It means they're outnumbered."

"What are you thinking? You don't expect me or Herb to do anything!"

"I wasn't counting you two. William and I should be enough."

"Enough for what?"

"I'm not sure yet. Let me give it some thought."

Chapter 14

Stephen had only a vague memory of the conditions along the road between Worcester and Evesham. He recalled that the land was open and cultivated most of the way, and so it proved to be, flat and easy riding, the road running fairly straight. He resisted the urge to look back to see if the followers were still there and he ordered everyone to keep their eyes forward. He didn't want to alert the pursuers to the fact they had been spotted.

Before long they reached a village with a stone church and two dozen houses strung along a single street; Witintune, Stephen remembered it being called. The road made a slight curve to the left as it entered the village and began a gentle descent, creating the appearance of a hump in the road behind them. Stephen chanced a glance backward here. The pursuers were out of sight beyond the hump and curve.

They came on an alehouse which sat flush to the street, its yard on the far side. Stephen turned into the yard, where a pair of travelers were resting at one of the tables.

"We'll take them here," Stephen said to William.

They both put on their arming caps, pulled up their coifs and settled their helmets on their heads. The travelers watched this with alarm. Arrays involving armored men were the stuff of stories, not the sort of thing that happened in tavern yards. Stephen put a finger to where his mouth would be if it weren't hidden by the face plate of his helmet.

"We're just planning a little surprise for some friends," he said.

"Stay where you are," Gilbert ordered with more authority than anyone might expect from so genial a face. "Make no sound."

"That means you, too," Herb said, who, dismounting, took the alewife's arm as she emerged from the house at this astonishing commotion.

Presently, they heard the muffled thump of horses' hooves moving at a trot.

Just before the leading horse's head came into view, Stephen spurred the stallion forward, sword at the point.

"Look out, Everard!" shouted one of the men behind Flat Nose.

Stephen's intention was to stab the leading rider and turn his attention to one of the men behind him, but the leader, Everard, reacted with unexpected swiftness to the ambush.

Everard swung up a crossbow hanging from his shoulder and deflected what otherwise would have been a fatal thrust. This parry turned into a blow at Stephen's head. Stephen blocked by swinging his shield across the cantle, pivoting the stallion to keep the leading man on his left, and, rising in the stirrups, cut at Everard's head. Everard avoided the cut with a duck and an elegant sideways movement of his horse, and used the space he obtained to draw his own sword and swing his shield off his back, the crossbow clattering to the road.

It would have been satisfying to kill Everard but that would take a lot of time and work: Stephen's adversary was clad in mail the same as he was, although he hadn't had time to put on his helmet, and it was hard to kill an armored man.

So Stephen did something he regretted even before it was begun. He cut with all his strength at the neck of Everard's horse, putting everything he had into it. The blow caught the rider by surprise, for Stephen made it first appear that the blow was aimed for him, but as it descended, Stephen changed its course so that it struck just behind the horse's ears. The blade went halfway through the horse's neck. It collapsed, almost jerking Stephen's blade out of his hand. Everard slid from the horse and stood in the road, then advanced on Stephen, sword raised. Stephen backed the stallion and made him dance to the left. This brought into view what was happening between William and the other two. Both those enemies were unhorsed. William was still engaged in an exchange of cuts with one man, and Gilbert was standing over the other after having struck him on the head so hard with a longstaff borrowed from an astonished onlooker so that his brains spilled onto the road.

Everard saw these things too. He gave up his attack on Stephen in an attempt to circle around behind him to aid his fellows. If he made it, Gilbert would be at his mercy.

Stephen dropped from the stallion and pushed it toward the alehouse's yard, where Herb, who was watching the proceedings with an open mouth along with the travelers and the alewife, caught the reins so that it could not run away.

Stephen, however, had no time to register what happened to the stallion. He got between Gilbert and Everard, his shield out to the left, the position for single combat, and sword raised, point toward the enemy.

Just as Stephen reached the distance to engage, Everard took a step back.

Gilbert came to Stephen's side. Stephen spared a glance at Gilbert.

"I killed that man!" Gilbert panted. "Dear God, forgive me!"

"Good for you. Get their horses."

Gilbert ran off to collect the loose horses, mindful to stay out of the way of William and the third man, who were still changing blows.

As Gilbert ran around behind Stephen with the two horses in tow, Stephen called to William: "Leave him be. You've done enough."

"He isn't dead yet," William said over his shoulder.

"Come on!"

William backed away from his opponent, who started to pursue, but stopped when Everard said, "Lay off, Dickie."

Dickie drew off to stand beside Everard. Then as Stephen backed away as well, and Herb led their horses into the road.

Stephen leaped aboard the stallion without benefit of a stirrup, "I'd like to be there when you tell FitzSimmons that you failed twice!" he said to Everard.

"I won't fail the third time," Everard growled.

"I'll keep an eye out for you."

Chapter 15

Carving needed patience and care. Gradually, the nose, eyes, brows and cheeks began to take shape. It looked like the girl at the weir, as best as Harry could remember. Although the face he had gazed on had been distorted by death and the onset of decay, he hoped that he was capturing how she had looked in life. He wished she might live, if only as a memory trapped in wood, eyes sad but the lips curved into a gentle smile.

He worked steadily throughout the day, not pausing for dinner, which he ate in snatches on the work table while the girl who brought it — there turned out to be an elder daughter in the house — watched without speaking.

No one else stopped by after the grandmother put the boys to work.

In the evening, Oswald brought candles down from the priory and lighted them for Harry so he could continue working in the dark, even though Harry had not asked for them. "The prior thought you might find them useful," Oswald said.

Harry stopped about midnight and slept on the table. It was a hard bed but he was too exhausted to get down.

Morning came too soon, as mornings do in the summer when the nights are short, and it seemed to Harry that he had barely shut his eyes then it was dawn and some fool was stampeding the sheep into the back pasture.

"Come on, lay-about," the eldest daughter Anne said, "time to get up. The day's wasting."

"Go away," Harry said. He knew he should get up, but even a hard table feels good after a short night. He was aware that someone had draped a blanket over him.

Anne snatched off the blanket.

Harry sat up, clutching himself as it was cold without the blanket. "You are a cruel little girl."

"I'm not a little girl. I am old enough to marry. Do you want some breakfast?" Anne held out a lump of cheese.

Harry reached for it. Anne retreated.

"Are you going to say something witless, like come and get it?" Harry asked.

Anne looked at Harry teetering on the edge of the table. She put out a hand to stop any fall in the offing. Her mischievous expression grew serious.

"Sorry," she said. She gave him the cheese and went back in the house.

Harry was chewing on the remainder of the cheese and considering what to do next about the carving when Anne returned with a bowl containing three hard boiled eggs. She put the bowl on the table where he could reach it and left.

"What, no salt?" Harry asked, but not loudly enough for anyone to hear. "What barbarian eats hard boiled eggs without salt?" Nonetheless, he took up two eggs and put one in each side of his mouth so that his cheeks puffed out like a squirrel's. It was the best breakfast he could remember in a long time. He loved hard boiled eggs and could eat a dozen if given the chance, although he had never had it.

He was shaping the hood surrounding the dead girl's face later in the morning, and was thinking how he would do her hair, when he got a visitor.

Harry glanced at the shadow in the doorway. "Well, hello, prior. Not finished yet, but almost."

Bertran advanced into the shed. He gazed at the statue's face for a long time without speaking. He seemed to be deeply moved by what he saw.

"It hardly looks like almost to me," Bertran said at last.

"I'm a professional. Trust me. I'll have her finished in time for your bishop."

"You've only got the face. What about the rest of her? Her hands? Her robes?"

"We're getting there. Don't you worry."

Bertran did not look convinced. "Nothing's ever easy, is it?" He turned away.

"Nothing that's any good. Oh," Harry said, "there's something you can help me with, I hope."

"What?" Bertran asked.

Harry fished in his pouch and produced the gold ring taken from the girl at the weir. He held it out to Bertran. "Have you ever seen anything like this?"

Bertran seemed stunned at the ring. His mouth fell open then shut abruptly. He extended a finger toward the ring but stopped short of contact. The hand withdrew to its sleeve. "It's Roman, I can tell you that much."

"There's an inscription. What's it mean?" Harry pointed to the ring's disk, LEG XIV GEM. He expected Bertran to take it from him to examine the inscription more closely, but Bertran's hand stayed within his sleeve.

"It means Legio the fourteenth, Gemina."

"What's that?"

"It's the name of a Roman legion that was stationed hereabout a thousand years ago. Why?"

"A girl who died recently at Ludlow was wearing it when she was found."

"She was dead, was she?" Bertran looked into the distance. "Do you know how she died?"

"Drowned in the river. We found her at the first Ludlow weir."

"Stephen Attebrook put you up to asking the question?"

"He meant to ask it himself, but as I said earlier he was called away on a more urgent matter."

"I find it hard to believe that Attebrook would come here after what he did to me."

Harry nodded. "Yes, you said. I've known many the odd reason for bearing a grudge, but that's one of the better ones. How'd it happen?"

"None of your business."

"'Course it isn't, but that's never stopped me asking before."

"You're impudent."

"People've said that about me."

"It's a wonder no one's cut out your tongue."

"Too much trouble to bend over to reach it, I suppose. That ring, you don't imagine it was passed down from ancient times in the girl's family, do you?"

"I doubt that. It would be more worn. This looks almost freshly made. There was a Roman horde found about ten years ago near Acton Burnell. It could have come from there."

"Any way to know for sure?" Harry had heard of Acton Burnell but it took a moment to remember exactly where it was: a place about twenty miles north of Ludlow. He had never been there, but that wasn't unusual since he hadn't been to many places.

"You'd have to ask the bishop."

"Which bishop would that be? There are so many."

"Of Hereford, of course."

"Why would he be so well informed on this question?"

"Bernard de Wellys, the lord there, contributed a goodly share to the cathedral, although I'm sure he's sorry about that now, given his situation. There's quite a bit still in store. You can compare the ring with what's been saved. A skilled smith could tell if the stuff came from the same hand."

"I'll pop over to Hereford straightaway, soon as I'm finished here."

"Will you, now?" Bertran asked. But he did not wait for an answer, and strode out of the shed.

Toward suppertime, two shadows caught the corner of Harry's eye. He glanced up and saw the tops of two tonsured heads just visible at the gap between the wall and the roof as the two figures made their way around to the door.

"Hello there," Harry said, playing the part of a jovial tradesman. "Come to see the progress we've made so far? It won't be long before she's done."

He had, in fact, made great progress. The face was complete, the robes about her head and body had formed, and he had just about finished the hair showing from beneath the mantle so that it had a lifelike, flowing appearance.

Edwin the monk stepped into the shed while the other monk remained in the doorway. He bent close to the face of the carving, then straightened up with an appalled expression. "That is not our Lady!" he exclaimed, directing a quivering finger at the carving's nose.

"What's wrong with her?" Harry asked.

"She's," Edwin struggled for words, "— she's not saintly!"

"What's a saint look like? Have you known many?"

"She is . . . ordinary!"

"What of it? Saints were people once, like us. On the outside, anyway."

"This is meant to represent the Mother of Christ! She should be — she should be different!"

"Different how?"

Edwin waved his hands. "As she was before. An angel!"

"Before? You mean like the old statue?"

"Exactly!"

Harry had not cared for the original statue. It was stiff, artificial, unhuman and unreal. He wanted something that seemed as if one looked on the face of the living woman. "I was not hired to be a copyist. I was hired to carve the Mother's likeness. I have a vision of her. It came to me on a beam of light. That's what you'll see when I'm done."

Edwin did not seem moved by Harry's claim to a vision. "I have seen enough to know that this is an insult to her memory. Ugly! A monstrosity!"

"The prior's seen her. He didn't find fault."

"The man has no judgment," Edwin snorted. He went out.

The smell of smoke was the first hint of trouble. The aroma of smoke by itself was not remarkable. Every house reeked of smoke from the hearth. But in the shed the reek should be a mere suggestion. Harry's eyes came open.

He saw that a corner of the roof was on fire. Sparks dropped from the corner as the size of the blaze grew and began to spread up the thatch.

He bolted upright and sat paralyzed on the table. The unreality of the moment left him unable to move.

"Holy shit!" Harry cried at last.

He fumbled to return the gouges and chisels he had been using into the toolbox, and let himself down from the table. He collected box, his blanket and satchel, and dragged them out the door. By the time he reached the threshold, the fire had consumed half the shed's roof. The heat was searing.

With his gear safe in the yard, Harry banged on the back door and shouted, "Fire!"

The shepherd opened the door, a groggy disbelieving look on his face that vanished as soon as he saw the shed. He disappeared into the house, crying for his family to gather everything they had and get out. This did not take long since they did not own much, and within a minute or two everything of value, including all the sheep, table, benches and stools had been pulled into the yard and ushered a safe distance away.

"How'd it start?" the shepherd asked Harry as he tugged a trunk through the back door.

"No idea," Harry said.

"Fires like that don't start by themselves," the shepherd muttered.

"No, they don't."

Anne emerged with an armload of blankets which she set on the trunk.

"The Lady is still in there," Anne said.

"What lady?" the shepherd asked.

"His lady," Anne said, nodding toward Harry. "Our Lady."

"A pity," the shepherd said. "You'll have to start over."

"We need to save her," Anne said. She pulled one of the blankets over her head and shoulders, and ran into the shed.

"Anne!" cried the shepherd, "what are you doing?"

He ran after the girl. They reappeared in a moment, lugging the block of wood that was the Lady. They dropped the block by the trunk, coughing and struggling for breath as the roof to the shed collapsed with a crash, throwing sparks into the air.

Anne stroked the statue's face. "She isn't even singed. It's a miracle!"

"I suppose it is," her father said.

The true miracle, Harry reflected, was that Anne herself was unscathed.

The monks came down from the priory by the time the house was no more than smoldering ashes and burning posts. The fire had drawn the entire village since there was nothing anybody liked more than a good house fire as long it didn't threaten your own, and the story of the statue's rescue had traveled from one set of lips to another, and grown larger in the process so that when the tale reached the ears of the monks it seemed that Anne had gone into the flaming cottage by herself to fetch the Lady, and that both of them were untouched by flames that would have consumed anyone else.

"Is that what happened?" Bertran asked Harry during a spare moment.

"Pretty close," Harry said. "She did go into the fire and bring out the statue."

"We can truly count it as a miracle, then?" Bertran asked with satisfaction.

"Yes, I think you can." He added, "You should reward Anne for her bravery. She deserves something. Her father, too."

"I'll take care of them."

The Bear Wagon

Yet there was something in the way Bertran said this that did not give Harry any confidence that a reward lay in Anne's future.

Chapter 16

Stephen figured the kidnappers' most likely entry into London was through Newgate, which opened onto Holborne Street and led to all the roads toward the west. Stephen, William and the others had come down that very street from Oxford and he was certain that his prey would also. So he and William stationed themselves at Newgate, while Herb and Gilbert went to Ludgate in the south just in case.

But after a day of observing how the gate wardens handled traffic through Newgate, Stephen began to wonder if the quarry would attempt the gates. The portals were wide enough to admit two carts at a time. However, the wardens forced people to enter single file so that no one avoided an inspection of the contents of their carts or pack horses and paying the entry toll. The kidnappers would have the girls tied up. No warden would fail to see this and to ask questions. A girl had only to call for help within the gate and wardens would tumble out of the flanking towers.

The day went by in dreadful monotony. The only break was when Stephen or William dared to leave their stools outside the tavern by Newgate to take a piss in the backyard cesspit. Otherwise, they kept their eyes on the gate, hoping for some sight of Ida, or a string of girls on horseback, accompanied by men with a pack of dogs. But there was nothing.

The bell heralding the close of the gate clanged at sundown.

Two of the gate wardens approached the tavern after the gates had closed, and Stephen and Willian were returning their stools through the tavern's street window.

One of the wardens paused at the tavern's door. "What are you two gentlemen doing here, if you don't mind my asking?"

"Waiting for someone," Stephen said.

"Bit odd, isn't it, for you to do it yourselves? I'd have thought it a task for a servant."

"We do what we have to do."

"Must be an important person, then."

Stephen directed a thumb at William who wore an impatient expression and was paying no attention to the gate warden. "His daughter."

"A runaway, is she?" The warden smirked at the possibility that she might have run off with a lover the father did not approve of.

"Worse than that."

"What could be worse?"

So Stephen told him.

The warden looked shocked when Stephen finished the story. "I can't believe anyone would do that. What are they up to?"

"I don't know."

"You know, a bunch like that will stick out like a sore thumb. I could keep a lookout for them for you, you know."

"You could?" Stephen had not considered this possibility.

"It'll cost you a bit, you know."

"How much?"

"Oh, let's say half a shilling a day."

"I don't think we have that much money left. We had to leave Ludlow in a hurry. We might be able to afford two pence a day."

"Five, and I'll promise you the eyes of the other boys." The warden hooked his thumbed into this belt.

"Five pence!" thundered William, whose attention apparently had found the conversation after all. "That's robbery!"

Stephen held out a hand. "Quiet, William."

William opened his mouth as if to continue protesting, but then he shut it.

"Five it is, if it buys everyone's eyes," Stephen said.

Stephen and the warden shook on the deal.

"Good, then. When can I expect payment?"

"Go ahead, William," Stephen said. "Pay the man."

"I pay him?" William sputtered.

"You're the moneybags."

"You son-of-a-bitch."

"Careful there, that's our mother you're talking about."

William looked ready to hit Stephen over the head with his purse rather than to dig into it for the agreed sum. But at last he poured out a palmful of pennies and counted five into the warden's eager hand.

"Thank you, sirs," the warden said as his fingers closed about the little silver coins. "Pleasure doing business with you."

"Just see that you do the service we've paid for," William growled.

"He do have a problem with his temper, don't he now," the warden said to Stephen, making sure to keep out of reach, since William, like Stephen, was carrying his sword.

"We had our differences over that when we were younger," Stephen said.

"What gave you leave to be so free with my money? It's almost all I have," William asked furiously as they turned toward their own inn.

"Do you want Ida back? Or are you just going through the motions to impress Elysande?"

"I have no need to impress Elysande. You trust that man? He'll just keep my money and say he's working. I've seen his kind before."

"I think I do trust him." Stephen stopped and grasped William by the shoulder. "It frees us to make inquiries in the city. What if they don't come through the gates?"

"How else would they come?"

"There are other ways."

"What other ways? Fly over the walls?"

"There is the river. The waterfront is a sieve and unwatched along much of it."

"And you didn't think of this before? When we decided not to try to catch them on the road? You, the clever one?

Not so clever after all, eh?" William pushed off Stephen's hand. "You've lost her! You threw away our one chance!"

The accusation stung, because it was probably right. Stephen had leaped to a conclusion because at the moment it had felt right. But like a lot of his conclusions, it was plainly wrong in the light of mature reflection. He had spent his life blundering from one thing to another, burying his mistakes under a show of cleverness. Now when cleverness really counted, he had come up short. He could almost hear Gilbert's reproach.

"I'll find her, William. I'll find her if it's the last thing I do," Stephen said, aware even as the words left his mouth how empty they sounded.

William gnawed his lower lip.

"We'll sell two of the horses," Stephen said. "We have spares."

William's brow furrowed. "I do not get to keep them, for my loss?"

"What gave you the idea they were both yours?"

"I am the elder brother, and the lord. What are you — a trumped up nothing."

"Well, the King has seen fit to make me coroner. That is something."

"Of a small part of a small shire. And if you live up to expectations, that will not last long."

"Do you even have enough money left for us to get by? Did you think vengeance would be cheap?"

William did not answer, his mouth a grim line.

"There's a place called Smithfield outside the city," Stephen said. "It's where the horse market is. Tomorrow we'll sell the two we took from those fellows."

William mused, "Those are good horses. They should fetch a good price. Quite a lot actually."

"It will likely cost more than a pair of horses to get her back before we're done."

They continued to the inn without speaking.

Chapter 17

The following morning Stephen and William sold the two horses, one for four pounds and the other for five. This was less than they were worth since they were made warhorses, but they were in a hurry to sell, never the best position to get the best price.

That much money was far more than anyone carried about. The buyer, a knight from Norfolk who gave his name as Godfrey de Hambleton, offered to sign over a letter of credit he held on an Italian bank. But William, not trusting that it was genuine since he had never heard of such a thing as an Italian banker let alone a letter of credit, required buyer and sellers to call on the banker to ensure he would stand behind the note. This meant a ride through London to the great bridge, where the banker had his house and place of business.

London could be a confusing place to anyone unfamiliar with it. Hambleton professed to bewilderment as the little party rode through the throng on broad Westcheap Street.

"I hardly ever come to London. Nasty, smelly place full of nasty, smelly people. Ordinarily leave directions to my man," said the knight, who seemed a hearty fellow. "Unfortunately, he's fallen ill."

"What's wrong with that one?" William asked, pointing to the knight's servant, who was riding before them to make a passage for his master, Stephen, William and Gilbert.

"He's a dolt," the knight said. "Aren't you, John?"

"Stupid as they come," said John, the servant. "Can't find my own head some days to put my hat on."

"Stupid as a fox, I'll bet," Gilbert muttered.

"What?" asked Hambleton. "What?"

"He said, isn't that a handsome old church," Stephen said, having to shout to be heard over the cries of the peddlers hawking merchandise in the street, from piles of old clothes, to shoes with holes in their soles, rusty knives, and even a fellow with a bar on his shoulders from which hung a dozen chickens by their feet which swung back and forth in a worrisome way and looked ripe for the stealing as he couldn't watch them all at once.

"Church?" Hambleton inquired. "That rancid old thing?" He gave a critical eye to the pile of grey stone from which much of the plaster had flaked off.

This church sat on the right at a fork in the street just beyond the ford of the Walbrook, a stream that ran straight through the city. The fork was unusual for the fact there were three streets fanning out from it rather than the usual two.

"What now, John?" Hambleton shouted.

"Not sure, sir," said John. "I think we take the middle one."

"It doesn't matter if you take the middle one or the one on the right," Stephen said. "You'll get there just the same. But the right is a bit shorter."

"I'm for shorter," Hambleton declared.

"So am I," Gilbert said, looking uncomfortable on his mule, even though people on their feet were moving faster than he was and he was in little danger of falling off; and if he had there were many bodies on either side to soften the impact.

Before long, they passed two more churches before the street dead-ended. John looked left and right, gauging whether to turn one way or the other, or perhaps cross over and take the street that came in across the way at another church, where there was a tavern on the opposing side. Whores sat on the upper floor window sills watching their little group and probably measuring how much could be drained out of their purses.

"Hey, boys!" one of the whores called. "Why don't you stop for a drink!" She dangled a leg over the sill and drew up her skirt so they got a good look at it.

Hambleton gazed at the questioner. She was a young thing, not more than sixteen or seventeen and rather pretty with freckles across her nose. But when she spoke it was evident that she had very few teeth and a split lip.

"Another day," Hambleton said in a tone that left no question that there never would be such a day.

"It's cheap!" the girl called back.

"That's what we're afraid of," William said.

"It's cheap because we know you won't take long!" the girl said, sticking out her tongue.

"I hate the city," Hambleton said. "Everybody's so impudent. Are you sure you know where we're going?" Hambleton asked John.

"'Course, I do, sir!" John said.

"Go right, and keep straight ahead," Stephen said. "We're almost there."

"I was about to say that," John declared.

"You seem to know your way around London," Hambleton said to Stephen.

"I spent some time here," Stephen said.

"You wouldn't happen to be the Attebrook who was apprentice to the royal justice Ademar de Valence, by any chance?" Hambleton asked with more shrewdness that he had displayed to this point.

"I am, why?" Stephen said.

Hambleton chuckled without humor. "One of my younger brats just signed on as a clerk not too long ago. He doesn't enjoy the experience, as if that's important! The young these days! He said Valence claims he is as bad as that fellow Attebrook when he does something that does not please him."

"It's hard not to displease Valence."

"Is it true that you cut off the hand of a fellow clerk?"

"It's one of the reasons I had to leave Valence's employ. He gave me an awful beating and then summoned the sheriff. I wasn't cut out to be a lawyer, anyway."

"A quarrel, I suppose — your dispute with the clerk."

"A stupid one, really."

"We usually see they're stupid once we're sober."

"Yes. It happened not far from here," Stephen said. "Just down there by All Hallows Church." He gestured to the right as they passed the intersection with Thames Street. "It was over the most foolish thing — who got first crack at a whore. We were a pair of hotheads. He hated taking second place. He pushed me, so I pushed him back and the next thing we knew we both had swords out. He swung at me, forgetting there was a roof above us. His blade caught in the cross beam."

"And you cut off his hand while he was trying to tug it free."

"I'm afraid so. It's nothing to be proud of. I've done many foolish things, but that's one of the worst."

Bridge Street, which passed in front of Saint Magnus Martyr Church and was the entrance to the great bridge, looked like most other London streets, which is to say it was only wide enough for a single cart or wagon to pass at once. And the bridge itself was so lined with buildings along its edges that it gave the impression at first of being on hard ground and not suspended in the air over water.

So Gilbert, who had been looking forward to experiencing the spectacle of the bridge, was unaware that he had even set foot on it until there was a gap between two houses that, rather than revealing an overgrown back garden, afforded a sweeping view up the Thames to the curve of the river more than a mile off; greyish green water covered with flat-bottomed ferries and small sailboats.

"Great God in Heaven!" Gilbert exclaimed as he realized where he was. "Why didn't you say something?" He would have stopped to admire this view, but there were pedestrians leading a pack train pressing close behind and they did not seem the sort who would suffer an interruption in their journey.

"My mind was elsewhere," Stephen said.

"Has anyone fallen off?" Gilbert asked. "I should have been warned so I could prepare for the possibility."

"More than once, I'm sure."

"Yet it feels steady. If I did not have the proof of my one eyes, I'd think we were still in the city."

"It is the city, yet," Stephen said. "The city controls the bridge all the way to Southwark."

"And it is quite steady," Hambleton said over his shoulder. "Stay in the middle and you're safe."

They came to a house just shy of a large stone chapel on the downriver side of the bridge. Hambleton dismounted.

"We're here," he said.

The others dismounted as well. Gilbert was drawn to the gap between the house and chapel, where he got an excellent view of the wharves downriver with ocean-going cogs tied up in a forest of masts all the way to the Tower and the green countryside beyond.

"Why does the banker keep his business here?" Gilbert asked. "It's a small house, hardly worthy of a banker. I expected a mansion."

"He probably likes to know when the ships come and go," Stephen said, himself admiring the view downriver. "Here he doesn't have to wait for someone to bring him word. He can see for himself." He pointed to a large indention in the city's coastline a short distance away where ships were moored one against the other so that it looked possible to walk across the harbor without a foot having to touch the water. This was Billingsgate, one of the city's most important and busiest wharves. "It's probably hard to burgle as well."

"I had not thought of that. But you're the one with first-hand knowledge of such things."

"That's enough."

"Right. Sorry."

John and Gilbert held the horses while the others entered the banker's house. The entry led to steep stairs rising to the first floor above. There was a door to the left that opened into the banker's office; Stephen could not rightly think of it as a shop, which is what it would be in another man's house. A counter separated the brief space beyond the door from the office proper where there were four clerks fiddling over accounts by the windows, which pierced three walls: front, side and back. The banker himself was distinguishable from the clerks by his flowing jacket with its embroidered sleeves that hung almost to the floor and his hat, which resembled a turban like the Moors wore.

"May I help you?" asked one of the clerks, approaching the counter. He was an Englishman by the look and sound of him.

"I have a letter of credit with your house," said Hambleton, "and I would like to sign it over to these gentlemen."

"Very good, sir," the clerk said.

The Norfolk knight drew out his indenture and handed it to the clerk, who examined it closely and then went to a chest in the far corner. He rummaged in there for a few moments, and returned to the counter with the indenture's twin. He held them together to ensure that the torn edges fit together so there was no chance of a forgery.

"What do I need to do now?" Hambleton asked.

"You've only to sign and seal, providing the names of the recipients of the note," the clerk said.

"Ah, certainly," Hambleton said.

The clerk dipped an iron stylus in the inkpot and handed it to the knight. The knight scrawled something that might have been a name and handed the stylus back.

"If you would be so kind as to put their names on it," Hambleton said.

"Of course, sir," said the clerk. "And you are?"

"I am William Attebrook and this is Stephen Attebrook," William said.

"Very good, sir," the clerk said and bent over the note to write down their names.

After that, the knight brought out his seal and applied it to the drop of hot wax the clerk dripped on the parchment.

"There," the knight said. "All done. Wasn't that easy? It's amazing how you can do business these days, isn't it?"

"I suppose so," William said with some suspicion, gazing at the newly sealed note. "So that's worth ten pounds? That little writ?"

"Good as gold," Hambleton said. "This is how I sell my wool clip now. Take a note, then come into town and spend it."

"Huh," William said. "Are you sure about this?" he asked Stephen.

"It's more common in the south, but there's no reason why we can't do things like this in England."

"Damned foreign stuff."

"Well, since we are done, gentlemen," Hambleton said, "I shall be off. Lots to do and not enough time in the day for all of it." He went out.

Stephen was about to follow, but stopped when William made no similar move.

"I'd like to redeem the note," William said.

"Now?" the clerk asked.

"All of it."

"That's not possible."

"What do you mean, it's not possible. It's my money, or it's supposed to be."

"Well, it is, but we don't have the means to redeem the entire note at this moment."

"You pledge a note and then don't keep enough on hand to back it up? Is this some kind of swindle?"

The banker looked up at this. He spoke rapidly in what Stephen assumed was Italian, although some of the words seemed familiar.

The clerk replied in the same language.

The banker looked irritated and replied.

"We have enough on hand to redeem half the note," the clerk said.

"Half!" William spat. "I want all of it!"

"I am afraid that is the best we can do. We will have the remainder next week."

"I have expenses!"

"I am sure you do."

"Half should be more than enough for now, William," Stephen said.

William's mouth worked. "Half now and half tomorrow, or I go to the sheriff."

There was another exchange between the clerk and the banker.

"Sir Bartolommeo agrees to produce the other half in three days," the clerk said.

William fumed. "Very well. Three days."

"What was all the shouting about?" Gilbert asked when Stephen, carrying a bag full of silver pennies, emerged from the banker's house.

"William being William," Stephen said.

"He is such a pleasant fellow," Gilbert said, daring to say this because William had already mounted his horse and headed back to the city. "It's a wonder you haven't killed him."

"He was too big for me when I was young."

"There is still time."

It was one thing to realize the nature of the problem — that entry into the city could be accomplished more easily along the water than through the city gates. It was another to do something effective about it. London's waterfront was a good mile in length from the terminus of the west wall to the Tower, and while there were perhaps twenty officially licensed wharves, hundreds of houses along the river had their own docks where boats came and went outside the control of the government.

Stephen and Gilbert spent the remainder of the day trudging along the waterfront asking the ferrymen, the wharf operators and workmen if they had seen anything resembling the gang that had taken Ida. They started at the ruins of

Baynard's Castle at the west wall, where there was still a wharf operating at the castle's water gate. Then they worked their way down Thames Street, often reaching wharves through lanes so narrow that only a single person could pass along them: a wonder how goods were brought up from the river. The wharves passed in tedious succession — Saint Paul's, King's Gate, the Fishhuthe, the Timberhuthe, Broken Wharf, Queenhuthe, Dow Gate, Heywharf, Wolseygate and down to Oystergate at the foot of London Bridge and many houses in between. They learned nothing. No one had seen anything. Many, palms graced with a penny, promised to send word to Stephen's inn if they did, but Stephen doubted anyone would. It was money thrown away, but in their desperation, had to be spent.

They returned to the inn between Ludgate and Saint Paul's Cathedral at dusk, footsore and hungry.

William was eating supper as they came in. He said nothing, his mouth full of salted cod, as they sat down. Stephen waved at a servant for ale.

"Seen anything of Herb?" William asked after swallowing the cod.

"No, why?" Stephen asked.

"He's not at his post." William sounded disgruntled. Herb actually had two posts. He had been left to shuttle between the gates in case any of the wardens had seen anything.

"And you're unhappy because he isn't here to wipe your ass for you?" Stephen asked.

William slammed the table. "Damn you! I have had about as much of you as I can stand!"

"Have a go, William. It won't turn out like before."

William's nostrils flared. The tables around them went quiet. The occupants sensed a fight coming on, and that meant entertainment.

The spectators were disappointed, however, for before William had time to do anything, Herb burst in.

"They're here!" Herb cried. "They've come!"

Chapter 18

Harry occupied a corner of the storeroom on the west side of the cloister since the fire. His lodgings were close to the gate so he heard the commotion when a visitor strode through, calling for Prior Bertran by name. Harry pulled himself to the doorway and looked out to see a man-at-arms hurrying across the cloister toward the chapter house. Edwin and a couple of monks spilled out to greet this commotion. They conferred briefly and then disappeared into the house, alarm on the monks' faces.

"What's going on?" Harry asked.

"I don't rightly know," Oswald said, coming out of the gateway. "Wouldn't tell me. Shouted something about he was a messenger for the bishop. Brushed right past in a great hurry to see the prior. Must be important. How's it going?"

"I'm done. She only needs painting now."

"May I see her?"

"Be my guest."

Oswald entered the storeroom and knelt by the statue which was on the ground since there was no work table. He was silent for a long time.

"Not a bad piece of work," he said.

"On time for the bishop, too," Harry said.

"The bishop will be pleased," Oswald said.

"Maybe that's what the messenger had to say — that the bishop's here."

"I hope that's what it was."

After the messenger had gone, one of the monks emerged and rushed to the cloister gate. Harry heard the doors shut and the bar bang into place. That was odd. The gates were never shut and barred in daytime.

As the monk rushed back to the chapter house, Harry called, "What's going on?"

The monk looked annoyed at the interruption. He halted and gazed at Harry. "The bishop and his canons have been taken prisoner by those opposed to the King," he said. "They are burning his estates."

This was alarming news. But the bishop, Peter of Aigueblanche, was not well thought of by many English people hereabout, especially the lower gentry who provided most of Simon de Montfort's support. The bishop tended to prefer foreigners for positions of wealth and power in his See. It meant the war was starting.

Harry said, "I suppose that means he won't be coming to see the Lady."

"That is blindingly obvious," the monk said. "Anyway, he wasn't coming to see that thing, he was coming to do something about the prior." The monk hurried toward the chapter house.

Well, Harry thought, here's one who put no stock in the talk about the miracle of the fire. One of Edwin's adherents?

"Hey!" Harry shouted at his back. "Do you think they're coming here?"

"That is a possibility!" the monk shouted back without turning around.

Harry had no experience that allowed him to gauge the strength of this threat, but people did all sorts of nasty things in wars. He imagined that some soldier, eager for plunder, might pause to lop off Harry's head for sport. Crippled people were often looked on as no more important than dogs, after all.

The prudent course was to collect his money and get out as soon as he could. It was still early in the afternoon. There was plenty of sunlight left to reach Ludlow before nightfall.

Harry put on the thick leather gloves that protected his hands from the ground, and began the long scoot across the cloister.

The monks were filing through the door to the church as he entered the chapter house.

"Can I speak to you, prior?" Harry asked, for Prior Bertran was last in line.

"Not now," Bertran said. "We are about to pray for the safety of my cousin, the bishop. He has been made prisoner by enemies of the King."

"I heard."

"Then you know the urgency of our task."

Bertran entered the church, ending the conversation.

Harry might have returned to the storeroom, but having to go back and forth could be tedious, so he waited by the door for the monks to finish.

They were in the church more than an hour, which suggested the bishop was in terrible danger and needed every ounce of divine intervention the monks could summon. But at last the monks filed back into the chapter house. A few seemed surprised to see Harry by the door, but most ignored him, except for one who patted him on the head.

"You're still here?" Bertran asked as he shut the door to the church. "What do you want?"

"I've finished, and I'm ready to be paid."

"Are you? Hmm." Bertran glanced at the other monks. He waved them away, and said, "Leave us alone, if you please."

Bertran crossed the floor to a sturdy, high-backed chair across the central hearth, the only one of its kind in the round chamber, the other monks having to make do with benches.

"I am not sure that the statue is needed," Bertran said.

"What do you mean?"

"Well, the bishop will not be coming after all."

"What difference does that make? What's broken needs to be replaced. I've made the replacement."

"I am not sure the calculation is that simple. Hard times are coming. I must look to the preservation of my house. That requires the careful management of its resources. I cannot now spend house funds on something that is not vital to the house."

"I see. We had a deal and now you're backing out."

"I could, I suppose, spare four shillings for the work."

Four shillings was a lot of money by itself, although only a fifth of the agreed price. Harry needed the money and had lost almost a week here, time he might have spent profitably in Ludlow, so the offer was tempting. But a certain stubbornness made him say, "Never mind."

Harry swung around toward the door to the cloister.

"I could give you another four shillings for that ring," Bertran said.

"Of the house money? You'd spend house money on baubles?"

"Of course not of the house money. I would pay for that with my own funds."

"You fancy the ring, do you?"

"It is a pretty thing. It is not often you come across artifacts like that."

"The ring isn't mine to sell. If you won't honor your bargain, then I'll take my leave."

Bertran leaned his head on a hand and nodded.

Harry went out.

Oswald had a couple of priory servants harness Harry's cart horse and lift the statue, wrapped in canvas, to the cart.

"It's too bad things did not work out," Oswald said after the servants deposited Harry in the cart as well.

"Yeah," Harry said.

"What will you do with her?"

"Stick her in a corner and wonder who she was."

"Do you think you'll ever find out?"

"I doubt it. Take care of yourself, Oswald," Harry said. "Looks like hard times ahead."

Oswald chuckled. "Good times, if you're a soldier."

"And hard on everyone else. Besides, you're not a soldier now."

"I have my memories, but you're right. I'll keep out of the way. Anyway, I'll be able to dodge faster than you."

"They'll never see me hiding under the table," Harry laughed.

He clicked his tongue and gently flicked the reins, and the cart horse stepped out toward the gate.

He turned right at the gate toward Bromfield village and the Shrewsbury Road. Although there was road to the left, where it crossed the Teme at the bridge and mill, it became a forest track and he did not know where it went from there. Better to stick with the road he knew.

Anne, the shepherd's daughter, was minding a flock in the pasture across the road. She waved and smiled when she saw Harry. The gesture made his heart flutter even though it was supposed to belong to another. She ran over and squeezed through the hedge.

"Just thought I'd say good-bye," Anne said as they reached the cart.

"I'm glad I got to see you before I left."

"Really?"

"That was a brave thing you did, saving the Lady."

Anne's eyes fell on the bundle of canvas behind Harry. "You're taking her with you!"

"The prior backed out on the deal."

"He didn't! The rat." Anne looked apprehensive at speaking this so loudly. Disrespect of a lord — and priors were reckoned as lords of their own small domains — could earn you a beating or a fine.

"Offered only four shillings rather than the whole pound he promised."

Anne shook her head. "Why didn't you take the money? It's a lot."

"A man should keep his word."

"So you've prided yourself out of four shillings. A man like you can't afford pride. Think of all the ale you could buy with that."

"Pride's all I've got, and I get my ale free."

"You're the lucky one."

"I have a friend who's a soft touch."

"Can I have a peek at her, now that she's finished?"

"I suppose."

Anne climbed into the cart. She fumbled with the ties and pulled back the canvas to have a look at the statue's face.

"The prior's a fool," Anne said, making sure to keep her voice low this time, since they were still in range of the gatehouse. "She's beautiful." Anne frowned, though. "She looks familiar. I didn't notice it before."

"How could she look familiar? She's someone you've never met."

"Is this a likeness of a real person?"

"A girl who was found drowned in the Teme."

Anne became more thoughtful. "I may have seen her then."

"How could you?"

"If I tell you how, you must promise first never to repeat it to anyone."

"I can't promise that. The coroner will want to know. He's on the case."

"The coroner?"

"Yeah, it's one of the reasons why I'm here."

"The coroner?" Anne repeated with disbelief. She crossed her arms. "You're acquainted with the coroner?"

"We're good friends. I live in his house."

"Get on!"

"So I must tell him. He'll want to know."

"Well, just so it doesn't get back to my dad."

"I'll swear the coroner to secrecy. He a decent fellow. He'll keep your secret."

"What about you?"

"Oh, me, too, of course."

"All right, then. There's this boy in the village. Outside of it, actually. He lives off the road down where the Onny joins the Teme. I slipped out one night to meet him about a week ago. There's a little copse on the river not far from his house. We used to meet there."

"Used to?" Harry asked.

"Yeah, I don't see him anymore. He wanted to go beyond kissing and playing with my tits, and wouldn't take no for an answer. But dad wouldn't believe me if he found out. He'd suspect the worst. But anyway, that night, there were some folks camped across the river. Weren't supposed to be there. That wood south of the Teme belongs to the priory. No one has permission to camp there. They had a big fire going, too, which is odd. Anyway, there was a girl there. They led her out from a big wagon. They told her to get on her knees and bend over."

"Who's 'they'?"

"The men in the campsite." She said this like it was a stupid question.

"All right. Then what?"

"The girl refused to get down, so they beat her with rods." Anne shuddered. "I've seen beatings before, but nothing like this. Two of them at once, swinging away as hard as they could over and over. Then they pushed her down. One of them, who never bothered to take off his hood and cloak, had her from the back. Another was about to have a go at her, when she got up and ran away — straight into the river.

"I guess she hoped to get away, but there's a deep hole there where the water is over everyone's head. We all know to avoid it. More than one person's drowned there. She went into the hole and under. And that's the last I saw of her."

"How can you tell if she resembles that?" Harry waved at the statue.

"I got a good look at her face in the firelight. I can't swear the statue's a likeness of her. But it's close."

"And you didn't tell the reeve?"

Anne shook her head. "I was afraid I'd be found out. Dad would kill me."

"There's one other thing."

"What's that?"

"Were the girl's hands tied behind her back?"

"I didn't think about that before, but I believe they were. She ran funny, not swinging her arms like a normal person, you know?"

"Thanks," Harry said. "I'll be seeing you."

Anne smiled. "That would be nice."

Chapter 19

"Where are they?" William growled, shooting up and casting his napkin on the table.

"Well, I'm not sure, exactly," Herb said.

"Damn it, man, what do you mean you're not sure!"

"I saw them at Ludgate and followed them into the city, I don't know where. Miles and miles it was."

"The city isn't big enough to go miles and miles," Gilbert said to Stephen.

"He got lost," Stephen said.

Herb nodded. "That's right, sir. I have no idea where I ended up. Or how I got back."

"That is not helpful!" William snarled.

Herb blanched at William's rage. "I did follow them."

"And the girls?" Stephen asked. "Did you see Ida?"

Herb shook his head. "I didn't see her, or any of the others. It was two fellows with a pack of dogs. They came through Ludgate, where I was watching like you said to do."

"Jesus Christ in Heaven!" William sank to the bench and rested his forehead on his palms. "A pack of dogs! And you thought it was them? Just because they had a pack of dogs? England's filled with packs of dogs!"

"Well, sir," Herb said, "one of the gate wardens pointed them out to me. He said he knew them. They had a bear wagon. He was surprised that they'd lost it."

"That is promising," Stephen said. "Do you think you could find your way back to where they went?"

"I'm not sure, sir," Herb said. "They went by a church that was in the middle of the street and turned off into a side lane. That's the best I can remember."

"And how many churches are there like that in this city?" William asked.

"Not that many, actually," Stephen said.

Years ago in another life, Stephen had gained a passing familiarity with London. When he wasn't traveling the circuit with his master, the royal justice Ademar de Valence, they spent their time adjudicating cases at the palace at Westminster, or rather, de Valence had adjudicated cases while Stephen fetched and carried and copied and made notes. Stephen had Sundays off, and he often went into the city, especially early in his legal career. That was where the best brothels were — along Thames Street — and he and Bertran Vardon had made a pledge to sample every one of them. However, there were times during their first year together that they had taken the full day just to walk around and see what there was to be seen. Usually these were days when they had no money, although Bertran was a master at finding ways to conjure up pennies seemingly out of thin air. So Stephen had a vague memory of a church standing in the middle of the street, the only such church he could remember in the entire city.

He wracked his brains for the name of it, a task made difficult by William's grasp on his arm and jabbering questions about this mystery church and its location.

At last he could stand this interference no longer, and he said, "For God's sake, William! Give me a moment to think!"

"He usually needs more than a moment," Gilbert said to Herb. "It could take a good hour."

"I hope not, for his sake," Herb said.

"You may think that out of loyalty," Gilbert said, "but I believe Sir Stephen's more than a match for your lord."

"It wasn't like that in the old days, when they were boys."

"So I've gathered."

"Oh, I remember. I was there. My lord gave him a good thumping, seemed like every week."

"I remember now," Stephen said, brow unfurrowing. "It's on Fenchurch Street."

"Where's that?" William asked.

"To the east. Near the Tower. We passed it on our way to the bridge."

"I don't remember any church in the middle of the street."

"We passed Fenchurch Street, not the church itself."

"All right, then." William strode toward the door.

"William! We can't go now. It's after nightfall. Curfew will start before we get there. The watch will fine us if we're caught."

William rounded on Stephen. "You're afraid of the damned watch? And a fucking fine?"

"Herb's not going to be able to find anything in the dark. We'll go first thing in the morning."

The morning arrived chilly and fog-shrouded, visibility reduced to thirty feet — no improvement on the night.

But William could not be persuaded to wait until the fog lifted, and they set off from the inn in twilight.

"Come on," William said as they stepped into Ludgate Street. "We'll catch their arses in bed."

"That's where I'd like to be right now," Gilbert lamented to Herb. "It's impossible to get enough sleep in the summer."

"Hush," Herb said.

They groped their way around Saint Paul's Cathedral and the bishop's palace, where the voices of the bishop's servants came through the open window as they began their morning chores. Vendors were setting up booths about the church, and a crowd of supplicants was already gathered outside the palace doors, waiting to be allowed in.

The street forked where an addition to the cathedral was under construction. The left led to Westcheap, the main street through the city which ran from Newgate to Aldgate, although it changed its name several times on the way. Stephen led them instead eastward down Athelingstreet, which was narrower and less busy. It was still early. Only a few shops had begun to open their windows and there were few people about so they were able to make quick time, despite the piles of rubbish people had tossed into the street.

After some meandering and a few name changes the street emptied into Bridge Street. Stephen turned left with the fog lifting. After about two-hundred yards, they came to a familiar looking intersection where a large church occupied the southeast corner across from a whorehouse which was closed up.

"This is Fenchurch," Stephen said.

"Now what?" William asked.

"That way." Stephen pointed down Fenchurch Street.

After another two-hundred yards and round a gentle bend they came on a small church sitting in the middle of the street.

"Saint Mary Fenchurch," Stephen announced, glad that it was still there and that he had been able to find it. He had not been sure about this and had fretted silently throughout the journey, knowing that William was certain to throw a tantrum if he was wrong.

"Is this it?" William demanded of Herb.

"It is."

"Get on with it, then," William said. "It's getting late."

"It's around here somewhere," Herb said. "I'm sure of it."

It was the lane he had a seen a man and boy on horses with a pack of dogs take the previous evening. There were several lanes to choose from east of the church, narrow defiles that wandered off from the main street, leading God knew where.

Herb examined the nearest of them, glancing nervously at William.

At last Herb said, "That one."

William strode into the lane. Herb hurried after him. Gilbert shrugged at Stephen and they followed.

Even at high noon on the brightest day, the lane would have been in deep shadow owning to the narrowness of the passage and tallness of the houses on either side. And with the overcast it was nearly dark as night. Visibility was not helped by the fact that ropes had been strung above their heads across the lane from house to house, and washing hung thick on them, some of it still wet and dripping on their heads.

The stink by itself was enough to drive any man away: a foul mixture of piss, shit and the gaggingly sweetish aroma of rotting rubbish, overlaid with the nastiness of a rotting corpse somewhere in the piles that littered the alley.

They startled a pair of black-maned hogs rooting in one pile. The hogs glared at them as if daring them to approach whatever prize lay there on which they had been dining. But William drew his sword, for a hog was never to be trifled with. The hogs, not being stupid, decided their meal was not worth the trouble, and trotted off, pausing at a corner to observe the progress of the men and to see whether they fancied the meal for themselves.

A woman carrying a large bundle of what looked like rags on her back came round the corner, heedless of the hogs, who paid her no more mind than she did them. She smiled at William and Herb as she drew up, and said, "Are either of ye kind sirs in need of a shirt?"

"No," William said with distaste, for the woman was obviously what was known as a forestaller, a dealer in second hand goods that were usually of questionable quality.

"How about a pair of stockings? Hardly worn at all."

"No," William said. "Get on and stop bothering me."

"Oh, you've a temper, I see. Is he always this bileful?" the peddler asked Stephen.

"Most of the time," Stephen replied. "You wouldn't happen to live around here, would you?"

"Me palace is just down the lane, sir. Did you fancy dropping by for a tipple?"

"Perhaps later. We've some business to conduct first."

"Can't imagine what that might be. Hardly anyone does business here. Not a shop in sight anywhere."

"Yes, it is a bit out of the way. That's no doubt why you are compelled to take your wares on your back."

The peddler cackled. "You've seen through me, have you? Say, what business could you have?"

"We're in the market for a fighting dog or two. We heard there was a fellow up this lane who has a pack."

"Well, there is." The peddler gestured back the way she had come.

"What's his name?"

"You've come here without knowing his name?"

"I am afraid so. I've only heard that he is a bear baiter."

"He is that, when he sobers up enough to work at all. I suppose it don't hurt to tell. He's always hard up for money and no doubt will be glad to entertain your offer. He's called Cross-eyed Wally."

"I suppose the name is descriptive."

The peddler laughed. "Yeah, he got knocked in the head as a boy and when he gets drunk he has a hard time keeping his eyes straight."

"How does a cross-eyed man manage a bear?"

"Oh, he ain't had a bear for months. The damn thing dropped over dead last Candlemas."

"I wonder what he's been doing for money, then."

The peddler leaned close. "I've wondered that myself, but it don't do to inquire too closely into other people's business, if you know what I mean."

"I suppose that's why Wally's put it about that he is willing to sell a dog."

"I hadn't heard that, but I suppose so. Sure you wouldn't like a spare shirt? Looks like you could use one."

"That may be, but I'll catch you another day."

"Yeah, sure you will, yer honor!"

"A pleasure to talk to you, my lady."

"Mine too, your lordship!" She laughed and backed away.

"Oh," Stephen said, "I forgot to ask where Wally's house is."

"Round the corner, fourth on the left."

"It's hard to imagine fitting a bear wagon up this lane," Gilbert said. "It's so narrow."

"Let's hope it's the right bear baiter," Stephen said as the group moved off toward the corner under the watching eyes of the hogs, who decided it was safe to edge past on the other side of the lane.

Stephen counted off four doors on the left and stopped before the fourth. William came around him with an expression that suggested he intended to break down the door.

"Let me handle this, William," Stephen said. "Kicking in the door will simply alert them to trouble."

"I suppose you have a better plan?"

"I've been giving it some thought."

Stephen rapped on the door and stood back.

Presently the top half of the door opened. A woman stood inside, her hair in a soiled linen wimple. "What do you want?"

"I'm looking for Wally," Stephen said.

"What for?"

"I've a business proposition."

"What business could a lordling like you have with the likes of us? If that's what you are. I have my doubts."

"I want to hire him."

"What for?"

"That's for his ears, not yours."

There was a long pause. "What should I tell him is your name?"

"Vardon." It was the first name that popped into Stephen's head.

The woman retreated into the house. Stephen could hear her speaking to a man, although the words exchanged were too muffled to make out. The white blob of a head could be seen for a moment peeking around a corner. It disappeared. Then there was the sound of feet pounding on stairs.

Stephen's heart leaped. "He's gone a runner!"

Stephen vaulted the lower half of the door into the entryway and ran into the hall at the rear of the house. He was just in time to see a man's feet disappear at the top of the stairway. Stephen dashed in pursuit, pushing aside the woman who had answered the door. She fell hard on her backside with a shout.

144

His long legs enabled Stephen to take the stairs three at a time, and he was able to get close enough to see Wally, if that's who it was, on his way up the stairway to the top.

"Bobby!" Wally shouted near the top. "Follow me! Now!"

"What is it, dad?" a boy's voice cried.

"We've been found out!"

A floor above Stephen, a boy of about twelve rushed out of a chamber and pounded after Wally up the stairs.

Stephen was within only a couple of arm's lengths of Wally and Bobby when he reached the top of the stairs.

The quarry fled into a chamber on the top floor and slammed the door. Stephen rammed into the door without a pause. The door gave way, but not without some injury to his shoulder, and he pitched forward onto the floor, the iron latch skittering into a corner.

Wally was already out the window, shimmying across on a rope connected to a house on the other side of the lane.

Bobby was on the rope, too, but Stephen was able to grasp a scrawny ankle. Bobby tried to kick free, but Stephen got another hand on the ankle and gave a terrific yank. Bobby came loose from the rope. He dangled upside down, only Stephen's grip on the ankle preventing him from plunging four stories to the sodden lane below.

"Don't hurt me!" Bobby shrieked. "I ain't done nothing! Leggo! I mean, don't leggo! Pull me in!"

"I'll pull you in in my own good time," Stephen panted. "After you answer a few questions."

Feet pounded behind Stephen and he feared that they might belong to the housewife, about to bang him on the head with a block of wood. But it was William.

"Where's that Wally fellow?" William asked.

"Gone across the way."

William saw Wally then, opening a shutter on the opposite house and slipping inside.

"Should I fetch him?" William asked.

"You can try, but I suspect he'll be long gone by the time you get over there."

"You're probably right. What do we do with that one? Hold him hostage?"

"We could. But perhaps he can tell us what we need to know."

"Sounds fair. Why don't you give him to me? You look tired."

"I am. He's heavier than he looks."

"You're just getting old."

"That's funny, coming from you."

"See, I have a sense of humor after all. You just never noticed."

William accepted Bobby's ankle while Stephen leaned against the windowsill. Bobby, meanwhile, had begun to squirm.

"That is not prudent, young fellow," William said, giving Bobby a shake. "I might lose my grip."

Bobby went quiet.

"So, Bobby," Stephen asked, "what have you and your old dad been up to that you're worried about being found out?"

"Nothing."

"Come now, Bobby, we know you've been very busy. Tell me about the girls."

"I don't know nothing about no girls."

"Yes, you do. This fellow here who has you by the leg, one of them's his daughter. He wants her back. You can imagine how angry he is about losing her, and what he might to do to anyone who is responsible."

"I ain't responsible!"

"You had your part to play. We already know this. The only way I can persuade my friend here to allow you to live is if you tell us everything, so we can get her back."

"You promise you'll pull me in?"

"I promise."

Bobby was quiet for a few moments. "All right. We was hired to snatch a few girls."

"What for?"

"To sell 'em."

"To whom?"

"There's houses in the city that buy virgin country girls."

"What houses are they?"

"Well, this batch isn't going to any houses."

"Where are they going?"

"There's a ship coming for them. That's what I heard, anyway."

"A ship? What ship?"

"I don't know. I just heard it was a Portugie ship. The captain was going to buy the lot. Dad said we were going to be rich."

"Do you know the name of this ship?"

"No."

"Has the ship got here?"

"I don't know. I don't think so."

"Why don't you think so?"

"Because the girls are still in hold."

"Where would that be?"

"I don't know. Some farmhouse outside the city."

"Could you find it again?"

"I don't think so. It was dark when we dropped them off. I'd fallen asleep."

"You're lying!" William shouted. He gave Bobby a vicious shake.

"I'm not! I swear!" Bobby cried. "I don't know exactly!"

"You little bastard!" William cried. He swung Bobby outward and then back so that Bobby bashed into the wall.

"William!" Stephen said. "Stop that."

But William did not stop. He swung Bobby out and back again.

As Bobby swung toward the house he arched his back, reaching for a rope just below him. As he reached he gave his trapped leg a wrench. William lost his grip. Bobby fell. It looked as though he would get the rope, but he missed it and cartwheeled to the ground. He landed on his head with a thud.

"Shit," William said, looking at the body below, for Bobby was clearly dead.

"We better get out of here," Stephen said.

He hurried toward the stairway.

Chapter 20

Stephen heard the first cries of "Out! Out!" as he descended the stairs to the hall.

"Well, that didn't take long," William said.

"I suppose it doesn't when you go dropping bodies in the street."

"I didn't drop him."

"I have a feeling no one will believe you."

"What now?" William asked as they reached the ground.

The cries were coming from the lane. So Stephen said, "Out the back."

They ran to the rear of the house and into the back garden, followed by Herb, whom they had met on the stairs. Stephen had not seen Gilbert and hoped that he had the sense not to enter the house and had got away at the first sign of trouble. He had no time to look for Gilbert. The cries of "Out!" meant that hue and cry was being raised, and that required everyone who heard it to turn out to apprehend the evildoers, which in this case meant them.

In his hurry, it did not occur to Stephen that the back garden might be the home of the dogs. He experienced a moment of fright when he discovered that it was, but the dogs were penned in a shed and not running free so that they could only howl at the appearance of the strangers. A pair of horses lifted their heads from a pile of hay at the men's appearance and watched curiously as they crossed the yard.

And there was, to Stephen's surprise, another bear wagon by the hay pile, newer and of a different color with fresher blue and yellow paint than the one abandoned on the road.

Stephen vaulted the back fence without breaking stride and raced across the neighboring garden to the house on the other side, Herb and William drawing away since he could not run very fast with his bad foot.

Herb pulled open the back door to the house. He and William disappeared inside.

When Stephen entered, he had to step over the legs of a woman on her backside, knocked over by Herb or William.

"What are you doing in my house?" the woman demanded.

"I beg your pardon," Stephen said as he dodged around a girl of four who was clutching a rag doll and sucking her thumb.

"House-breaker! I'll have the sheriff after you!" the woman shouted at his back as he stumped across the hall to the front door.

"The least of my crimes, I'm afraid," Stephen said.

The front of the house was occupied by a small shop, the usual arrangement with town houses, and Stephen glimpsed a man and boy crouched over a wooden foot on which they are shaping a shoe but watching the entryway because of the commotion.

Stephen tossed the cobbler a penny. "Sorry about the trouble."

The cobbler gaped and then dove for the penny, which was a good thing because he could not then see which way Stephen went.

This house sat on a street rather than a lane, the difference being that one was wider than the other. Stephen had no idea where he was. Herb and William were just disappearing around a bend to the left. So Stephen went right toward a larger street in the distance, judging that it was best to split up. A cart laden with wood was just ahead. Stephen slipped around in front of it in case the cobbler felt compelled to stick his head out of the shop to see which way Stephen had gone.

After a hundred yards or so, this side street emptied into a wide and busy thoroughfare. Stephen recognized it, although he could not recall its name: Corn something or other it was called here. But he did remember that it ran straight through the city from Newgate to Aldgate.

He turned west toward Newgate, getting his breath under control, trying not to attract any notice and listening closely for any sound of pursuit.

When William and Herb vaulted over the lower half of the door after Stephen, Gilbert hesitated. The vaulting of objects was something for which he had little aptitude, even in his youth. He could have lifted the latch, but his hand lingered over it. Nothing good is going to come from this, a voice said in his mind. One key to living a long life was not taking foolish or unnecessary risks, and while he did not want to be thought a coward any more than anyone did, he did not want to throw away the chance to see his grandchildren, and since he had married late in life he would be in his dotage before any arrived unless Jennie could be persuaded to give up her insane infatuation with Harry and make a decent marriage. It's not that Gilbert didn't like Harry. In fact, he was fond of him, although he would never admit this. But despite the fact that he had risen to a profession from beggarhood, Gilbert could not imagine that Harry would make enough to provide more than a precarious future for Jennie.

So instead of following the others into the house, he slinked down the lane to an alley between two houses where a rain barrel stood guard over the opening. Here he had both a view of the house in question and concealment from any casual observer who might glance his way.

There were shouts from the house and then a man appeared at the top story window. He clambered onto one of the laundry ropes stretched over the lane, and crawled across it to the house on the other side. Gilbert gawked at this in amazement, having never seen such a thing before and, had he not seen it, he would have considered it impossible.

A boy appeared moments later who attempted the same feat, to be snagged by Stephen, who passed his grip to William.

Gilbert heard the questioning and then saw William drop the boy, who struck a rope below which made him cartwheel to the ground.

"Oh, God!" Gilbert murmured. "Better get out of there."

Someone in a house across the way must have seen the boy dropped because that person, a woman, emerged from her house and shouted "Out!" over and over.

An impulse to flee wracked Gilbert's ample frame, but he suppressed it. His appearance in the lane and the fact he was a stranger meant he would certainly be detained, and he did not want that. So he remained in his nook and watched as a crowd gathered, mainly women but a few boys and old men too, as they clustered around the body and discussed matters. The absence of men in their prime puzzled Gilbert until he connected this with the absence of any shops in the lane: it was all houses for men who were probably day labor and worked elsewhere.

Presently, the man who had crossed on the rope came out of the house across the lane.

The man ignored the crowd. He went into his house. While he was there, the howling of the dogs ceased, and he came back to the street.

"Who were those men?" someone asked the man, who had to be Wally.

"No one," Wally said. "No one came."

"But Sarah says —"

"I know what Sarah says, but I don't want anyone saying a thing about them to the coroner when he gets here, or any of the jurymen, either. Bobby fell. He was trying to get across on a rope when he fell. Everybody knows how that fool liked to play on the ropes. He got careless and fell."

"You're sure?"

"I'll take care of my visitors in my own good time. Can't depend on the law for it, anyway."

Wally's questioner spat. "That's true. You can't depend on the law for shit."

"Remember! Tell them he fell!" Wally strode away from the throng coming directly at Gilbert.

Gilbert sank behind the rain barrel, certain he would be seen. But Wally's eyes were on the ground before him, for good reason given all the rubbish that was there to cause any careless person to trip and fall into the muck, a mishap that could be fatal, since disease lurked in the mire. Indeed, with so many rubbish piles about it was a wonder Wally had got his wagon up the lane.

It puzzled Gilbert why Wally would be in such a hurry to leave the scene of the boy's death. It must be because of some matter of supreme importance. Whether this matter had anything to do with the reason why Gilbert was in London could not be determined from behind the rain barrel, so Gilbert pulled up his hood, slipped around the rain barrel and gave chase. He half expected someone in the throng about the body to call out for him to stop, but nobody seemed to have noticed his sudden appearance and rapid retreat.

Wally hurried down the lane and turned right onto Fenchurch Street. Gilbert dashed to the corner in case Wally ducked into a house or a shop before he got there. But Wally had something else in mind, for he was striding by Saint Mary Fenchurch. Gilbert did the best he could to keep Wally in sight.

They passed by the church of the whorehouse, as Gilbert had come to call it in his own mind, owing to the fact that Stephen had not told him the church's actual name, and into the street beyond. Even though it was still quite early the girls were at their places at the windows. One spotted him and called out.

"I'm a married man!" Gilbert called back.

"She'll never find out!"

"Oh, yes, she will!"

Although Gilbert still had very little idea of London geography and was in danger of getting lost if he made any turns, he remembered this street because he had been down it not long ago. It came out at the fork of the three roads where there was another church and beyond that a ford over a rather substantial stream that flowed through the city, the only one of its kind, he remembered Stephen saying.

Gilbert kept expecting Wally to turn this way or that — or worse, to look behind and find he was being followed. But Wally marched with determination, in a hurry to get somewhere fast.

They reached the stream and splashed through the ford, a dead cat riding the current by Gilbert's legs.

The great street they were on, one of the city's grandest, ran all the way to Newgate: Gilbert was proud he remembered this and it gave him some comfort that he could find his way to the inn and his dinner before long.

However, instead of making for Newgate, Wally turned down a street where a big stone cross stood before a church. They went down this side street, which marked the east edge of the grounds of Saint Paul's Cathedral and through the gate onto the road south of Saint Paul's.

Ludgate loomed ahead, and Wally passed through, squeezing by a cart full of goats, the gate wards occupied in counting the goats, a process interrupted when one of the goats realized this was his chance for freedom and leaped the rails to dash off into the crowd to the shouts of encouragement from some and dodging the grasping hands of others who perhaps saw an opportunity for a free dinner.

Between Ludgate and the River Fleet was waste ground, open and covered in long grass that was often employed at sheep and cattle grazing, except for the squat stone structure that Gilbert had been told was the new prison, the gaol at Newgate having proved inadequate to the task of housing the city's criminals. Such open ground might have given Wally the chance, had he looked back, to see Gilbert. But fortunately, a line of carts and pack horses waiting to get into the city crowded the road.

The road was lined with houses and shops beyond the Fleet Bridge as in the city, so there did not seem much likelihood Gilbert would be spotted as they trudged west, the pace having slackened to a middling walk as Wally grew tired, although he got one fright when Wally paused to look in his direction, causing Gilbert to pretend interest in a set of iron pots on display at a shop.

The road forked at Temple Bar just beyond a large, imposing palace of some sort set back from the road. Wally took the left fork. They continued along this way until the road forked again. This time, Wally took the right fork, the left one leading southward, where the spires of a large cathedral could be seen over the tops of the houses and the trees. Gilbert had heard of Westminster and he surmised it lay in that direction. He had hoped to see it, but this would not be his opportunity.

They were in the country now, which forced Gilbert to fall back so that he only had a distant glimpse of Wally since there wasn't enough traffic to conceal him.

The most notable thing about entering the country, apart from the pleasant sights of barley, green and tall in well-tended fields on both sides of the road, was the odor. Gone were the stenches of town, the shit; the sweet gagging rubbish; the acrid snap of piss; the sodden, dull oppression of horse manure; and the reek of bodies that had gone too long without a bath. Instead, the breeze brought the aroma of moist earth, healthy and life-giving, and grass, and as they passed an orchard that of ripening apples.

Gilbert, who enjoyed a walk in the country if it wasn't made too quickly or too long, could not fully savor this one, for Wally gave no indication he meant to stop any time soon. Mile after mile seemed to pass under Gilbert's feet and he wished for a bench to rest his feet and a pot of ale to soothe his thirst. But still Wally pressed on with an unseemly urgency.

While it felt like hours and hours and miles and miles, at last a small village came into view ahead, thatched roofs of ordinary people's houses clustered about a stone church and a stone manor house.

The main road cut straight through the village and Gilbert reached the green separating the church from the manor house in time to see Wally pass through the gate to the manor house. Gilbert could not, of course, follow Wally any farther and he stuck out like a sore thumb standing there on the green. However, there appeared to be an inn on the green beside the church, or at least an ale house, with tables and benches in the yard under a large, friendly oak.

Gilbert seized a seat on a bench, glad to rest his feet. A servant, a boy with a face spotted with pimples, came out of the house with a pitcher and a cup.

"Ale for you, then?" the boy asked.

"Yes, please," said a grateful Gilbert. "What is this place?"

"Knightsbridge, of course. What did you think it was?"

"Oh, yes, it certainly is." Although Gilbert saw no sign of any bridge.

"Last stop before London, it is," the boy said. "We got the finest ale and cheese in the region. Made right in our own back garden. Won't get any better even in the city than here, except where they sell our stuff."

"That sounds excellent. I'll have some of the cheese, I think."

"I'll be right back."

"You can leave the pot," Gilbert said, reaching for it to replenish his cup.

An hour or so elapsed before Wally appeared again. He was not alone. He was at the tail of a procession of four other men surrounding six girls shrouded in cloaks, their heads down so that Gilbert could not see their faces. Gilbert's heart clenched with fear and excitement at the sight of them. This had not been a wasted journey after all.

The procession hustled across the green, the leader of it casting a suspicious glance in Gilbert's direction. Gilbert pretended to be more interested in a wren above his head, the picture of a man taking his ease on the way from here to there, or so he hoped.

Wally broke away as the procession departed, heading southward. He hurried back up the road to London.

Gilbert dropped some farthings on the table and followed the procession.

There were open fields south of the village, which made pursuit a dicey proposition, if Gilbert hoped to remain undiscovered. And he really did. This bunch was capable of murder and he didn't want to be found out.

The procession was following a path that ran along a stream. Gilbert waited until they had rounded a bend and disappeared from sight, then hurried after them.

He proceeded this way, from bend to bend, until at last he detected the metallic odor of the river. He moved more carefully now, for they had to have halted at the bank, which meant he could stumble on them at any moment.

He heard voices, a girl protesting, a snarl in response, a girl's yelp, and then a hollow thump — the unmistakable sound of an oar knocking against a boat.

After a couple of heart beats, Gilbert crept closer.

His suspicions were confirmed as he reached the river bank, where a house stood under a brace of willows.

A ferry boat was pulling away from the bank into the middle of the river, headed down stream. Two men were rowing, there was another at the tiller, and the four men and the girls were clustered about the mast.

Gilbert hurried back up the path to Knightsbridge. It was a long way to London and he had to get there as soon as he could.

Then he stopped.

There had been a rowboat pulled up on the bank by the house, a small thing for only a few people.

He swallowed hard, thinking about this rowboat. The audacity of the thought blossoming in his mind made him giddy with fright. He could not do it, he should not do it.

He went back to the house.

Gilbert stood above the rowboat waiting for a voice from the house to ask his intentions.

No one said a thing.

He stumbled down the bank, pushed the boat into the water, stepped into it, and settled on the rowing bench.

He looked over his shoulder. The ferry boat was still in sight, drawing away.

He rowed after it.

Gilbert's experience with rowboats was limited to small rivers like the Teme where the water was slack in most places and the objective had either been to get across or go a short distance at a leisurely pace to see the sights and enjoy oneself. Neither had required much effort.

Here, however, the water was not slack, and in fact it was running in the wrong direction: upstream. So not only did he have to struggle to keep the kidnappers' boat in sight over his shoulder, but he had to fight the river itself. It wasn't long before his arms and back ached and sweat dribbled down his forehead — his hat having been removed early on — and stung his eyes. It grew so hot that he even had to take off his coat. He hoped no one saw this indignity and mistook him for a common working person. While he had been awed by the majestic size of the river when he had first seen it, it wasn't long before he began to loathe the greenish brown monster.

The only good thing was that the kidnappers did not seem to be getting away, even though their boat had two men at the oars.

The upshot was that Gilbert spent so much attention on the rowing of the boat — it was harder to keep on course over a long distance than he remembered — and casting glances at the target that he had little opportunity to spare for admiring the sights along the way.

And then, after what seemed like half a day of rowing, the glory of the Westminster palace and the abbey cathedral appeared on his right. It was such an overwhelming sight, one of the grandest things Gilbert had ever seen, that he almost stopped dead in the stream. Boys in a boat heading upstream saw him gawking and snickered. Gilbert looked over his shoulders and applied the oars.

His appreciation of the shore had shown him something else. The stream was now flowing properly downriver, for Gilbert was making much better time than he had been.

It wasn't long before he came to a great bend in the river, where houses grew more thickly along the northern bank, most of them palaces of the rich cloaked with beautiful gardens, and he realized he had reached the outskirts of the city.

The struggle was not yet ended, however. The river had grown choked with boats ahead going every which way, requiring him to change directions often to avoid a collision, which he feared because if his boat overturned he might fall in and drown. Like many English people he had shrunk from learning to swim owing to the perpetual coldness of the water. He regretted that decision now.

Gilbert suffered several moments of panic when he had trouble picking out the kidnappers' boat from the throng of others in his way, but somehow he managed to keep it in sight as he reached the city at last, and it slid along on his right, more deserving of his attention that he could give it. But there was one moment he allowed himself to marvel at the spectacle: the entire city from Baynard's Castle to the Tower stood before him, in its chaotic yet mesmerizing jumble, a gorgeous sight captured in a single glimpse, the entire great city lying whole before his eyes. Wait until he told the people back at Ludlow about this.

Then the moment passed when a ferryman fended his boat off with a pole. "Observe the right of way, jackass!" the ferryman admonished. The cow standing in the back of the ferryboat did not seem the least perturbed by the incident, however, and did not lift its head from the pile of hay before it.

"Sorry! Sorry!" Gilbert stammered. He had no idea what the right of way was, but he suspected he was violating this law at every stroke.

The kidnapper's boat was nearing the great bridge now, and Gilbert stopped rowing to admire the scene. He had got a view before when he and Stephen had trudged from wharf to wharf but that had been nothing to compare with this — the stone arches marching across the water supported by little islands shaped like boats with prows and sterns, the houses rearing impossibly high and seeming about to topple over.

When he brought his attention back to the business at hand, he saw that the kidnappers' boat was making for the broadest arch of the span about halfway across where there was a drawbridge. There were boats clustered about the span and people visible on the little islands of packed earth holding up the supports. Gilbert wondered what they were doing there as he rowed toward the drawbridge.

He heard a dispute break out on the kidnappers' boat, something about running the bridge. Gilbert wondered what that meant. It must be another nautical term. He would have to ask about it when he got off the river, in a way that did not reveal his own ignorance, of course.

As he drew closer, he became aware of shouts and calls of derision from the people on the boats and the islands, and behind them the rushing of water.

This latter sound puzzled Gilbert. Why was there the noise of rushing water? It reminded him of a stream going over a weir.

He glanced over his shoulder for the source of this mystery in time to see a boat enter the span occupied by the drawbridge. To his amazement, the prow of the boat dipped from view and the stern tilted into the air. Then it shot out of sight.

Barely a heartbeat passed and the kidnappers' boat entered the span as well, and its prow too seemingly dipped into the water while its stern tilted skyward.

It was only then that Gilbert appreciated his danger. Ahead there lay the froth and fury of rapids. He could not imagine how they had got there. And he was about to go over them.

Gilbert dug his oars into the water, determined to avoid this fate. But in his haste and inexperience at watercraft, instead of turning the boat safely away, it only slewed about. There was the sensation of a great suck on the boat as the water, its pull increasing and inexorable, drew him toward the fatal gap. Distantly he heard hoots and laughter from the spectators. Was that for him?

He did not waste any effort considering this possibility. He was too busy trying to avoid going over the cliff.

But try as he might, he succeeded only in driving the prow of his boat hard against one of the islands.

The impact and the effect of the rushing current caused the boat to tip. There was a moment when it seemed as if that would be it, but brown and swirling water came over the sides, causing the boat to flip over all the way, pitching Gilbert into the stream.

The rushing current threw him forward, and he tumbled end over end, a child's rag doll tossed away. Then he came to calmer water where he felt no sensation but perhaps one of suspension, engulfed by brownish green goo with a silver shimmering light above. But it was cold and there was death within it. The shimmering diminished, a sign he was sinking deeper. He imagined hands reaching from the murk to grasp his ankles and pull him down.

It was only then that he began to panic.

He had no idea what to do, but some instinct made him claw toward the surface which now seemed impossibly far away.

No matter how hard he struggled he seemed to make to progress at all. He lungs burned, eager to take a breath, even if was only of water. His head was about to burst, his eyes were about to pop out of his head.

And then he broke the surface. No air ever tasted fresher, even if it was filled with the aromas of the city; that is to say, rubbish, shit, horse manure and piss and faintly of tar and pitch, not to mention the stink of smoke.

Having no experience at staying afloat in water deeper than he was tall, Gilbert continued his thrashing in the hopes this would have some good effect. But these hopes seemed a trifle optimistic, even from his distressed vantage point.

However, a voice quite close said, "Look what I've found! It's a fooking mermaid!"

"Ugliest mermaid I've ever seen," another voice said.

"How're you doing there, mermaid?" the first voice asked Gilbert.

"I'm not a mermaid," Gilbert burbled with a mouth full of water. "Can you help me out? I can't swim."

"You are a master of the obvious," the voice said. The owner of the voice grasped Gilbert's collar.

Gilbert realized the voices belonged to two men in a small boat.

"If you twiddle our wands we'll take you to shore, all safe and sound," the man with the second voice said.

"Throw me back," Gilbert said.

The man with a grip on Gilbert's collar gave him a shake. "Got any money?"

"A little."

"Let's see what you got."

Gilbert handed over his purse.

The man who had held his collar released him, but Gilbert was able to cling to the side of the boat. The fellow inspected the contents of the purse.

"The fooker's a fooking lord," the fellow declared.

He hauled Gilbert into the boat.

"More like a whale that a mermaid," his companion opined as Gilbert flopped over the gunwale.

"Where can we humble lads take you, sir?" asked the collar grabber.

Gilbert gestured toward the London end of the bridge. "There."

"Row quickly, churl," the fellow said to his companion. "His lordship needs to return to the sweet bosom of his lady."

"She'll appreciate that he's had a bath," the other fellow said. "I bet it's been some time."

"I bathe every week, thank you very much," Gilbert said clasping his knees.

"Oooh. He *is* a lord!" the purse snatcher said. "Bathes every week! No friend of lice and fleas, you are! They deserve a home, too, you know."

Gilbert looked around for some sight of the kidnapper's boat, some indication where they had gone. But there was nothing. They had as good as vanished from the river. He had failed, and never so spectacularly.

"I've lost my coat and hat," Gilbert said to no one in particular.

"And a perfectly good boat! What were you thinking, trying to run the bridge like that? I've never seen such a pathetic effort."

Chapter 21

"I'm sorry," Gilbert said into his cup after he had finished his account of what had happened to him that day.

"You should be," William growled. He upended his cup. "We'd have Ida by now if you'd been more careful."

"I don't know," Stephen said, waving to the servant to replenish the cheese platter, all there was on offer at the inn for supper, since the dinner traffic had consumed everything at that meal and there were no leftovers, the usual fare at supper. "We're a step closer. So, they ran the bridge, eh?"

"What does that mean?" Gilbert asked.

"When the tide changes, the bridge's pilings act as a sort of dam," Stephen said. "The buildup on one side rushes between them and it's very dangerous to run the bridge then. People usually wait for slack water to avoid the rapids. It suggests a bit of desperation on their part. Most only take the risk for the fun of it."

"They know we're after them and that we're close," Gilbert said.

"Yes, I'd say that's true."

"Do you think the ship is here?"

"I suspect it is. I can't think of anywhere else they would have taken the girls. If they had a hiding place in London they would have used it straightaway."

"How will we find this ship? There are so many."

"The usual way, I suppose. Ask around."

"Oh, my aching feet. I wish there was another way. Will you buy me a new coat and hat first? I was relieved of all my money by those robbers on the river."

"You gave them more than the usual charge. They're only supposed to get a penny for pulling you out."

"How do you know this?"

"I've run the bridge a few times."

"Why does that not surprise me? No doubt gambling was involved."

"It was innocent fun, nothing more. The exuberance of youth."

"I am not deceived. You've led a wastrel's life." Gilbert sighed. "What a day, dunked and fleeced. I shall never live this down."

"I'll be sure you don't."

"I knew I could count on you."

"What else are friends for?"

"I wish there were another way …" Gilbert's words echoed in Stephen's mind the next morning as they all set out to find the ship. His initial thought had been to do what they had done before: talk to people at all the wharves, this time below the bridge, where the ocean-going ships tied up. But that would take time since tedious footwork was the usual way of finding things out. However, he had a feeling that they now did not have the luxury of time.

So when the party reached Bridge Street, Stephen turned on it toward the bridge.

"Where are you going?" William asked.

"Playing a hunch," Stephen said.

"Oh, dear," Gilbert said.

"What?" William said. "His hunches aren't reliable?"

"Sometimes they are." Gilbert hurried after Stephen. "Half the time, anyway, I'd say. I hope this doesn't take long."

"It shouldn't," Stephen said over his shoulder as he shrank against a house wall to avoid an oncoming cart piled high with building stone.

Stephen stopped at the Italian banker's house that stood by the gap just before Saint Thomas' Chapel. He knocked on the door. One of the functionaries opened it after a minute or so.

"What can we do for you, sir?" the functionary asked.

"I would like to see Sir Bartolommeo," Stephen said.

"He is not up yet."

"But it's well after dawn."

"He was up late last night. He will be down in an hour or so. Have you come to redeem the remainder of your funds? We have an extra day."

"It's not about that. I need some information."

"What sort of information?"

"About a ship."

The functionary pursed his lips in thought. "Edmund is here. He keeps track of the shipping."

Edmund turned out to be the Englishman who had translated for them during their earlier transaction.

"Good day to you," Edmund said when he came to the counter. "Harold tells me you want information about a ship."

"That's right," Stephen said.

"What for, may I ask? No offense intended, but you do not seem the sort to need a ship."

"I don't need anything but to find it."

"I feel compelled to ask why, for some reason, but I think I will leave that question aside. What is its name, this ship?"

"We have no idea."

"That isn't helpful."

"If it has a name, we'd like to know it. Also, if it is in port, and where."

"I don't see how I can be of any help."

"This is a Portuguese ship. Do you know of any that has arrived recently?"

Edmund's brow furrowed. "As a matter of fact, yes. Come with me."

Harold opened the counter and allowed them to pass to a stairway at the rear of the house. They all climbed to the top floor, where there was a dormitory for servants, and a porch at the rear, overlooking the river. Edmund went out to the porch. It was a small porch and thus a tight fit for everyone, so Herb and Gilbert had to watch from the doorway.

Edmund pointed downriver to a spot shy of the Tower. "It's that cog without a forecastle at the Watergate," he said.

Stephen peered through the haze toward the indicated spot. There was such a jumble of ships moored along the eastern wharves and about that spot in particular that even with Edmund's pointing finger he wasn't sure of the vessel he meant.

"It arrived two days ago," Edmund said.

"What's the ship's name?"

"The *Sao Jorge*."

Stephen had never heard of a wharf called the Watergate, but the place Edmund had pointed to lay beside the London shipyards, where shipwrights built vessels above and on the broad tidal flats just west of the Tower.

The Watergate lay five-hundred yards from London Bridge where Thames Street dead-ended at the shipyards. It was long, narrow, and canal-like, with revetments made from old ships' hulls. The tide was out and the place smelled of mud, brine and rotting fish.

The boats within the canal itself were for river traffic. They lay on their keels in the mud, masts tilting every which way.

The big ships were farther out at the end of the wharf, where the water was deep enough to float them; even at low tide there was enough river under them that they didn't lean much when their keels were on the bottom.

There a crane operated by a pair of men on a treadmill was lowering a pallet of what appeared to be lead ingots toward the forward hatch of the ship nearest the wharf, the others being tied up gunwale to gunwale, a full half dozen big ships bobbing and creaking together in the current. And there was a line of carts laden with more ingots waiting to be unloaded, the drivers standing around looking bored, one of them shagging broken pieces of wood at something out of sight in the canal.

The party could not stand here long without attracting attention, so Stephen led them a couple of doors back up Thames Street to a tavern.

"What are you doing?" William protested. "We're here! Let's not tarry."

"We don't know they're here," Stephen said. "And we can't go barging onto a ship unless we're sure. We won't get a second chance. So I want to have a look around first. You stay here. One person snooping about is probably one too many."

There had been a forestaller selling old clothes a few streets back at Billingsgate. Stephen went out to find him, and he was still there. Stephen bought a shapeless woolen hat that was hardly more than a sock for the head, an old green shirt and worn orange stockings that had lost almost all their color, but were in better condition than his own in that they had fewer patches and holes that had been mended. He carried them back to the tavern where he changed in the back garden.

"You look a sight," William snorted. "Like some poor workman or even a beggar. You should be ashamed of yourself."

"Well, I'm not, and that's the idea. Wally will have told them a couple of knights were after them. This way, I won't be spotted, at least I hope so."

William shook his head at this madness, for dressing as a person of a lower class was a grave embarrassment for a person of the gentry.

"Well, I do think you look handsome," Gilbert said.

"Thank you, Gilbert. I feel almost regal. A feather in the cap ought to do it, don't you think?"

"It is a pity you spared the expense."

"Sacrifices sometimes must be made. Try not to wander off. I don't think I'll be long."

At the wharf, Stephen strolled all the way out to the end by the bow of the ship being loaded, and watched proceedings with the air of a man who had an appreciation for the loading of ships.

The ship was commonly called a cog, now coming into general use on the seas. It was a good seventy-five feet long, broad and imposing. A yellow and black sail was furled to the yard of the single mast. There was, as he had been told to expect in the *Sao Jorge*, no forecastle, nor even a proper sterncastle either. The structure at the stern was more of a raised platform for the steersman with the upper deck serving as the ceiling for a covered area on the main deck. Stephen had been on similar ships before and this was where the crew sheltered, the hold being a dank, dark and unpleasant place reserved for the stores, the cargo and the ship's rats.

The two hatches, which gaped before the mast, were open and men were visible in the openings wrestling armloads of ingots out of sight below deck, singing a chant of some sort. It was hard, dirty work, and he was glad he did not have to do anything like it for a living. There were two fellows on the sterncastle. Both had thick black beards and wore brown coats. They looked so alike that they could be brothers, distinguishable only by the fact that one was older with grey flecking his hair and a receding hairline. The younger one poured ruby-colored wine from a pitcher into a cup for his companion, and they sipped together while watching the proceedings.

There was no sign of Ida or any other girl. But there would not be, of course. They would be hidden away below decks if they were anywhere at all.

Stephen started to ask one of the workmen which of the ships at the wharf was the *Sao Jorge*, but the question stuck on his tongue, unuttered. If he was the captain of the ship and if he had stolen girls in his hold, he'd be sure to see that anyone snooping about for the *Sao Jorge* would be reported to him. The last thing Stephen wanted was to alert the crew of the *Sao Jorge* that he was on to them.

An officious-looking man topped with a purple felt hat bearing a silver badge striding toward him, followed closely by a fellow who had a clerkish look about him, marched down the wharf toward the ships. That badge meant something important, but what?

"Who is that?" Stephen asked one of the cart drivers.

"The Weasel," the cart driver said. "Customs agent for this part of the river. A real turd."

Customs! Stephen should have thought of that before. They would know the name and location of every ocean-going ship in the river. There were times when he was an idiot, and this was one of them, when he could least afford it.

Stephen was about to ask the Weasel, but another group appeared behind him: four women with yellow hats led by a man wearing a red cap embroidered with yellow, a long cloak with slits in the sides for his arms and yellow stars painted on his shoes. The yellow hats meant the women were whores and the man had to be their pimp.

The Weasel glanced at Stephen without a sign of interest as he passed by. The Weasel mounted the gangway to the ship and crossed it to the next one. He kept going until he reached the last ship.

Meanwhile, the pimp stopped at the gangway. "I say," he called to the men on the sterncastle. "Is this the Sow Horhay?"

"It is," one of the men said in heavily accented English.

The pimp bowed elaborately. "I have brought your entertainment, gentlemen."

The men on the sterncastle grinned and descended to the main deck.

The younger of the pair drew a canvas curtain across the open space beneath the sterncastle.

"Welcome aboard," said the other one that Stephen took to be the captain.

The whores went aboard and vanished behind the curtain with the two men.

The pimp climbed to the sterncastle where he poured himself a cup of wine and leaned against the railing.

Now that Stephen had identified the *Sao Jorge* at no risk to himself and without alerting the crew, he still had to establish that the girls were aboard. A small rowboat passed by the mouth of the canal heading down river. One man was rowing and the other dangled a fishing line in the water. The sight of the rowboat sparked an idea in Stephen's mind.

He hurried back to Little Wales Street which ran above the shipyard and along it toward the Tower. There were only a few houses on the river side and they soon gave way so that the road ran along the tidal flats where ships were on blocks in various stages of construction, the frames of uncompleted ones looking like the ribs of enormous dead sea creatures. Not too far away, the rowboat had put ashore. Stephen went down to the two men in it.

"I'd like to hire your boat," Stephen said.

The two looked him up and down. The man who had been rowing said, "With what? A kiss and a promise?"

"I have money," Stephen said. He emptied half the contents of his purse into his palm. "Would two pennies do it?" This was an awful lot to hire a small rowboat, but he did not want to waste time dickering.

"Where'd you steal that?" The boatman stared in amazement.

"It's not stolen, and how it was earned is none of your business."

"What you want me boat for?"

"Also none of your business. And if you can throw a drill into the deal, I'll add another penny."

"You're mad."

"People have said that before. But I'm really just in a hurry."

"Billie, fetch this fellow a drill. Mick's got a spare one he ain't using."

Stephen pushed the boat into the river and rowed upstream. He rowed slowly around the press of ships at the mouth of the wharf and those anchored not far from it or tied to mooring stakes driven into the river bottom. He turned between two cogs and headed into the thicket of vessels. The ships were too close together here to allow Stephen to use the oars — in fact, there were spots where he could hardly fit the boat through — but he was able to make progress by standing in the boat and pulling it along by grasping the bows or sterns of the ships on either side.

The Bear Wagon

At last he reached the stern of the *Sao Jorge*. He held onto the rudder, careful not to turn it, which he feared would alert anyone above on deck. He listened to the captain and the mate say a few words to each other over the racket made by the loading of the ingots; it sounded like Portuguese to him, but he wasn't sure. When the two men gave no sign they knew Stephen was there, he worked his way around the rudder so that he could press an ear to the stern planks, reasonably sure that the overhang of the sterncastle would conceal him from anyone who did not lean over the rail. In the cogs he had traveled in, there had been a compartment just before the rudder where valuables were kept separate from the cargo hold and where the crew could not pilfer them. He was gambling that if the girls were on the ship, they were imprisoned there. He could hear knocking about inside, and feel vibrations, which had to come from the loading. Above, the pimp tapped his foot to the rhythm of the song.

Then there was a faint knock close by and the sound of voices. They were too faint to tell if they belonged to men or women.

Stephen applied the drill to the side of the ship. The plank was only an inch or two thick and it did not take long to put a hole in it. He listened at the hole. There was silence, then rustling. He had the sensation of someone pressing close.

He put his mouth the hole and whispered, "Is anyone there?"

"Yes! Yes!" a girl said. "Who are you?"

"Hush," Stephen whispered, fearful that those above might hear despite the racket of the singing. The tapping foot did not break its cadence, however. "Don't let them hear you. Is Ida there?"

"Help us!" the girl said. "Please help us!"

There were footfalls above Stephen's head. Someone hawked and spat over the side. Stephen froze, petrified he would be discovered. The footfalls retreated, and the tapping to the song returned, but he was afraid to speak any further.

"We'll come for you," Stephen breathed into the hole. "Don't worry. Now, be quiet, as if nothing has happened."

Chapter 22

Stephen plugged the hole with a scrap cut from the hem of his shirt. It would not escape detection if seen from outside, but that seemed unlikely. However, if one of the crew looked into the compartment from the hold, it should still be dark, the hole undetected.

He eased out from between the ships into the river. His heart pounded and his mouth was dry, and he had to force himself to go carefully and not be in a hurry. Even so, once he was out of sight of the *Sao Jorge*, he rushed things, banging several times into this ship or that until he was free of them.

He rowed for all he was worth once he was in the current, a sense of mad urgency taking over his mind.

He beached the rowboat where he had got it and ran up the mudflat as fast as his bad foot allowed, slipping a few times until he reached the street, ignoring the amazed expressions on the faces of the men who had rented the boat.

He broke down to a walk only at the top of the Watergate canal, his sense of prudence momentarily asserting itself at the realization that someone from the *Sao Jorge* might see him running and wonder what was up. They had to be desperate men and the slightest suspicion might arouse them to action.

The same sense of prudence caused him to pause at the tavern door. It now occurred to him that members of the *Sao Jorge's* crew might be in the tavern, given its proximity to the Watergate, even though it was not the closest one, a possibility that had not occurred to him when he had chosen it earlier. He cursed himself for a fool. He could have already ruined everything. So he only stuck his head in. He caught Herb's attention and waved him to the door.

"Have them come out now," Stephen panted when Herb reached the street. "Quietly, as if nothing is the matter."

"Right, sir," Herb said. "Is everything all right?"

"Just go — quickly!"

"What is it?" William asked when they had all emerged and gone up the street after Stephen some yards from the tavern. "Did you find her?"

Stephen grasped William by the shoulders. His voice failed him at that moment. He nodded.

"Dear God!" William exclaimed. In his excitement he embraced Stephen. "Dear God! Thanks be to God!"

They stepped back from their embrace.

"Now we have to get her out," Stephen said.

It was fully dark by the time the hired boat pushed away from Southwark and headed into the river. Stephen wanted the protection of the night and it gave the crew of the *Sao Jorge* a chance to settle down to sleep. He savored the prospect of catching the bastards in their sleep. It was a clear night, the stars bright, and there would not be a moon for an hour or so yet, it being a quarter past full.

The jagged outline of the roofs of London drew closer as the boat crew pulled at the oars, the captain having declared a sail unnecessary for the mere crossing of the river. Peter, the captain, was experienced at smuggling goods into the city during the night to avoid the tolls, and oars were preferred to sail. It attracted less attention. Moreover, there were obstacles in the way, lines of ships anchored side-by-side here and there that could be better avoided under oars than sail.

At last the keel scraped bottom at the shipyard above the Tower on Little Wales Street. Stephen leaped from the bow, shield on his back, helmet in hand, mail jingling. William, Herb and Gilbert followed. He would have preferred to leave someone with the boat to ensure it would be there when they got back. But he needed every one of them for the attack to succeed, and so he had to trust that the amount the crew was expecting to be paid would hold them still.

They reached Little Wales and turned west toward the Watergate.

The Bear Wagon

Stephen paused at the top of the canal. "Here we go, lads," he said. He put on his arming cap and helmet. William and Herb did the same. Gilbert, who had no helmet or armor, hefted an axe and gulped in apprehension even though he was not expected to fight. His job was to hack into the prison compartment when the time came.

He drew his sword, swung his shield from his back and marched toward the wharf.

It wasn't apparent that something was amiss until Stephen put his foot on the gangway.

The outline of the ship tied up against the wharf was different. There was a forecastle of a sort, a raised platform with a railing at the bow, and the sterncastle was higher than he remembered, also with railings rather than a solid low wall.

"Wait here," he told the others.

Stephen crossed to the deck. He expected there to be a watchman, but no one challenged him. He went around the mast to the sterncastle, where he heard snores of sleeping men.

He prodded the foot of one of the sleeping men.

The sailor sat up, rubbing his face. "*Hoe is het?*" he asked.

"Speak English," Stephen said.

"Who are you?" the sailor asked in a Dutch accent.

The others began to stir at the commotion.

"What ship is this?" Stephen asked.

"*De mus*, out of Ostend."

"Where's the ship that was here this afternoon?"

"She finished loading."

"And?"

"They towed her to anchorage to make room for us."

"Where?"

"How would I know? Middle of the river somewhere, I suppose. Why?"

"We have some business with her captain."

"And you thought to do it in the middle of the night?"

"It isn't the middle of the night. Sleep tight. Sorry to disturb you."

Stephen returned to the wharf.

They spent the night in the rowboat at the shipyard. In the morning, Herb went up to a cookhouse on the street and brought back breakfast for everyone, fresh bread, slices of bacon that were still hot enough to burn the mouth concealed in a loaf that was soaked with delicious grease, butter and apples.

Stephen chewed on his portion without tasting it as he surveyed the river, looking for the *Sao Jorge*. Until this moment, he had not appreciated how busy the Thames was. Even this early, hundreds of boats where on the river, crossing from London to Southwark or going the other way, some under sail, others under oars. And everywhere on the water there were great clumps of ocean-going vessels moored side-by-side, swing on their anchors from the bridge to beyond the Tower. It fact it was so clogged with these clumps of ships that it was a miracle that any one of them could fit through one way or the other. The *Sao Jorge* could be anywhere.

"No sign of her?" asked Peter, the boat captain.

Stephen shook his head. "She could have gone already."

"I doubt that. Few captains dare the river in the late afternoon. Tide's coming in, but it's nearly slack water. It'll turn in an hour. I'll wager he's waiting for the morning ebb. That's when most ships depart: the morning ebb, if they can. You can get almost to the sea if you leave on the morning ebb."

"Almost to the sea?"

"Yeah, it's near eighty miles with all the twists and turns. The ships go as far as they can, then anchor and wait for the next day's flood. Captains don't like to do it because there's pirates toward the mouth. But they don't really have a choice if they want to keep their ship. No pilot in his right mind runs the sands after dark and at low water."

Stephen had no idea what Peter meant by the sands, but he didn't pursue the point. Yet what Peter had said gave him an idea. "What will it cost to follow her, if she's still here?"

"More than we've been paid so far." Peter grinned, naming a sum. "And we'll need provisions if we're going downriver."

Stephen poured out the contents of his purse and gave Peter a handful of coins.

"Get what provisions you need."

Peter stirred the coins in his hand. "All right. Nothing like a little river cruise."

"I trust it has been profitable so far."

Peter grinned and turned to his mate.

"Herb," Stephen said, holding out a few more pennies. "See if you can get us a ladder."

"A ladder, sir? What do we need a ladder for?"

"Never mind that now, just find one. Eight or ten feet should do."

The tide turned at dawn and since then the river had flowed upstream. Slack water arrived about five hours later, and the river seemed to stand still. Shortly after, the flow reversed and receded from about the boat with surprising rapidity so that where she had floated in the shallows, her keel had come to rest on the mud.

Gilbert shaded his eyes against the rising sun. He pointed across the river near the far shore opposite the Tower. "Isn't that it?"

Stephen peered in the direction indicated. A pair of rowboats was towing a cog from a thicket of vessels. The mast bore a yellow and black sail which fell from the yard as he watched and flapped free.

"That's her," he said.

"All right!" Peter said. He put a shoulder to the gunwale of the boat. "Everyone now! Push! And that means you, too, sirs! She's a heavy bitch when she's on the bottom. Let's get her in the water!"

Everyone put their backs to an oar, even William, until they had got beyond the congestion of the anchorages at the first turn of the river. Then Peter raised the boat's sail and they had nothing to do but enjoy the breeze, watch the green fields on either side roll by and worry about what came next.

The *Sao Jorge* lay ahead, but she was vanishing around another turn of the river, where a small village was visible at the top of the curve.

"She's getting away," Willian growled. "Can't we go faster?"

"This is the best we can do," Peter said. "She has more sail than we do. We'll never catch her in a race. But we'll find her by dark, when she has to anchor."

The wind died in late afternoon, and for a time the boat drifted downstream on the current. But then the tide turned and to avoid being pushed back the way they had come, Peter insisted that everyone, crew and passengers alike, take to the oars again. Within minutes the rowers were sweating so that hats and coats found themselves in piles at the men's feet. At least the deck boards were dry.

"Take heart, boys!" Peter said. "They have no oars! We may stumble on them at any moment."

"I am comforted by the fact we are drawing closer," Gilbert muttered to Stephen. "But only a little."

"They may even drop anchor!" Peter said.

"Do you really think so?" asked Stephen, who was squeezing as much hope from this possibility as he could. He dreaded the thought they might escape to the sea with Ida.

There'd be no getting her back then. This was their only chance.

"Ships have been known to do that to avoid drifting into a bank when becalmed in the river," Peter said with the air of complete authority. "Without headway, they can't steer. So keep rowing!"

"What is headway?" Gilbert asked Stephen.

"I think he means going forward. It's nautical stuff."

"Ah, a good thing about travel is how it opens the mind to new things. But I wish I was home just the same."

"Look at it another way. You will be able to pretend expertise on ships and boats, like you do in other things. Imagine the rapt attention you will achieve in the hall on winter evenings. People will think you are a world traveler."

"It is not all pretense. I have traveled quite a lot. Who else in Ludlow besides yourself can boast of running the London Bridge?"

Stephen chuckled. "That is something to boast about. Will you mention your swim?"

"I'm sure you'll do that for me."

"Of course. If you forget to do so."

"Do you think you could spell me?" Gilbert gasped to Peter after they had been rowing for an hour or so. "I can take the tiller." This was another nautical term he had picked up.

"You'll just run us into the bank," Peter said giving the steering oar mounted to the stern post a swish so that the boat rocked to and fro. There were clearly privileges to being boatmaster that he was loathe to give up.

"It's a broad river. I think I can manage to stay in the middle of it."

"Can you afford to pay for my boat if you sink it?"

"How much does a boat like this cost?"

"Probably forty shillings just in workmen's wages. And then you have the cost of timber and nails, the sails, rope, goat hair for caulking, tar. It's a long list. What did you think, that a shipwright just slaps things together?"

"I had not thought about it."

"I've a big investment here. I have to protect it. Now, get on with it and quit complaining."

At sundown the tide turned again and began another runout to the sea. A breeze picked up as well, from the northwest. The river turned sharply north beyond the town of Gravesend. Before them were three cogs anchored straight ahead where the river bent eastward. As they drew closer, they could make out that one of them had yellow and black sails bundled to the yardarm.

"There she is," Peter said with satisfaction. "Told you."

He turned the boat into a stream entering from the right as if that had been the boat's intention all along.

"We can wait for full dark here," Peter said to Stephen and William. "You best get what rest you can."

It had been brisk on the water, but now it started to grow very chilly as the sunlight faded and night descended.

Peter had moored the boat close enough that Stephen and William were able to splash to the shore.

Stephen waded through tall marsh grass to the head of the inlet, for it was too broad to be called a stream, even though that is what Peter had named it: Cliff Burn.

William and Peter joined him.

"They'll be anchored right at the edge of the flats," Peter said. "There's a village over there." He waved to the east. "Cliffe, it's called. The villagers love to take a vessel now and then, same as the people of Canvey and around Benflot. They swarm out in the night and attack the shipping at anchor waiting for the morning. This reach of the river is filled with the hulks they've ravaged. Can't blame, them. Piss poor, this place is. The ship masters like to gather together when they can. Makes them feel safe. Might do some good, too, if the ships have boats of their own."

Stephen squinted down the river in the failing light. "I can't tell if they have any boats of their own."

"What's your plan, then?" Peter asked. "Swoop in and kill everyone aboard?"

"Something like that."

"A subtle plan. Well, it's worked for others, so there's no reason it shouldn't work for you. Have you given any thought what you'll do with the ship after you've taken her?"

"No," William said. "We haven't. I'm not interested in the ship. Just what she's carrying."

"Yes, precious cargo, I understand," Peter said. "They'll be waiting for you with a watch out, you know. You'll have a better chance of taking her if you have a few more men."

"Where are we going to get them?" Stephen asked.

"Right here." Peter thumped his chest. "Give me the ship and her cargo, except for your precious bit, of course, and we'll be happy to help."

With the deal struck, Peter went off to the village of Cliffe. He returned in an hour with five men from the village armed with two bows and forty arrows, short swords and small round shields. They also had two grappling hooks, a pair of axes and rope.

"This is my cousin, Fred," Peter said by way of introduction, "and a few of his in-laws, reprobates, I'm sorry to say, every one."

"That's right, we are," Fred said with a grin that even in the dark revealed front teeth the size of shovels and the smell of onions.

"Well, they should be fast asleep by now," Peter said. "Maybe even the watch. So let's be off before daylight."

"Yes, I love summer," Fred said, "but there's never enough dark for any meaningful work."

Everyone clambered into the boat. The Cliffe men took over the oars and rowed into the river while William, Stephen and Herb struggled into their gambesons and mail.

"Nice and easy, boys," Peter said.

"We know what to do, you lunk," said one of the Cliffe men. "It ain't like we haven't done this before."

"You do know how to steer this thing, right?" another of the Cliffe men said.

"I am surprised he managed to get this far down river," said another of the Cliffe men with a grin. "The oaf."

"Couldn't sail a cake of soap in a tub," said Fred with gusto.

"Stop it, boys," Peter said. "You're scaring our guests."

"Ooo, begging yer pardon, sirs," Fred said. "Don't want to upset you."

"You're not upsetting me," Stephen said as he slipped by the rowers to the bow. "But watch out for William. He has a temper."

"Quiet, you," Peter said. "They'll hear us."

"Right," Fred muttered, but it was a whisper.

It was hard to make out anything ahead, even though the shore could be distinguished from the sky, stars winking above scattered clouds. Stephen fretting, wondering how Peter knew which way to go. But presently, three bulky shapes loomed ahead. Peter hissed. The rowers held their oars above the water. The boat glided forward, accompanied only by the sound of lapping at the bow and a few minor creaks and groans.

They were headed toward the middle ship. There was a cough from the ship to the right. Stephen cringed, expecting a voice to call the alarm. But the night was silent.

Peter turned the boat side-on as it reached the *Sao Jorge*, and the rowers on the left side of the boat brought in their oars.

In the instant before the two vessels bumped together, two of the Cliffe men tossed their grappling hooks into the air. The hooks caught on the gunwale of the ship.

Stephen and William raised the ladder and rested it against the side of the ship. Stephen was about to mount the ladder when William put a hand on his shoulder.

"No," William breathed into Stephen's ear. "I'll go first. I must do it."

There wasn't time to protest. Every moment was precious now and could not be wasted. So Stephen slipped aside so that William could take the ladder.

William had ascended no more than halfway up with Stephen at his heels when a voice above on the Sao Jorge shouted "*Estamos sendo embarcados!*" At least, that's how it sounded to Stephen.

There was a drumroll of feet on the deck and heads appeared at the gunwale as William reached the top.

One of the heads aimed an ax blow at William's head. William raised his shield in time to deflect the blow, but it was so powerful, he staggered and would have fallen had he not grasped the gunwale with his sword hand, the sword itself dangling from a wrist strap he had put on at Stephen's recommendation, and Stephen gripped his belt from behind.

Blows rained down on William. He sheltered under his shield as best he could but many of them fell on his helmet and shoulders. But it is hard to kill an armored man and he did not go down, although he was staggered several times. He recovered his sword and began to deliver blows of his own, which killed one man and drove back the others for a step or two, but they were on him again in a flash.

"Up! Up!" Stephen shouted from below and pushed at William's buttocks, for the best way to mount a wall was in a sudden rush that pushed the defenders back and created space for those behind to follow, no matter how terrible the risk to the first man. And make no mistake, being the first on the wall was the most difficult and dangerous task there had to be in war.

William climbed one rung, then another. Before he could get any higher, one of the ax wielders delivered a powerful blow that William did not see coming. It struck him on the head. A helmet will protect you from having your head cleaved in two most of the time, but it will not entirely soften the concussion of an impact, and it was clear that this blow had dazed William. He swayed, then toppled off the ladder.

Stephen tried to hold him by the belt, but William's weight tore him from Stephen's grip.

A small gap had opened between the boat and the ship, and William plunged into it. He struck the water with a great splash.

"Get him!" Stephen cried.

But even though Gilbert and one of the Cliffe men lunged for William, he sank like a stone before they could get a grip on him, dragged down by the weight of his armor, leaving only a circle of froth.

Stephen had less than a moment to contemplate the cold enormity of what had just happened. He had lost friends before, but even though he had had his differences with William, differences that had bordered on mutual hatred, it was a terrible thing to lose someone you had grown up with and had known all your life.

Yet he had to put these thoughts out of his mind. If he dwelt on them for more than a heartbeat, the cause might be lost.

He gripped his sword and climbed the ladder.

They were waiting for him.

Stephen cut off the hand of one sailor who was trying to push the ladder away. The return cut took a man raising an ax under the chin and sent him staggering. A third sailor drove at Stephen with a spear. Stephen deflected the point with his shield.

Stephen leaped over the gunwale and parried a thrust from a sailor on his right with a downward cut — a perfect barrier guard his instructor would have praised — then his point slipped under the sailor's sword and took him in the gut. It was not enough to stab someone, though. The man did not die immediately from a thrust and could cut you down as he perished. Stephen knew this danger well. He yanked his sword free with a kick and clove the sailor's head into two parts to the collar.

He was aboard now and had to create space for the men behind. So Stephen laid about, swinging his sword almost artlessly to drive back the sailors on deck who had crowded around.

They knew that their only option lay in getting someone behind Stephen to drag him down. But as two maneuvered to do that, the Cliffe men and Herb thumped onto the deck and got beside him.

Although the numbers were even, seven to seven, the fight did not last long. In only seconds, five sailors were on the deck, dying. Two retreated to the shelter of the cabin under the sterncastle. Stephen stalked them, swept up in that strange euphoria of battle.

One of the sailors, the black-bearded man Stephen had taken to be the first mate, held out his sword and said something that Stephen did not understand. This was not a time for talk; once the battle frenzy had taken hold talk was impossible. Stephen drove his point into the man's heart, the vision of that coil of dark water in his mind.

The remaining sailor, the captain, shouted and stabbed at Stephen's head, but it was a fool's blow. It changed as Stephen raised his shield to take it. But he saw the sword alter its course and he slipped his leg, the target, out of the way. The sword hissed by. The sailor was off balance for a moment, and Stephen filled that instant by slamming the cross of his sword into the man's eye.

The man screamed and fell to his knees, clutching his face.

A bubble burst in Stephen's heart then and all the bitter sweetness of the battle fury passed away.

He panted as if he could not catch his breath. His grip on the sword loosened, and it slipped from his fingers. It would have clattered to the deck had it not been for the thong around his wrist.

Peter and Fred grabbed the captain by the shoulders and dragged him toward the gunwale. Pirating could be a nasty business.

"Wait," Stephen said.

"You're not going to let him live, are you?" Peter asked, incredulous.

"I have a question for him."

Stephen stepped up to the captain. He wiped the blood from his sword on the tail of the sailor's shirt and sheathed the sword. The captain was a well-dressed stocky man with a blunt nose and a strong chin. It was the hard face of a man who endured a hard world, and had a thin cruel mouth surrounded by a thick black beard.

"Where were you bound?" Stephen asked in Spanish.

The captain frowned at the question, a hand over his damaged eye.

"Lisboa," the captain said, surprised at being addressed in a language he understood.

"And then?"

"What do you mean, and then?"

"What were you going to do with the girls?"

The captain's eye flitted from Stephen to a point over the water.

"I know they are below deck," Stephen said.

"We were going on to Tangiers," the captain said, reluctant to say more. But it was enough.

Stephen nodded and turned away.

He did not see Peter and Fred cut the captain's throat and throw the body overboard, but he could not avoid hearing the splash. There was even some satisfaction in the death of a man who would sell young girls into slavery in a foreign land. He had got what he deserved.

Gilbert and Herb already had the hatch open and had gone below. It wasn't long before Gilbert reappeared with six shrouded figures, slim and small. It was odd that Herb did not show up with them. Stephen wondered what had got into Herb but he lost that thought at the sight of the girls.

Stephen went to each girl, throwing back her hood as they crowded around him, weeping.

She was not there. She was not one of them.

"Where is Ida?" Stephen cried out. "Where is she?"

"Ida?" one of the girls asked.

"She was among you, wasn't she?"

The girls nodded.

"What happened to her?" Stephen cried. It felt as though invisible hands were tearing his heart apart, and he could not stand the pain.

"She was with us until that house where they kept us for a time," one girl said. "Then she was sold to someone."

Relief drenched Stephen's ravaged heart. "Who?"

"We don't know. We just heard them talking about it — the men with the wagon."

"I know the place," Gilbert said. "It has to be the manor house at Knightsbridge."

"We'll go there, then," Stephen said.

There was a loud thump on deck at the hatch to the hold.

"Gilbert," Herb gasped, "can you give me a hand with this?"

"What is it?" Gilbert asked, kneeling by Herb, who was struggling for breath over a chest about two feet long, a foot high and a foot wide, with a lock securing the lid.

"It's a chest," Herb said.

"I see that," Gilbert said.

"I found it below. I want to see what's in it. It's really heavy."

"Something valuable, no doubt. That's why people usually put locks on chests."

Herb took one of the boarding axes lying on the deck and broke the lock. He lifted the lid.

"Good Lord!" he exclaimed. "Look at that!"

The chest was filled to the brim with silver coins.

"It's not cargo," Stephen said. "Any more than the girls."

"That is your interpretation," Peter said.

"We can fight over it," Stephen said. "Or you can take a share. A small share."

Peter glanced at the Cliffe men. Greed and fear played on their faces. Yet they had seen what havoc Stephen could make and they were not eager for a fight in which some of them would surely die, even over such a fortune as lay in the chest.

"We'll take a share," Fred said. "The ship's more than enough."

Chapter 23

"What will become of us, sir?" a girl called Eleanor asked as the river boat pulled away under sail from the *Sao Jorge* in the twilight before dawn. Like the others, she was fifteen if a day, slender, blonde, and quite pretty.

Stephen was in no mood to talk with anyone. But he pulled his eyes from the ship, which was weighing anchor, the sail already down and flapping in the light breeze, and his thoughts from the bitter memory of what had happened there. It was odd how you could hate someone all your life and then, when he had died, not hate him at all. In fact, how you could miss him.

Why had William wanted to go first? Stephen had been turning that question around in his mind when the girl interrupted him, but he could not find a good answer. Was it because of pride? William was indeed a proud man, even overly so. But he had not been much for actual fighting, despite being a bully, and like most bullies Stephen suspected that he was not very brave. Could it have been for love of Ida? Stephen wanted to believe that somewhere in William's black heart there had been room for love. He would never know the answer but he knew which one he preferred.

"I'll see you home," he said. "I'll see you all home. It may take some time. But you'll get there just the same."

"Thank you, sir," Eleanor said. She went over to sit with the other girls by the base of the mast. They put their heads together as she told them what she had learned.

"Thank you, sir!" the girls chorused.

"That was good of you," Gilbert said.

Stephen rested a hand on the chest. "We can afford it. We can afford a lot of things now."

"I'd say so," Gilbert said. "We could probably buy the entire town of Ludlow with that treasure."

"A good portion of it, anyway," Stephen said.

"I had no idea ship's captains were so rich."

"Neither did I."

Stephen mulled about the future and the contents of the chest as the boat made its slow way up the river to London. He was so morose that no one approached him. The girls chatted with Gilbert and Herb and avoided Stephen other than throwing furtive glances his way.

Stephen, however, could not avoid overhearing the conversation and learning about them. There was Eleanor, whose name he already knew, from Church Stretton who had been taken on her way to church for a Friday evening Mass. She was the daughter of a butcher who had a shop on the Shrewsbury Road at the north end of the village. Stephen had ridden by it, in fact, although it had escaped his notice. There was Mary from Stanton Lacy, the daughter of a tanner; Henrietta, from Richard's Castle, whose father was a tailor; Juliana from Leintwardine, fatherless and whose mother took in laundry to make ends meet; Eloise the daughter of a village reeve and Mabb's wife; and Amice from Bitterley who did not mention her father's work. It was curious that they all came from north Herefordshire or southern Shropshire, but Stephen did not know what to make of this.

They reached London in the evening and put in at Southwark below the bridge. Stephen paid off the three boys Peter had left behind to crew the boat, giving each a little extra than had been promised for their good service.

They spent the night at an inn beside Saint Olave's Church not far from the landing spot, Stephen and Gilbert sleeping on either side of the chest. Stephen woke up often in the night to make sure it remained there.

In the morning, they found a carpenter and locksmith to replace the lock, and hired a boy with a wheelbarrow to help take it to the Italian banker's house on the bridge, since the box was much too heavy to carry any distance. If the banker or Edmund, his clerk, had any suspicions about where the money had come from, they did not show it. The chest went into a vault carved into the stone support pillar below the main room of the house.

Stephen held back a large sack of coins and the last amount paid for the horses he had sold. He, Gilbert and Herb, concealing the sack in Stephen's saddle roll, rode through the city and out Ludgate to Westminster.

The houses along the road to Westminster grew grand and large the closer they got. These were the houses of great lords who built them to be close to the King. At the bend itself and just outside the palace gate, however, there were more humble houses where people rented rooms to the lesser folk: servants, clerks and such, but also to out-of-work soldiers hoping to be taken on by a lord.

At the bend and the village of Charing where there was a market cross, Stephen went to every tavern. There were a lot of them owing to its proximity to Westminster. He hired ten soldiers there.

He hired twenty more in the taverns outside the palace gates.

The next morning the little army rode to Knightsbridge.

It was a couple of miles to Knightsbridge from Charing, where they had assembled, and the army was nearly there before the bells of the abbey in Westminster rang the hour of Prime, the arrival of full daylight, which could be heard even this far out in the country as faint bongs from beyond the horizon.

Stephen halted the formation at the ford of a stream a quarter mile short of Knightsbridge. It was as close as he could hope to come without being seen from the village, for the land was treeless apart from a copse here and there. Any large body of armed men was certain to be suspect in these troubled times. People locked themselves in until such a host had passed. He wanted to surprise the holder of the manor.

Stephen sent Herb ahead on foot to reconnoiter, Gilbert having been left behind to watch over the girls.

Herb returned shortly, looking grim.

"He's not there?" Stephen asked.

"Oh, he's there all right," Herb said. "About to sit down to his breakfast, according to the servants."

"What's his name?"

"Gerald Ilbode."

Stephen's nostrils flared as he took a deep breath against the jitters that always preceded an action. He felt more nervous than he had before boarding the *Sao Jorge*. At the ship, he had thought the crisis was nearing its conclusion and chilly rage had driven off the anxiety. Now Ida felt as far away as ever and in danger of slipping away for good.

"Get your gear on," Stephen said.

Herb's lips tightened at the tone, as if he had received a rebuke. "Right away, sir."

Stephen led the column at a brisk canter on the last quarter mile. The center of the village lay at a fork in the road where there was a wide space for a market and a small stone church. A tavern lay beside the church with a broad oak in the yard, and across from the tavern and church was the manor house. It was surrounded by a stone wall about the height of a man and not meant for defense. The house itself, rising behind the wall, was three stories of stone and no more a fort than the wall: a prosperous looking house with a tiled roof painted blue. There was money in that house, and money in the fat and tidy village that lay about it.

They had arrived so quickly that word of their appearance had not reached the manor house. The front gate stood open. Stephen brushed by porter who attempted to block the way.

"Sir! Sir!" the porter stammered, rushing up to Stephen as he dismounted. "What is your business?"

Stephen ignored him and climbed the stairs to the first floor, the ground being an undercroft used for storage.

To his relief, no one had barred the door. He burst in and passed through the wooden screen separating the hall from the pantry and buttery. The household was at breakfast, although a few had risen and gone to the windows to see about the commotion in the yard.

A tall, slender man with shoulder length black hair rose from a tall-backed chair behind the high table. He was too thin to be a fighter and his hands, the fingers studded with expensive gold rings, were long and reedy. A girl sat beside him, young and pretty, a fair-haired girl, her hair down and braided in the fashion of an unmarried maiden. Her eyes were on her lap and her expression was frightened.

The slender man, who had to be Ilbode, glanced at a stairway at his rear, as if considering flight. But he remained still as Stephen marched up, sword drawn. A few of the men-at-arms who had followed Stephen came round the table and cut off any possibility of retreat in that direction.

"You are the lord here?" Stephen demanded of Ilbode.

"I am a King's man," Ilbode said, his voice high and cracking a bit with fright. "I will not yield to you!"

"We have other business besides the differences between the barons and the King," Stephen said.

This did not alleviate Ilbode's fright.

The girl's eyes rose from her lap. She stood up. "Help me, sir! For the love of God! I am kept here against my will!"

A burly fellow standing behind the girl gripped her shoulder as if to force her into silence and back to her seat.

"Take your hand off her," Stephen said, "if you want to keep it."

Ilbode and the burly fellow exchanged glances. Ilbode nodded. The burly fellow stepped away.

Stephen waved to the girl. She dashed around the table to his side.

"Where are you from?" Stephen asked.

"Barlby, sir," the girl said. At Stephen's frown, she added. "It's in the north, sir. A small village of no account."

"Is there a place below for keeping prisoners?"

She nodded.

Stephen indicated Ilbode and the burly man. "Bring them. The rest of you, make sure no one leaves the house or grounds."

The place for keeping prisoners was a small cell in a corner of the undercroft. There were no windows but the light admitted by the doorway revealed the ground to be covered with rotting straw that smelled of shit and piss. Iron rings were spaced about the walls. Lengths of rope dangled from the rings.

Stephen had Ilbode and the burly man secured to one of the rings.

"I hope you are comfortable," Stephen said.

"What do you want?" Ilbode asked.

"Information. If you provide it and are truthful, I'll let you live."

Ilbode licked his lips. "All right."

"A week ago, eight girls were brought here and put in this cell," Stephen said. "Girls not unlike this one here. Am I right?"

Ilbode hesitated, then nodded.

"Six of them were taken to London after a man who used to own a bear wagon dropped by with a warning."

Ilbode did not reply.

"What happened to the last girl?"

Ilbode took a deep breath. "I sold her."

"To whom?"

"To a passer-by."

"Liar!" the girl shouted from the doorway.

"Do you want to amend your statement?" Stephen asked.

Ilbode's mouth twitched. "I dare not give his name. On my life."

"Very noble of you," Stephen said. He drew his dagger and grasped Ilbode's right hand by the thumb. "One more chance."

Ilbode shook his head.

Stephen sliced off the thumb.

Ilbode squealed and clutched the wounded hand to his chest.

"That is only the beginning. For each lie, you'll lose a part. Next time it may not be a finger."

"There is no need to go any further," the girl said. "I know who he was."

"You'd care to save him?"

"I'll tell you, if you give me the dagger."

Stephen pondered this statement for a moment. It led to a dark place. "Before I do so, I have one question of you. The seventh girl, the girl who was sold, what was her name?"

"Ida. I heard the others call her Ida."

Stephen held out the dagger, pommel forward.

"Don't!" Ilbode cried. "Don't give it to her!"

The girl grasped the weapon. "His name is Richard de Frenze."

"Where can he be found?"

"His hold is south of Norwich near a village called Diss. He raped me. Like that one," the girl indicated Ilbode, "raped me."

"Did this Frenze rape Ida as well?"

"Not while he was here. But I doubt she stayed pure long after he got her back to Diss."

"Is this true?" Stephen asked Ilbode, although he did not doubt it.

"Please," Ilbode said, "I'll pay if you just go away and do no more harm! I have money! What is she to you anyway?"

"Ida is family," Stephen said.

"Shit," the burly man said. "Those stupid bastards snatched a gentry girl. I warned them."

"His name was Frenze?" Stephen asked the burly man, who nodded.

"Best make your peace while you have time." Stephen turned away and left the cell.

"You said you'd let us live!" Ilbode cried.

"You have a debt to pay to another. I cannot speak for her."

Ilbode died screaming and kicking. The other died silently.

The girl emerged, her gown smeared with blood. She wiped the dagger on her skirt and gave it back to Stephen.

"It's a good thing you came," she said. "The servants taunted me about what happened when Ilbode got bored with a girl. They said he had them drowned in the river."

"I wonder why he didn't just sell them," Stephen mused.

"He feared they would speak of what he did to them and of his business. What will you do with me?"

"I'll have you escorted to London. You'll be safe there with the other girls. I have business in Diss."

Chapter 24

Stephen had never been to Norfolk and consequently had no idea where Diss was. Fortunately, one of the men was from King's Lynn and knew the way. He said it was a good hundred miles, a journey that in ordinary times would have taken four or five days. But Stephen pressed them hard, and they reached Thetford on the afternoon of the second day, Thursday the fifth of July.

Because of the long days there was still a lot of daylight left, but Stephen ordered a pause to rest the horses, since they had only ten miles or so to go, and he wanted them fresh in order to make their getaway.

They were on the road before sun up, the pre-dawn twilight providing enough illumination.

Diss itself was nothing to speak of, a dozen houses north of a large pond. A few hasty questions to a woman cutting firewood in her yard told Stephen where to find Frenze Manor and its village, and they were off at a brisk trot on the indicated path, anxiety and triumph at the coming success at the conclusion of this awful business warring in his mind.

The village of Frenze gave itself away as they approached by a haze of smoke drifting above a copse of oaks. The path entered the copse, crossed a sluggish brown stream and ended at a fine stone church where the houses of the village clustered on the other side.

The manor house lay to the right, a long stone building of two stories behind a wicker fence. A round kitchen stood apart from the house, belching smoke, with a smithy beside it, the smith already at work with two boys who stopped work and gawked at the appearance of the host. Stephen rode into the yard, scattering sheep grazing on the grass. He dismounted and pushed open the front door, followed closely by the men immediately behind him while ten others went round the back in case anyone sought to escape.

Stephen had expected to surprise Frenze at breakfast, as he had Ilbode. But all that greeted his appearance in the hall were the frightened expressions on servants' faces.

"Where is Frenze?" Stephen demanded.

"Gone," a servant said, clutching his broom which he had been applying to the floor as if it might provide some protection.

"Where, gone?" Stephen asked.

"I'm not sure."

"Where's the steward?"

"Gone to Thetford."

"Then who's in charge here? Where is Frenze's wife?"

"He's got no wife. Least ways, none who lives here. She ran off long ago. We don't speak of it."

"Did he come back from London with a young girl?"

The broom wielder looked frightened. He nodded.

"Does he often enjoy the services of young girls?"

"Please, don't make me speak of it."

Stephen grasped the broom wielder by the throat. "If you do not satisfy me, I will lay your guts on the floor."

"He kills them when he's done," the broom-wielder said in a shaking voice.

"And you do not speak of it."

"My lord will kill us, too, if we do. He is terrible. You have no idea."

Stephen drew his dagger. "Have you ever seen a man gutted before? Because you are about to."

Before the broom-wielder could reply, two soldiers entered the hall with a priest.

"What is the meaning of this outrage?" the priest cried.

Stephen let go of the servant and turned on the priest. "How long have you served here?"

"What has that got to do with anything?"

"I know about the girls. And so do you."

The priest's demand had been fueled by bluster more than courage, and he paled so that the freckles on his face stood out.

Stephen put the point of the dagger in the priest's mouth. He could barely contain his fury. "I am sure he pays you a handsome sum to keep your mouth shut, but I will widen it if you do not tell me what I want to know."

The priest nodded, the whites of his eyes showing.

"Frenze came back from London with another girl," Stephen said. "Where have they gone?"

"Buckenham Castle," the priest stammered. "He's gone to Buckenham Castle. He is constable there."

"And he took the girl with him?"

"Yes."

Stephen patted the priest's cheek with the dagger. "Search the house and grounds. Make sure he's not lying."

There were two Buckenhams in Norfolk, the soldier who had been their guide told Stephen, one old and one new. The castle was the New Buckenham, the soldier said with some awe, and it was the most formidable castle in Norfolk, if not all of England apart from the Tower of London.

"Its walls are round as an apple," the soldier said, "and forty feet high! The great tower is sixty at least. They say you can see the sea from the top of it."

Stephen doubted the walls were forty feet high. He had seen many castles including the remains of Gaillard in Normandy, and some of the grandest walled towns in Europe when he was in Spain. Twenty feet was the best they had, although Byzantium was rumored to have walls of a similar height. Even so, it would be a formidable place.

"What's the size of the garrison?" Stephen asked.

"Twenty hired men," the soldier said. "And five knights doing castle service."

"And I suppose you want us to take this place," said Guy Cookson. He was bald and grey with protruding front teeth and a split lower lip that had healed poorly, leaving a permanent notch, like a harelip in reverse. He was twice Stephen's age, yet he had impressed Stephen as the most experienced soldier of the lot for all his unlikely appearance. The others knew him and deferred to him, so Stephen had made him second-in-command. "A castle with twenty-five men or more."

"I'll think of a way," Stephen said. A thought stirred within the darkness of his mind, not fully formed but half visible. "He'll feel safe there."

"Who'll feel safe?" Guy asked.

"Frenze. He'll feel safe in that castle."

"I would if I were him. You'd need a real army to take a place like that. And it would likely take months."

"Yes, you would." Stephen gestured toward the manor house. "Burn it. And the barn too."

"No plundering first?" Guy asked.

"There's no way for us to carry it away. Besides, we've a castle to take. Don't worry. You're well paid."

Guy chuckled. "That we are. You there! Fire the house and that fat barn besides!" He turned back to Stephen. "I've always loved the smell of a burning house."

In the end, the enthusiasm of the soldiers for setting fire to things got out of hand, and they ran through the little village beyond the church torching the thatch roofs so that flames were soon shooting fifty feet or more into the air all around, giant bonfires snorting columns of black smoke into the sky. It was all Stephen could do to restrain them from firing the church as well, although he would have taken pleasure in it if that oily priest was inside. He closed his ears to the crying of the women who were losing all that they owned, while the village men hustled away what they could save of their possessions and their livestock.

With the fires burning so furiously that they could not be put out, the raiders mounted their horses and rode back southward. When they were out of sight of the house, Stephen turned westward toward Diss.

The column cut across fields short of the village, heedless of the damage they were doing to the rye crop. They crossed one road the guide said was the wrong one and after passing through another field, they turned north on the next road out of the village.

Stephen set a punishing pace, alternating canters and trots. He hated treating the horses this way, but it could not be helped. They passed through a village strung along the road about five miles from Diss, then a mile onward the road turned sharply right. There was a large patch of forest here. Stephen turned into it.

"This is as good a place as any," Stephen said to Guy.

"For what?" Guy asked.

"Waiting. You can have the boys undo the girths and feed the horses. They can eat themselves, but no fires. I don't want to give any sign that we're here. And have them keep away from the edge of the wood."

"Right, sir."

Guy went away to carry out the orders while Stephen settled down where he could watch the road from Diss.

After about an hour, a horseman appeared on the road from Diss, coming fast. Stephen was surprised to see it was the priest from Frenze. He had not expected that. But it was a good sign. A good sign, indeed. He ducked down behind a beech tree as the priest cantered by.

A couple of hours after that, a column of soldiers came from the north.

A mailed knight rode alone at the head of the column, his helmet tucked under an arm and his arming cap stuffed in his belt. His face was grim and angry.

Stephen smiled at the sight of him, for his plan was working so far.

Chapter 25

Stephen counted twenty men in the column besides Frenze. As he ticked them off on his fingers, he had begun to worry about that priest, who could undo his plan, which was shaky enough to begin with. But the priest followed at the end of the column.

When they had gone round the bend and were vanishing into the distance, Stephen stood up from his hiding place. He went deeper into the wood where the horses were tethered and the men gathered around sacks of bread they had brought from London.

"Tighten your girths, boys," Stephen said. "We've a castle to take."

"I've been part of some daft schemes in my life," Guy said, "but this is one of the craziest. I just hope it's worth it."

"Me, too."

"Have you ever taken a castle before? I hope you don't mind my asking."

"Several times. I've been first on the wall twice."

Guy blinked. "I say. That is something. Can't say as I've had the honor. Not that I want it. Dicey thing scaling a castle's walls."

"At least we don't have to do that."

"They'd swat us off like flies if we tried."

Not too long after leaving the wood, they came on a track crossing the road. Stephen was glad to bump into this track, for the road they were on lead directly to the castle, according to their guide. He turned onto it, heading east.

After proceeding along this track for some distance, he cut into the field on the left, keeping to the paths along the edges of the field strips.

It wasn't long before they came on the town. It was surrounded by an embankment which was crowned with the usual palisade, but like many such earthworks, it was in need of repair. Parts of the palisade looked as though they could be brought down with a sneeze.

They broke up into parties of six and, one at a time, approached the town's eastern gate. Stephen's party entered first, followed at intervals by the others so that, hopefully, the gate wardens might not think they were together. Anyway, it wasn't the town's gate wardens Stephen worried about alarming. They were unlikely to know that anything was afoot or amiss, and so they shouldn't be paying close attention to anything but the collection of the toll charged for entry into the town. Besides, Stephen had everyone remove their mail and stow their helmets. His party also had left their shields with the second group. It was risky engaging in any sort of fight without armor, but people would notice an armored party, wonder, worry and be on their guard.

Stephen went straight through the town to the west gate. His group dismounted here. One man remained to hold the horses. Stephen and the others hefted their saddle packs and swords, and walked out of the gate.

The castle lay a hundred yards from the town across a pasture where sheep and horses were grazing. It was round without any towers along the lime-washed wall, which were not forty feet high. They were twenty or so, but the wall sat on the crown of a steep embankment so that the top could well be forty feet above the surrounding ground. It looked impregnable. Stephen wouldn't have wanted less than five-thousand men to carry the place by direct assault.

The main gate lay out of sight on the other side of the castle. It sat within an old style gate tower, tall and square. Stephen approached it on foot, heart pounding and mouth dry. This was the biggest gamble he had ever taken in his life and he was dizzy at the prospect of failure.

Then the gate came into view and he nearly cried out with relief: the drawbridge was down and the gate was open, although one gate door was shut. Two men with shields on their backs and spears stood in the gap. He had counted on the man left in charge thinking the castle so formidable that the burning of a manor nearby still did not put it in direct danger.

Stephen crossed the drawbridge over the ditch, trying to look tired, as if he had come a long way. The others straggled behind him.

"Good afternoon," Stephen said, his heart pounding again. He was surprised he could even speak. His parched tongue felt three times its normal size.

"What do you boys want?" one of the guards asked, hitching his thumbs into his belt.

Stephen glanced back at his companions. One had come up to his side. The others were leaning against the rails of the bridge a few paces away pretending not to pay attention.

"We wondered if you might have a need for more men," Stephen said.

"For what?" the guard smirked. "Cleaning the shithouse?"

"No, we're soldiers."

"You don't look like soldiers to me. Where's your gear? Where's your horses?"

"We were robbed. South of here. A band of thirty or so. Surprised us at camp. Took the horses and most of our stuff. What you see is what we were able to save."

The guard frowned. "There was a bunch like that who burned a manor south of here this morning."

"What about it?"

"What about what?"

"Can you use us or not?"

"Na, I doubt it. We're full up."

"How about a bite to eat, then? You can spare that, surely. Put yourself in our shoes."

The guard considered this. He nodded. "Hank," he said to the other guard, "see if the cook can spare a couple of old loaves for this sorry lot."

The guard addressed as Hank withdrew into the bailey.

Stephen made as though to say something but grasped the guard's right arm, instead. The soldier behind Stephen grabbed the soldier's left arm and, before he could call out, rammed a dagger into his throat.

They lay the body down.

"You take his shield," Stephen said. He drew his sword and, carrying his saddle pack for protection in his left hand, went through the gate.

He stopped within the gate passage. His role was to guard the passageway in case anyone from within tried to retake it. No one, however, seemed to have noticed any threat. The soldier sent to the kitchen could be seen at the doorway talking to someone inside. No one else was in sight apart from a man tying up his drawers at a privy and a woman feeding pigs from a bucket.

The others in Stephen's party ran by and turned up the stairs. Their job was to secure the winch room so that no one could raise the drawbridge. There was no portcullis at this castle, as it was built before they came into use.

There was the sound of a scuffle audible through the murder hole in the ceiling above Stephen's head. Then one of his men said through the hole, "We've got it."

Stephen went out of the gate and brought out a small horn that Guy had given him. He blew three blasts of the horn and then went back into the gate passage.

One of the enemy guards staggered out of the tower onto the wall walk to the left, blood streaming down his face from a cut on the head. He opened his mouth to cry out, but then one of Stephen's men emerged as well. The enemy backed away and stumbled. Stephen's man pushed him off the wall walk. The enemy guard crashed through the roof of a shed and hit the ground with a thump.

"Hold the gate!" Stephen called to his man on the walk.

Stephen then dashed across the bailey to the wooden stairway leading to the entry to the great tower, a monstrous round thing that reared forty feet if an inch above the ground. Now that he had secured the gate, he needed to ensure that the people in the great tower did not succeed in locking themselves inside where he would not be able to get at them.

The soldier had turned from the kitchen door at the sound of the body's impact with the ground. He spotted Stephen, dropped the two loaves in his hand, drew his sword and gave chase.

Stephen could not run very fast, owing to his bad foot, and he just beat the soldier to the stairs.

Stephen did not pause to dispute his right to the stairs. He leaped up three stairs and bounded to the top, a swipe of the soldier's sword nearly severing an ankle.

At the top, he threw his shoulder to the doors and they swung open: the attack had unfolded so rapidly that no one had yet barred the door. As in most circular great towers there was no screen separating the door from the hall proper, and no one was inside but a man sweeping the floor and what appeared to be a knight in the lord's high chair with his feet propped up on the great table and a cup on his lap. The knight's feet hit the floor and he bounded to his feet.

Stephen ignored him for the moment, since the knight had no sword that he could see; the only weapons in view were a rack of spears against the wall. He turned back to the entrance to face the soldier who was just arriving at the top.

The soldier had his shield in front of him now to force his way in. Although Stephen's leather bag provided some protection, he backed up as the soldier edged forward.

The soldier raised his blade and Stephen realized what he meant to do: a great downright blow from above.

When it came, Stephen parried with the left bow while stepping out to his left to get out of the way. He whirled his blade around in a furious cut from the left of his own. He aimed at the soldier's neck, but the aim was off. Stephen's sword clanked against the soldier's helmet. The force of the blow, however, stunned the soldier. He staggered and Stephen took advantage of the moment to drive a stamp kick into his ribs. The soldier went down.

Stephen glanced at the knight now to see what he was up to. For surely he would not sit still and watch.

The knight had not. He came across the floor, a spear in hand.

Spears were clumsy looking weapons, but dangerous as a viper in the hands of a man who knew how to use one. And this knight looked as though he had had some schooling, for he seemed to glide across the floor, his feet hissing on the floorboards, approaching carefully yet quickly, and measuring his options.

Stephen gave him space, backing away and moving to the right, ready to parry with the saddle pack.

Then there was a thunder of footfalls on the stairs and Stephen's men crowded into the room.

"There you are, sir!" Guy cried. "I had wondered where you had got to!"

The knight stood up from his fighting crouch. The spear point sagged to the floor. He dropped the shaft. "Quarter?" he asked.

"Quarter," Stephen said.

"Your servant," the knight said. He bowed.

"There is a way you can be of service," Stephen said. "Frenze brought a young girl with him. Where is she?"

The knight pointed upward. "In the top chamber."

"She better not be harmed, for your sake — for everyone's sake. Tie him up, and the others. And bar the gate and set out a watch."

The door to the top chamber, at the end of a spiraling staircase, was locked.

Stephen hammered on the door with his fist. "Ida! Are you in there?"

There was no response.

Stephen went back down to the hall. "The door's locked," he said to the knight. "Where is the key?"

"My lord keeps it."

"Is there a spare?"

The knight shook his head. "There is only the one."

"Is there a blacksmith here?"

"Yes."

"Get him. Have him bring a hammer and chisel."

Stephen could not wait for the blacksmith. He took a battle ax from one of his men, and remounted the stairs. They led beyond the top floor to the roof, where the day and night watch could keep an eye on the countryside from a small watch tower that projected from the battlements like a chimney, although today, there was no watch here.

The roof was tile covering wooden shingles. Stephen cleared away the tiles and hacked a hole in the shingles. He let himself in through the hole, dangled a moment and dropped to the floor.

The light was dim in here. The only windows were narrow arrow slits. No one seemed to be in the chamber and Stephen wondered if he had been lied to. Then there was a rustling from the other side of the poster bed.

Stephen crept round the bed. He could make out two figures in the gloom.

"Come any closer," a harsh female voice grated, "and I'll cut her throat!"

"If you do, you will surely die," Stephen said. "For I'll kill you."

"I'll die if I succeed, I'll die if I fail. It makes no difference."

Stephen could see the two better now as his eyes adjusted to the dark. The woman who had spoken was broad and beefy, with a broad and beefy hand clamped on a much smaller and slighter girl's mouth. Stephen could not tell if this was Ida, for her features were distorted by the strength of the beefy woman's grasp.

Stephen took a step forward, heart pounding, panic surging, at a loss for what to do.

Then the young girl took matters into her own hands. She grasped the beefy woman's elbow and thrust her head onto the pocket formed by that elbow so that the dagger under her chin could not be drawn across her neck.

Stephen leaped forward and grasped the beefy woman's dagger arm. He twisted the dagger from her substantial grasp and it clattered across the floor. The girl ducked down and away and slipped behind him.

He expected the beefy woman to give up the fight, now it was clear she had lost. But instead she came at him, arms outstretched, hands curled like claws.

She so caught Stephen by surprise that he did not react, and she had him by the throat, driving him backward with the force of her rush.

Stephen's reflexes took over. He gripped the beefy woman by the elbows, pivoted about and threw her over his outstretched right leg. She landed at his feet, and he pounded her on the face. She went limp. He straightened up, breathing hard.

The girl came up to him and peered into his face. She was a beautiful thing, one of the most beautiful creatures he had ever seen in his life. But he did not recognize her.

"Ida?" Stephen croaked.

"Uncle Stephen!" she said. "It's really you! I thought it was you!"

She embraced him about the waist, her head barely reaching his shoulder. "You came!" she said, voice muffed as they held each other close, and choked with sobs. "You came! I thought no one would!"

"We'd go to the ends of the earth for you," Stephen said. "You know that."

Ida looked up. "Daddy's here?"

It was a moment before Stephen could bring himself to answer. "He's gone, Ida. He was killed trying to save you."

"And Mother?"

"What about her?"

"I heard she was ill, that she was dying."

"Your mother is fine."

"Dear God, thanks! Father's really dead?"

Stephen nodded.

"I cannot believe it."

"Nor can I, really. Much as I wished him dead from time to time, I am sorry he's gone."

Ida wiped tears from her cheeks. She stepped back. "Then you are lord of Hafton now," she said.

Another long moment passed before Stephen could speak. He had not thought about this at all. His mind had been too intent on achieving the result that had just come to pass.

"I suppose I am," he said at last. "Although I have a feeling I won't be for long, after all we've had to do to find you."

Chapter 26

In the end, the blacksmith was not needed to break the door hinges. Ida retrieved a bronze chain from around the beefy woman's neck which held the key to the chamber.

"She was my minder," Ida said as she gave Stephen the key. "I couldn't go to the privy without her. She stood by even when . . . he . . ." She could not say more, but Stephen understood her meaning.

"We will not speak of it," Stephen said. "It did not happen."

"You won't tell Mother?"

"No."

"Thank you. I could not bear the shame if it became known."

Stephen opened the chamber door. Guy was waiting in the curved stairwell with the blacksmith and other soldiers.

"My lady," Guy said in a hushed tone, not meeting her eye. He and the others had known this was about a girl, but to see her whole, beautiful and self-possessed nonetheless rendered him speechless. "You are well?"

"I am, thank you," Ida replied.

The men edged to the walls to make room for Ida and Stephen to squeeze by and followed them to the hall.

They were gone within the hour, however long it took to find and tack up a suitable horse for Ida.

They headed west from Buckenham Castle on a wide and well-traveled road, turning south about ten miles out at Great Hockham to Thetford, which they bypassed, reaching Newmarket in the evening, where they stayed in a barn and rested the horses for a day. Then it was on to Cambridge and down to the southwest to Dunstable, ever mindful of the possibility of pursuit, but finding none. Beyond Dunstable, they kept to the western shoulder of the Chiltern Hills on the ancient Icknield Way before cutting back toward the southeast on a road that brought them to Windsor, where they crossed the Thames. A footpath used by locals led along the river to Chertsey, where they spent another night. And then it was a long but easy ride up to Southwark, apart from a wet fording of the River Wey, for there was no bridge where Stephen decided to cross out of sight of a nearby town.

The men put up in a barn outside Southwark so as not to attract untoward attention while Stephen, Ida and Guy went into the town.

Gilbert saw them arrive at the Dancing Robin through a window and rushed into the street. "Oh, thank Heavens you're here!" he cried.

"Is something wrong?" Stephen asked, alarmed.

"Wrong? Of course, something's wrong! Nothing's been right since you left! You'd think that young women who've just cheated death would be more sober and better behaved, but those girls have been anything but well-behaved! Three have gone off again and I've no idea where! Yesterday I caught one at the riverside with a sailor! A sailor! I know enough about that lot to know none should be trusted, especially with a fresh young girl. I shall not answer to their parents for them, I tell you! I shall not!" Gilbert paused to catch his breath so the rant could continue, but then his eyes focused on Ida, who was just dismounting. "Oh, dear, I am forgetting my manners myself. You must be Lady Ida!"

"I am," Ida said. "And you must be Master Gilbert. I've heard all about you."

"Have you, my lady?" Gilbert said, eyes wandering with suspicion to Stephen. "I doubt you've heard all, and none of it was good, if the source of your knowledge is any indication."

"It was good enough to my ear."

"Well, whatever you have heard, I am deeply glad you are safe and sound. I had doubts about that, I must tell you. They were dark days on your trail, dark indeed."

"Let's not stand here in the street," Ida said as a groom emerged to take care of the horses. "You must tell me what you know of my father."

"I know precious little, my lady," Gilbert said glumly.

They took a table in a corner of the Dancing Robin and Stephen ordered a pitcher of wine. Pitchers of wine were a wild expense, but ale seemed too common a drink to mark what he felt was a celebration of their survival.

"Is he really dead?" Ida asked as she gripped her drinking bowl, goblets being an affectation not common in this part of town. "I cannot believe it."

"He is, my lady," Gilbert said. "I tried to catch him when he fell, but we weren't quick enough. He went under like a stone, weighted with his armor as he was."

"And he insisted on going first up the ladder?"

"He was certain you were on the ship and he wanted to be first aboard, so that you would be made safe. It was what any father would do."

"Or should do," Ida said. "I will miss him. He was not an easy man, but I never doubted his love. I wish I could say the same thing for my mother."

Stephen recovered the chest from the banker and paid off the soldiers, giving each a bonus for their success. He had a vain hope that it would help the men keep their mouths shut about what had happened, but he had scant expectation that they would. The truth would get out somehow, or a version of it, and certainly one that was not favorable to him. He wondered how much time he had left in England before he had to flee. The fact that he had now come into the manor with William's death did not mean that he would get to keep it. William's death would have to be proved and then his succession approved by the King himself, since that little manor was held directly of the King. But before any of that could come about, the rumors would destroy any hope Stephen had.

"It's been a pleasure, sir," Guy said as they shook hands at parting. "Any time you need to rescue a maiden, look me up."

"I'll do that," Stephen said, although they both knew it was unlikely they would run into each other again. "Take care, and good luck."

"Same to you, sir."

No one but fools wishing to die or be despoiled traveled alone from one town to another. And the unrest brought on by the conflict between the King and the supporters of Simon de Montfort that was spreading like a wildfire across the country gave excuse to the unscrupulous to indulge grudges against their neighbors or to prey on the unwary traveler. Rumors abounded about this, lurid tales of rape, pillage and slaughter — why, just a short while ago, Montfort supporters had attacked the sleepy manor of Knightsbridge, bringing murder to that quiet place — so the need for mutual protection was more acutely felt than it had been.

Thus, when it was time to return to Ludlow, Stephen and his party went to the Southwark market, where St. Mary's Church Street joined the high street leading to London Bridge, where the traveling parties gathered in the morning to make arrangements for company on the journey and inquire of the travelers gathering there. They had no takers, however, because most everyone was heading to Canterbury to the southeast, while they meant to go westward.

Consequently, it was rather late in the morning before they were able to set out, and they had to do so on their first leg without company apart from two wagons carrying barrels of salted eels and cod to Guildford some thirty miles away down a road they did not wish to take.

The girls, who rode in the cart Stephen had bought to carry them on the journey, did not seem aware of the danger. But Joan, who was with them, looked worried, and Ida, riding her stolen horse, kept near Stephen, the crossbow he had given her on the saddle pommel, ready for use.

"I am a dead shot with a crossbow," Ida had said the day before, "and I would like the comfort of one."

"You don't trust me to take care of you?" Stephen asked.

"I trust you," Ida said, "but I am concerned that neither that fellow Gilbert nor Herb will be able to watch your back as well as could be."

"Gilbert's managed well enough before," Stephen said, "although I'll give you, he doesn't look like he would be up to it. But if it will make you feel better …"

"It would make me feel better to think that I might take one out before I go down."

Stephen had hesitated to fulfill this request, for the thought of a woman fighting was out of the accepted norm. But gentry women hunted with crossbows, so in the end he could see no good reason not to grant her request. And when he bought her a bow, he picked up two others on impulse, one for Gilbert and the other for Herb.

Gilbert had never shot a crossbow before, but Herb took him to a field at the edge of Southwark and showed him how. Gilbert came back enthusiastic from the experience, and now walked with some swagger, the bow on his shoulder as if he thought he was a man of danger.

The day was warm and sunny for a change, and the ride would have been pleasant except for the worry about whether a band of robbers might leap into the road from some nearby copse that had not been trimmed back as it should have, or the fact that Stephen's mail and heavy gambeson had begun to chafe and made him sweat. He should be used to the fear and the discomfort, but for some reason, both bothered him a great deal, the anxiety perhaps because he now had so much to lose from a sudden attack.

Stephen's group parted from the barrel haulers beyond Kingston-On-Thames, passed over the River Wey at the appropriately-named village of Weybridge, and took a back road to Windsor, this time not concerned about being tracked.

The road passed through Chertsey, which they had visited before. The next day, where the road turned northward toward Windsor and the great castle could be seen in the distance across a broad rye field, Ida abruptly halted her horse and dismounted.

Stephen turned back to see what was the matter while the cart, with Gilbert driving seated on the money box, kept going.

Ida glanced about but there was no traffic. A few workers in the fields were far off and paid no attention.

"Uncle Stephen, please look away." As Stephen turned his back to Ida, she reached under the skirts of her gown and removed a soiled rag from her under drawers. She dropped the rag on the ground and pushed it into the roadside ditch with her foot.

"That is a relief," she said. "I don't know what I would have done if . . ."

She left the "if" hanging in the air between them.

But Stephen knew what she meant, and he was glad, too.

Ida gave Stephen the crossbow so that she could mount the horse. He returned it when she was settled, and they continued up the road to Windsor.

Ludlow had not changed a whit when they finally saw it almost a week later, although the world seemed to have done so. And it was a great relief to halt before Stephen's house on Bell Lane across from the Broken Shield Inn.

Gilbert eased off the cart, moving stiffly, while the girls hopped off in the street, giggling and talking.

Mistress Bartelot watched the proceeding from her window perch above their heads, consternation on her face at this unruly mob.

"Come down and let them in," Gilbert called to her. "Don't be rude to your visitors!"

"My visitors, indeed!" Mistress Bartelot shot back. But she disappeared from the window.

"Well, Harry," Gilbert said to Harry, who had pulled himself up to see over the counter what the commotion was all about. "What have you been up to?"

"Making a living, of course, like always. Did you find her?"

Gilbert gestured to Ida who was dismounting her horse. "Safe and sound, by the grace of God."

"Huh," Harry grunted, peering around a stack of bowls on the counter. "Go speak to your wife. She has news for you."

"Oh? About what?"

"You'll see."

Gilbert was miffed at Harry's reticence. "All right, then." He laid his bow on his shoulder and swaggered toward the inn as much as the stiffness in his back allowed.

Meanwhile, Mistress Bartelot had made it safely down stairs and opened the front door to the teeming mob of young women at the doorstep. She held the door for the girls, bewilderment on her face at the invasion of her house by so many strangers. She followed them to the hall, alarmed at Stephen's announcement that they would be staying for some days, but calling to their backs to take seats around the hearth and be comfortable, and that she would fetch something to eat and drink for them.

Stephen brought the chest down from the cart and paused at the door to the shop as he went in, while Herb led the cart and the other horses into the inn's yard.

"You're back," Harry grunted. "Gilbert says you found Ida."

Stephen nodded, wondering briefly what was the matter. Harry was prone to moods, so he put it off to that. "We did. At the cost of her father's life."

"What happened?"

"He fell into the Thames and was drowned."

"That's a sad end. Well, anyone but you would think it sad, given what you've had to say about him."

Stephen spotted the statue of the Virgin in the far corner. "The prior not like your work?"

"He decided that it wasn't needed," Harry said. "The whole thing was a waste of time."

"I'm sorry," Stephen said.

"It was good practice. Never done anything like her before. A few people have been coming by for a look at her. So I suppose it wasn't a complete waste. I may yet find a buyer. Just have to let the word get out. Ah, here's one now."

A woman and a skinny little girl with an oozing sore on her lip stood at the door to the street. The woman dipped in a brief curtsey to Stephen. He had seen her before around town: the wife of a charcoal seller, although he did not know her name.

"Begging your pardon, sir," the woman said. "Can we have a moment with the Lady?"

Stephen staggered back from the entrance to the shop, almost dropping the chest. Even after spending a fortune to hire the soldiers there was so much left that it still nearly killed him to carry it. What a mess that would have made: all those silver pennies strewn on the dirt. And what questions it would have generated. Chests heavy with silver don't just turn up anywhere and pauper knights do not stumble on them through honest efforts. Explanations would be demanded, and, when there was no ready answer, they would be created out of nothing.

"It's not my place to give you permission," he said. "It's Harry's shop."

"Thank you, sir," the woman said as she led the little girl by the hand into the shop, taking this as permission and not waiting for Harry.

"For the Lady," the woman said. She put a coin in Harry's hand.

Harry nodded and waved her into the shop.

They knelt before the unpainted carving, the wood a glowing yellow in the afternoon sunlight streaming through the front window. They touched the face, then pressed their hands together in prayer. Stephen hoped they found the comfort and the hope that was eluding them. In a harsh world, there was little enough.

Harry went back to the spoon he was carving. Except he asked, "What have you got there?"

"Nothing," Stephen said. "It's nothing."

"That nothing looks about to break your back."

Harry was subdued and withdrawn during supper, which was a more lively affair than the house had seen in some time. The girls were loud and talkative, full of stories about their ordeal, as well as laughter about little things. Even Ida came out of her melancholy.

By the time they had finished, night was falling. They sat around the fire for an hour until full dark, and then everyone went to bed. Stephen gave up his chamber to the girls for a pallet in the hall with Harry.

Mistress Bartelot retired to her chamber after fussing about making sure that the girls were taken care of, and the house fell silent. Only Stephen and Harry remained at the hearth.

"So you're a pirate now, in addition to your other crimes," Harry said. "It won't be long before the sheriff comes for you. At least I'll get a new landlord out of it, and Mistress Bartelot will have to find a new arrangement."

"Perhaps you're the one who will have to find a new arrangement."

"That's probably true. The new man will want rent. So far I've made precious little enough to pay it." Harry dug into his pouch and handed over the dead girl's golden ring. "Here, you can have this back."

"Did you find out anything?"

"Only how she died." Harry told him what Anne the shepherd's daughter had seen.

"That makes sense. Her body could easily have floated down the river from there. It isn't but a few miles."

"With only a half dozen sandbars to get in the way." Harry shrugged. "You think she was taken by the same lot that snatched the others?"

Stephen nodded. "I would say so."

Harry smiled for the first time that day. "We'll have to see what Gilbert thinks of it."

"I thought you didn't care what Gilbert thinks."

"Normally, no. But from what I heard from those girls, you've taken leave of your senses, so I doubt you're capable of puzzling it all out."

"You know, all the girls came from around here, close by, anyway. The girl at the weir probably did, too."

"A splendid guess. You have some wits left after all."

"I don't see you spending any on the problem."

"I have too thought about it."

"And not got anywhere."

"My, you are testy!"

"Me? Testy? What's got into you? You've done nothing but mope around all evening and now this."

Harry stared into the dwindling fire, which had burned down to coals and ash. "Edith has found a husband for Jennie. The son of the apothecary at the Beast Market. Edith was waiting for Gilbert to get back to have the banns announced."

"I am sorry, Harry."

Harry waved a hand. "It was bound to happen. What mother would want her baby to marry a man without legs or anything in the way of prospects?"

"You can't do anything about the leg part, but you've got a business going."

"Not much of one."

"Give it time, Harry. Things will turn around."

Stephen wrote letters the next morning to the parents of all the girls telling them that they were safe and where they could be collected, except he did not need one for Eloise, whom they had dropped off at Bromyard to be with her husband, who was, surprisingly, still alive and mending. Stephen had hoped to leave immediately afterward with Ida for Hafton, but the departure was delayed by coroner work. There had been two deaths while they were gone. An old woman had died in her bed surrounded by her family and a workman had fallen from a scaffold at the Saint Augustine Priory and broken his neck, to the prior's dismay, since he owned the scaffold and was forced to pay the fine. And although these were simple affairs, the inquests were not completed, owing to the need to summon two separate juries, and the reports written down until very late in the afternoon so that there was not enough light left for the journey.

They made the fifteen-mile ride through Wigmore rather than Mortimer's Cross to avoid reviving a bad memory, and arrived shortly before dinner.

Stephen had not been to Hafton in years — since he had gone to London for the clerkship with Ademar de Valance — and it had changed: it was still surrounded by an embankment and palisade but the wood on the embankment was in good repair, the stone manor house rising behind the wall with the ancient square tower at one end normally needing a lime wash at the top where rain had worn it away but now fresh and bright white with new lime, smoke curling up from the round kitchen beside the house, the buzzing of bees as they crossed the pasture between the Lugg bridge and the house, sheep and cows grazing in the long grass. William had obviously taken more care of the house than their father had done. Yet it was an ordinary house at an ordinary village that would not have impressed anyone else who happened to see it, but Stephen's heart swelled with an affection for it that he had tried hard to put away while he was gone. Once he saw it, he could not avoid realizing how much he had missed it. Nowhere else felt like home.

A boy watching the sheep ran to the house shouting that Ida had returned, and they were met by the entire household staff as they rode through the gate.

Elysande waited on the stairs as they came across the yard, and descended when they stopped at the foot and dismounted.

She took Ida's face in her hands and asked, "You are well, my dear?"

"Yes, Mama," Ida said, her voice shaking and tears beginning to run.

Elysande embraced her. "That is good to know." The embrace was quick and perfunctory. Elysande stepped back. Her eyes lingered on Stephen. They were cold, perhaps mingled with a bit of worry and a dash of resentment. But she had always been reserved, and had never liked Stephen any more than William had.

"Wipe off your face, my dear," Elysande said to Ida, "and come in the house."

Ida held out her hand to Stephen.

He took it, and they climbed the stairway after Elysande.

"So that is how William died," Elysande mused as the servants took away the platters and trenchers from dinner. Her fingers drummed silently on the arm of her chair. "I'd not have thought him capable of such a thing."

"In the end, he was," Stephen said. "Braver than I thought he would ever be."

"But I have only your word that's what happened," she said. "And there is no body."

"Herb was there. He saw it. So was Gilbert Wistwode."

"They are of no account. Their testimony counts for nothing."

"Not so. Their oaths count as much as any man's in a court of law."

"Oh, I forgot. You were a lawyer once, or almost one." She made a noise that was between a snort and a sigh. "It's something of a relief, in a way, but I suppose we must leave now, if you're to be lord of Hafton. Although we have nowhere to go." She was the fourth daughter of a knight from

The Bear Wagon

Rochford southeast of Ludlow. Being that low on the ladder, she had not brought any land to the marriage and very little money. William had taken a fancy to her when they met at the Ludlow fair and pursued the marriage against Father's wishes, the only time he had stood up to the man. But the marriage had cooled soon after it was consummated as it turned out William had a wandering wand and could not keep his hands off the village girls.

Stephen had given some thought to this matter on the way back from London. "You can remain here as long as you like. Someone will need to run the place while I am away. Who better than you?"

"I see. I will be a caretaker. Better than being tossed out on an ear with little to my name but a few embroideries. And Ida?"

"I'll provide for Ida. We can't give land but I have come into some money that will go toward the dowry. But it's up to you to find her a suitable husband."

"And she is clean. Nothing . . . untoward happened?"

"No. Nothing."

"You're sure?"

"I am."

"We should have her examined to be sure. Suitors may be frightened away by rumors of her experience."

"I will take her back to Ludlow and have it done if it will put your mind at ease. The priest at Saint Laurence's Church has experience in such things."

Elysande smiled. "Once that is taken care of, I will put out some feelers. There have been a few families who have taken an interest, although I am sorry to say most of them are merchants. I should hate to see my Ida married to a draper or some such thing. But it may be the best we can do."

She turned to Ida, but not to ask for her opinion on what to do about a marriage; the children were not consulted about such things. Instead, Elysande asked, "Ida dear, tell me. I've been puzzling on why you decided to come home so suddenly. Were you unhappy for some reason at the Iverys? Did something happen?"

"Why," Ida said, "you summoned me! You wrote that you were dying and asked me to come home right away."

"I wrote? I sent no such letter."

"I don't understand," Ida said.

"I was ill but it was a passing thing," Elysande said. "It was my arm. For some reason it had grown weak and I could hardly lift a wine cup." She flexed her left arm. "But it is better now. I prayed for Our Lady the Virgin's protection and she interceded, and I am healed. But I did not tell anyone about it. I certainly did not write a letter to you about it."

"Then who would have sent such a letter?" Ida cried.

"That is a good question," Stephen said. His thoughts rushed: Ida's kidnapping had not been an accident, the consequence of a chance encounter on the road? "Someone wanted to lure you away from the Iverys so you could be taken easily."

"Frenze?" Ida said.

"It would seem so. Is it possible he saw you somewhere, or met you?"

"I had never seen him until that moment," Ida said, leaving unsaid what "that moment" was.

"Someone planned it," Stephen murmured.

And a small voice whispered in his head: as he did for all the other girls.

Chapter 27

So Ida rode back to Ludlow with Stephen the next day.

She was quiet until they passed through Wigmore. "You will have me examined, then?" Her voice dripped hostility.

"I will pretend to have you examined. I will take you to the priest at Saint Laurence's. I will give him money. You will go into a room. You and he will sit there. And when you two come out, he will declare you untouched."

"Oh! He will do that?"

"He will be persuaded to do it."

"But he will have to lie."

"But he will not have to swear an oath on it. And the church will be a little bit richer. Once it is done, no one who hears about your ordeal will care if it is the truth or not. They will take it as the truth. And if they don't, they will have to answer to me."

Ida had her doubts that it would be this easy, but the following day she and Stephen walked up to Saint Laurence's and the thing went off as he had predicted.

He offered to take her back to Hafton that afternoon, but she declined to go.

"I am tired of all the traveling," Ida said. "I could use a few days of rest."

Since the girls lacked the demure deportment that Mistress Bartelot prized and filled the house with rancorous speech, too much laughter and joking, Stephen did not pursue the subject. Besides, he liked her company. She reminded him of Margaret de Thottenham, with an exterior as soft as a flower but iron beneath. He wished to have a daughter like her someday.

Within the next few days, the parents of the girls responded to Stephen's letters and arrived to take their daughters away. So before long, there was only one girl left, Joan, the one from Barlby in Yorkshire, whose parents had farther to travel to collect her.

"I doubt they'll be coming for me," Joan said one evening, however. "They'll not want to incur the expense. They don't care about me enough."

"I'll take you back then," Stephen sighed, not relishing a journey to faraway Yorkshire with its mists and moors.

"Don't you bother, sir," Joan said. "Say, you could use a housekeeper, can't you? Care to take me on?"

"That depends on what you cost," Stephen said.

"Why, sir, you're fairly rolling in money. I've seen the way you spend it!"

"And it won't stretch."

"I'll work for cheap. Bed and board and two pence a week."

"We could use her," Harry said, staring into the fire. "It's getting to look like a rubbish yard around here. As if the Thumpers had moved in."

"How are you with children?" Stephen asked.

"I am good. Why?" Joan asked. "I don't see any about — unless you're interested in making some." She swung her shoulders in a saucy way.

"Careful there," Harry said.

"I've a son," Stephen said. "I've lodged him elsewhere, but now that I have a house of my own, it's time I brought him back."

"Ah, well, then," Ida said. "I think Joan is just the one to help me look after him."

"Help you?" Stephen asked.

"Yes, I am staying as well. I shall help manage the house."

"I wonder what Mistress Bartelot will say about that," Harry said, for she had retired early, leaving the others about the hearth.

"What will she say, my lord?" Ida asked.

"If that is your desire," Stephen said. "But I think it is a good way to recruit her into the search for a husband for you."

"I have a feeling she'll be better at it than my mother," Ida said. "At least she is more likely to listen to me about what I want in a man."

"You have a shopping list?" Harry asked.

"Yes," Ida said with a smile. "And he must be taller than me, for one thing."

"Careful," Harry said. "I've been known to bite ankles when I attack."

Ida laughed. "Joan will protect me. She is handy with a knife."

"So I've heard," Harry said darkly.

"What we have not heard is the story of how you came to be taken," Stephen said. "We've heard from the others. But you've been oddly silent."

Joan hugged her knees, her expression wistful, which struck Stephen as a strange way to feel about something as awful as the girls had suffered.

"There was this boy," Joan said. "A right handsome lad. He was a peddler. He came through our village, stayed a couple of days. He was a sweet-talker, that one. Told me I was the prettiest girl he'd ever seen and that he'd fallen in love the first time he laid eyes on me. I liked him, so I went off with him. We landed in Chester, where his dad lived. They made a living collecting rubbish, stuff people threw away, fixing it up and then peddling it in the country villages. It was a decent enough living, I suppose, better than what I was used to at home. I thought I'd found a good deal, but then I caught him rolling with another girl."

"Did you stab him too?" Harry asked.

"No," Joan said. "I thought about it. But it seemed like too much trouble. Although I did feel right sore about it. I thought I loved him, see? I thought he loved me too, but it was just a lie so he could dip his wand. So I lit out, thinking to wander to Bristol. I had a hankering to see the great sea, which I have heard so much about. And to find a place for myself, eventually. I'm handy at all sorts of stuff, cooking, cleaning, making things for around a house. Baskets, I'm especially good at baskets. I can do that for you if you let me stay on."

"All right," Stephen said. "Then what?"

"Well, I was on the Ludlow road. I had just crossed over the bridge of this little river, and the bear wagon caught up with me. I'd disguised myself as a boy. It had fooled most people, if they didn't look close. But when the bear wagon came along I was taking a piss. No boy squats to take a piss by the road, and they knew me for a girl right away. I tried to run, but you can't outrun a man on horseback and a pack of dogs. It was the dogs got me first."

"Did you come through Shrewsbury?" Stephen asked.

"Yes."

"How far out from Shrewsbury were you?"

"I don't know, about a long day's walk. I can make twenty-five miles on a good day, especially when I'm by myself, as I was then. And it was toward the evening."

"Was there a mill above the bridge?"

"Yes, there was. Why?"

"And how far from the bridge had you come when the wagon caught up with you?"

"A couple hundred yards."

"And there was a grove of trees to the east?"

"How did you know?"

"Sounds like Onibury," Harry said.

"Right," Stephen agreed. He asked Joan, "Were all the others in the wagon? Except for Ida?"

"No. There was just one girl."

"That night, did they take a girl out who didn't come back?"

"We camped in a wood. It was by a river. I know because we could hear it. Someone came to the camp, a stranger to the group. He wanted to dip his wand. There was an argument about it, but finally they agreed. They pulled out Wanda because she was closest to the door. I heard her refuse, and then them beating her. There was a commotion, a splash, and cursing. They reckoned each one of us as valuable, like a bag of money with shoes or a cow or horse, and they were angry that they had lost one. The stranger told them not to worry about it, that he knew where they could find another girl who would make up for the loss."

"That would be Ida," Stephen said.

"I don't know. I suppose."

"She was the last one, though."

"That she was."

"Wanda was her name?" Harry asked.

"Yes," Joan said.

"Did she say where she was from?"

"She never did."

"Did the stranger have a name?" Stephen asked.

"If they said it I didn't hear," Joan said.

Chapter 28

The problem of the girl at the weir had receded to the back of Stephen's mind during the struggle to get Ida back. And once he had Ida safe Stephen had not thought about the girl. Now, however, the girl had a name as well as a face, and the problem of who was responsible for her death gnawed like a sin left unrepented. He had supposed that Ilbode was the center of things. But hearing Joan's story, he was no longer sure of that. There was this stranger, of course. And there was also the fact that every one of the girls came from villages that lay no more than fifteen or twenty miles from Bromfield. Part of the gang, perhaps even a significant part, lay at Bromfield. How or why it would have a connection with Ilbode and London men he could not guess.

Gilbert gave voice to Stephen's thoughts the next day when they shared a tub at the Wobbly Kettle.

"If that fellow at Bromfield is still on the loose, it means the bear wagon may roll again," Gilbert said.

"I have the feeling that it might roll again no matter what we do," Stephen replied. "Where there is money to be made, you'll always find unscrupulous men." His fingers played with the pommel of his sword, which leaned against the tub as a precaution in case that assassin made an appearance. He had gone armed everywhere in town these days, worried that the killer would show up again. But so far, nothing. Yet Stephen did not doubt he would make another try.

"You should do something about this end of it, at least, surely."

"Me? You're proposing that I do this alone?"

"Well, I, er, uh . . ."

"We'll go up there tomorrow and see what we can see."

Early the following morning, Stephen saddled his stallion while Mark tacked up Gilbert's mule. Gilbert stood by watching with a long face. But he brightened a bit as he and Stephen rode out of the yard and turned toward Dinham Gate. The usual route to Bromfield was across the Corve Bridge, but Stephen decided to go the back way, through the manor of Priors Halton to the west, where the road pettered out to a cart track through a forest on the south of the Teme. Its three ruts, outer two for the wheels and center for the horse, were much overgrown by grass and weeds, even though the people at Priors Halton walked its mile-and-a-half length to reach the church at Bromfield for Sunday services. Stephen kept a sharp look about to make sure they weren't being followed.

The forest was thick, of old oak and elm and an occasional ash distinguishable by its slender leaves, with high canopies that held back the light so that the air was dim, damp and cool. There was little in the way of undergrowth. They spotted several deer north of Priors Halton, which started and scampered away. A fox, an unusual sight during the day, ran into the path, paused to watch them, then leapt away. A badger rooted against the base of an oak, ignoring them since they had no dogs. A pair of wrens battled in the air while several crows feasted on some dead thing on the ground. A feral house cat watched from a high limb as they passed beneath it.

After some time, they heard the creaking of the priory mill. Stephen turned off the track and took a path leading eastward. The path curved with the bend of the river and presently they reached the place where the Onny flowed into the Teme. Here and there along the way were signs that at least two wagons or a wagon and a cart had passed through: there were wheel ruts in the margins. The ground must have been soft from rain, even muddy, at the time for them to have been left behind and still visible.

There was the remains of a fire by the riverbank. The ash pile was large, indicating that it had been kept going for several days. A pile of fire wood cut from fallen trees was stacked by the remains of the fire.

Stephen dismounted and searched among the fallen leaves. Old horse droppings were scattered a short distance from the fire, gone grey and flaky with age, and there were dog signs, as well.

He stood beneath two large willows on the riverbank gazing across to the mouth of the Onny. This was where Wanda had died. The bank was three feet high, thick with Loddon Lily whose flowers had fallen. It was a quiet, peaceful place that looked to offer good fishing. He imagined Wanda running into the blackness of night and then feet striking only air, to plunge into the dark water and then not come up. He had nearly drowned once himself when his boat had overturned running the London Bridge. If it hadn't been for a catcher below the bridge who had snagged him by the sleeve, he might have died. Drowning was not a pleasant way to go. It was not quick and you had ample time to contemplate the end if your mind wasn't consumed by panic.

He turned back into the wood. A flicker of movement from deeper within the forest caught his eye. An arrow whipped by his head and rattled through the branches behind him.

Stephen ducked behind a tree. "Gilbert! Take cover! Archers!"

"What?" Gilbert cried.

"Get your arse down!"

Stephen glanced around the tree trunk. He spotted at least two men with bows advancing toward them. One saw him and loosed another arrow. It made a *zipppp*! sound as it passed and buried itself into the earth.

He ran for the stallion as well as he could with his bad foot and encumbered by the sword. The stallion provided momentary protection as he pulled his own bow from its case and grabbed a half dozen arrows.

Now that Stephen had his own bow, he felt much better. He chanced a look around a tree and loosed an arrow at one of the attackers. Stephen's arrow ricocheted off the tree protecting the attacker, broke in two and the parts spun away.

Meanwhile, Gilbert had left cover and collected their mounts. Without being told, he pulled them toward the river, where they descended the bank.

Stephen approved of this. The sensible thing now was to follow Gilbert and withdraw across the river. But he was angry. It was always thus for him in a fight: first the anxiety beforehand, then the anger when the enemy struck his blow, followed by a calmness, almost a serenity but one of iron determination, and a feeling that another mind was directing his motions.

The battle calm settled on him and he loosed two arrows in quick succession as he had learned to do from horseback in Spain. The first arrow missed, but the second took his target in the throat, and the man sat down with a choking sound, hands on the arrow as if he meant to pull it out, even though that would not save him.

That left only the other one, for there had been but two attackers. The second man was more cautious now. He did not expose himself needlessly, nor shoot haphazardly. He and Stephen maneuvered around each other from tree to tree, seeking advantage. For his part, Stephen had only three arrows left, and from what he could see, the other man had the same number. Neither could afford a wasted shot.

Then the other man's nerve broke. He had not reckoned on such resistance. He turned and ran.

Stephen came from behind his tree and loosed an arrow. It arched through the wood and struck the fleeing enemy in the lower back. The man staggered on a few steps and collapsed. He pulled himself to his feet and staggered on some more. But he could not move fast enough to elude Stephen.

When the enemy heard Stephen drawing close, he turned. He could not stand up and sank to his knees. He nocked an arrow and tried to draw.

"Go ahead," Stephen said, training his own arrow. "Let's see what you can do."

The effort was too much for his adversary. The man dropped his bow.

Stephen came at him, stooped and pulled the bow out of his reach.

"Who are you?" Stephen asked. "The forester here?"

The man nodded.

"I thought as much," Stephen said. "Why did you shoot?"

"We were told to look out for people snooping around here, and get rid of them."

Foresters were protective of the lands they were hired to patrol, but usually they settled with capturing trespassers and letting the law take care of them. There had to be another reason, then. Stephen said, "Because of the bear wagon. It was camped here."

The forester nodded.

"And you didn't want anyone connecting it with the priory because it could not have stayed here without permission."

"Yes."

"How long was it here, that wagon and the fellows with it?"

"Three, four days," the forester muttered. It was an effort for him to speak.

"Did you ever have the chance to speak with them?"

"I might have."

"Was one of them called Huck?"

"He was the leader, such as they had one. He was a surly one. I never could see why anyone would follow him to the privy let alone on their business."

"Who else knew? They couldn't have camped there without permission. You'd have run them off, otherwise."

"The porter, Oswald, and Brother Bertran."

"Anyone else?"

The forester shook his head. "You'll get me some help, won't you?"

"That's a death wound you have. I'll send someone to collect your body."

"Those men!" Gilbert gasped as he clambered up the bank with the stallion and the mule. "They tried to kill us! Why?"

"They saw us snooping around the campsite," Stephen said. "They wanted to keep it a secret."

"They were in on it?"

"I have no doubt they were."

"Were . . ." Gilbert said, his voice faltering as he spotted the man who had been shot in the throat. Further on the other forester was crawling on hands and knees toward the mill, the arrow protruding from his back. "Oh dear, that looks painful."

They reached the bridge over the Teme, and thundered across at a fast canter, Gilbert holding the mule's mane and bouncing in the saddle, legs flapping disgracefully, frightened at the pace but determined not to be left behind. Above the weir on the right the river was placid, and a swan and a pair of female ducks were cruising on the stillish water, heedless of the danger in the air. Just up from the bridge was the burned out remains of a house, a pile of ash surrounded by charred posts, probably the one where Harry had labored. A pretty blonde girl washing clothes in a pail outside a tent behind the ruin watched them go by with a frown.

It was only a short distance from the bridge to the gatehouse. The gate was open, as Stephen had hoped it would be. He checked up the stallion and turned in, catching a glimpse of a burly man with a couple of missing fingers watching with alarm from the doorway that opened into the gateway passage, the usual station for porters. This had to be Oswald. Stephen did not pause for him. There would be time to deal with him later.

Stephen leapt from the stallion at the door to the chapter house, drawing his sword.

He pulled the door open and entered. Bertran Vardon was seated in a high-backed chair with a book on his lap. He had been reading from it and halted in mid-sentence. A dozen faces swiveled toward Stephen, shock and horror at the intrusion on them. One of the monks rose and snapped, "Get out! You defile this place of peace!"

"Shame! Shame!" other monks shouted.

Stephen crossed to Bertran, who looked flustered, afraid and filled with indecision. Stephen grasped Bertran by the collar of his black habit and lifted him to his feet. The book fell from his lap, the wooden cover clattering on the stones.

"What is the meaning of this?" Bertran blustered.

"You know," Stephen growled.

"Edwin!" Bertran cried as Stephen towed him across the floor to the doorway. Although Bertran had been lean and muscled like Stephen, he had let himself go when he entered the clerical life. He was not as fit and strong as he had once been, so his struggles came to nothing. "Bartholomew! Help me!"

Stephen threw Bertran on the cloister's ground and put the sword point to his throat.

"You had Ida kidnapped and sold her as a slave," Stephen panted.

"I didn't!" Bertran cried. "It wasn't me!"

Bertran looked across to the gateway, where Oswald the burly porter entered the cloister carrying a quarterstaff. He was followed by two other men.

Stephen recognized them, Everard and Dickie, the two he had driven off at the little village near Evesham on the rush to London.

"It was him!" Bertran pointed to Oswald.

Oswald scowled at the accusing finger.

He and the other two men, who drew swords, advanced across the cloister toward Stephen.

Chapter 29

Bertran took advantage of Stephen's distraction. He scrambled to his feet and put distance between them.

"Kill him!" he shrieked. "Everard! Kill him!"

"Don't worry your little head about that," Everard said. "We'll take care of him." He grinned. Yet he did not rush. He stepped out, sword up and before him in the long point position, ready to parry whatever came his way.

It was clear they meant to attack as they had in the orchard outside Leominster. Everard occupied the center. The other two, Oswald with his staff and Dickie, who had a pug nose, a suggestion of a double chin and crooked teeth, spread out to get to Stephen's flanks and rear.

This was the time when a sensible man would cut and run. Stephen had been lucky before, but luck can only stretch so far. No faith can be placed in it. A man stood virtually no chance at these odds when his opponents were trained men, as these were.

But Stephen was beyond thinking about the sensible thing. His mind had gone to that high, calm place where he seemed to float, where he could feel nothing but an odd surge of what seemed like power flowing into and through him, and yet where the world was as still as the surface of a pond on a windless night.

He walked toward Everard, while Dickie closed in from Stephen's right, sword resting above his right shoulder in the wrath guard, poised for a downward stroke that could slice a man from the collarbone to the navel.

Two steps away from Dickie, Stephen sifted his sword to his left hand, drew his dagger, and threw the dagger at Dickie. Throwing a dagger was a chancy thing; there was never any real certainty that it could connect and do damage; and he had not practiced this move much, although he and Rodrigo had occasionally played a drinking game where they threw their daggers at a plank and the one whose did not stick had to take a drink. Stephen had lost this game far more often than he had won it.

But this time, the dagger went home, the point entering Dickie's chest just below the left shoulder.

Dickie gasped and faultered.

Stephen cut down lefthanded at Dickie's head. The sword blade went in above Dickie's left ear and stopped below his nose, a poor cut with bad edge alignment, but good enough. Stephen pulled the blade out.

Both Everard and Oswald gaped at Dickie's demise, for it had been so unexpected. But they came on, Everard staying in front and Oswald edging behind Stephen.

Stephen returned the sword to his right hand as he slipped to one side to keep Oswald from getting his back.

Meanwhile, all the monks had spilled into the yard to watch the fight. As much as they might disapprove of such violence in their precinct, they could not resist the spectacle.

For his part, Gilbert was not going to stand there and do nothing but offer useless encouragement and moral support. He worked the lever to draw the crossbow's string and nocked a bolt from the quiver hanging from his belt.

He aimed and shot. The bolt burst across the cloister and hit Oswald in the leg.

"What the fuck!" Oswald cried. He turned to the source of his torment. Stephen would have to wait until this menace was eliminated. He rushed at Gilbert as if he had not been wounded.

Gilbert backpeddled, pulling the lever on the bow. The next bolt took Oswald in the upper chest at the distance of a single stride as he raised the staff to strike Gilbert down. Even then the wound did not seem to inhibit him.

Gilbert, not having any real idea what to do, held the bow above his head as protection, ducked under the descending quarterstaff and grabbed Oswald around the waist. He lifted Oswald and they fell together, Gilbert on top.

Stephen saw these developments out of the corner of his eye. An ordinary person might have felt a surge of relief at this unexpected adjustment in the odds. But Stephen felt nothing. He was empty.

Another man might have mocked Everard with something like, "Just you and me, now, eh?"

But the emptiness did not allow for words, only iron concentration on what stood before him.

Everard did not seem fazed by the change in circumstances. He relaxed his guard and began to strut about, sword twirling in circles, wearing a lazy smile. Stephen had seen this kind of behavior mainly from the hired champions in judicial duels. Like mercenaries, they fought for money. And like mercenaries, they didn't take unnecessary risks. Business was business and should be carried out at the least cost. But that did not mean he didn't relish a good fight. And it meant that Everard was probably very formidable when single combat was forced on him.

They circled each other, Everard's sword twirling slowly, Stephen's at his right leg, point toward the ground as he had been taught to stand by an Italian mercenary who had passed through Rodrigo's lands many years ago.

Stephen shifted his posture, bringing the sword to his left side with the point directed behind him. He pursed his lips to make himself look nervous and unsure.

Everard's smile widened to a grin, then subside as intent welled in his mind. Stephen, however, paid no attention to Everard's face. Some fencers advocated watching a man's eyes, but the Italian mercenary had been adamant that you kept your eyes on the sword hand. Stephen had found this to be excellent advice and had followed it ever since.

The sword twirling was meant to confuse and intimidate people and deceive them, for they could not usually anticipate when the blow would come or where it would fall. But there is a weakness in it, a pattern that can be exploited.

Stephen waited for the moment: when the sword came around and started its descent.

Then he attacked.

Stephen's blow came upward from his left at Everard's sword arm. But Everard was fast. He drew back slightly and parried to his right.

Stephen did not let the blades clash. He moved his sword around Everard's blade and cut down at Everard's arm.

Everard parried left.

This time the sword tinged together as they clashed. Neither man noticed how the sound echoed in the cloister. For a moment there was a pause, one less than the time it takes to blink, as the swords remained in contact and each man measured the other by the pressures they felt from the swords.

Then Stephen cut around at Everard's head.

Everard stepped back to avoid the cut and sent forth one of his own from above, which Stephen avoided by lunging left and covering in the right bow.

Although the exchange had taken only a second, both men were panting as if they had been struggling for a long time.

They began their dance again. This was how single combats went, each man cautious, careful, measuring, looking for an instant of weakness. They often dragged out with nothing seeming to happen, boring to those who watched except for the deadly tension that permeated the air, until there was a moment of furious action.

Everard saw an opportunity, or thought he did, and launched an attack from above that turned into an attack on the leg. Again, the men danced to make their blows and to avoid them, and the swords tinged with that odd, low and rather musical sound that did not seem to signal death, which was only whispered with the hissing of the blades in the air.

Again there was a pause, again the slow circling about the cloister, and then again the clash, blades sweeping about in frightening arcs and flashing in the late morning sunlight, the men dodging and twisting, which by a miracle left both untouched, a truly remarkable thing because when men gave and received blows with such intensity in the usual case one of them lay stricken and dying by this time.

Then they rested. They did not move around as much as before, but regarded each other, sword points on the ground as if thinking about what to do next.

Everard began the next engagement by raising his sword into the right bow, hand extended before his face, point toward Stephen. Keeping this position, he edged into distance.

Stephen countered with his sword in the wrath guard, over his right shoulder.

As Everard came into distance Stephen cut a horizontal blow at Everard's left. As Everard moved his blade to parry, Stephen pulled the blow and cut a horizontal blow to Everard's right. The cut was so fast that Stephen was sure it would hit Everard's right arm, but Everard dropped his hilt and caught Stephen's blade. Everard thrust over and Stephen barely managed a parry of his own.

Stephen raised his sword above his head to cut from above. He had intended to cut at Everard's head, but Everard was faster, sending a tremendous blow to Stephen's right. Stephen turned his downward cut into a parry which ran off and he cut horizontally to Everard's head. Everard parried again while Stephen drew back into the right wrath guard.

Then Everard cut from above. Stephen parried left with a half cut. Everard's blade slid down Stephen's to catch on the cross and the blades bound for an instant.

Stephen grasped Everard's blade near the point. He tried to kick Everard in the groin, but Everard set it aside with his knee. Everard wrapped his left arm around Stephen's sword hand at the wrist and stripped the sword away. Everard punched Stephen in the face one, twice, three times with his free hand. Stephen stumbled and fell backward. The only thing that saved him from a quick death was a deft back roll. Stephen regained his feet, but he was some distance from his sword, while Everard was only steps away with his blade raised for the final, killing blow.

The yawning gate to the cloister beckoned. The thought of making a run for it sped through Stephen's mind. But he discarded the possibility of escape as he backpeddled while Everard advanced. His bad foot wouldn't allow flight, and in the time it took to turn around Everard would be on him. He could only fight or die, probably die. He wished he had not thrown away the dagger.

"Do it!" Bertran shouted in a voice that was so high-pitched it was almost a scream. "What are you waiting for!" He waved the stump of his right arm. "Do to him what he did to me! Then finish him! Earn your money!"

"Bertran!" cried Edwin the monk. "What are you saying! That's murder!"

"He's got it coming," Bertran snapped.

"You're paying that man to commit murder?" Edwin asked. "This cannot stand!"

Edwin grabbed one of Bertran's arms. Bertran was stronger than the slighter man and would have pulled away, but other monks joined in.

"You have used the priory's money to buy murder!" Edwin shouted.

Everard watched these developments with some concern.

"It looks like you'll not get your fee after all," Stephen said.

"Huh," Everard grunted. But his sword settled to rest on his shoulder.

Bertran had not forgotten the wrestling lessons of his youth and he shook off the monks. He ran for Stephen's stallion, but it shied away and he turned to catch the mule. He vaulted into the saddle, gathered the reins, and turned the mule toward the gate. The mule resisted, but Bertran forced it first into a trot and then a canter, and they vanished through the gate.

Everard watched Bertran go with narrowed eyes. He looked at the monks. Then he sheathed his sword. "Looks like you're right. Fucking waste of time. I should have known."

The Bear Wagon

Despite the fact that Everard had sheathed his sword, Stephen gave him space as he edged around to collect his own. But he needn't have been so cautious. Everard knelt beside the man whom Stephen had struck down.

"You died for nothing, Dickie," Everard said. "I'm sorry."

He stood up. "You're not bad," he said to Stephen. "But I'd have killed you in the end."

"I don't know." Stephen smiled, glad that part of the business was over and he was still alive. "I had a few tricks left."

Stephen turned toward the prostrate porter, whom Gilbert was still holding down. He kneeled on Oswald's right arm. Even though that was the one with the missing fingers, he had shown he could still wield a weapon with it. And Stephen was still wary despite the arrow in his chest, for he had seen men pierced by arrows to go on to kill many others before they finally fell.

"You knew about the bear wagon," Stephen said.

Oswald grimaced. Having a man put his full weight on an arm like that was painful. "What of it?"

"Were you the one who raped the girl in the wood? Or was it Bertran?"

Oswald's lips pressed together.

"You might as well tell me." Stephen flicked the bolt with a finger. "You're going to die anyway. No one survives a wound like this."

"I don't know what you're talking about," Oswald whispered.

Stephen flicked the bolt again.

Oswald flinched.

"One of the girls they took was my niece," Stephen said. "I have a special interest in the matter. Who was it in the wood?"

"It was me."

"How did they come to take only girls from around here?"

"They came to see the Lady and seek her intercession," Oswald gasped.

"You remembered them and told Huck and his wagon men where to find them?"

"Yes."

"And Ida?"

"Her mother came, complaining of some illness. She spoke of a daughter."

"Yet there is something odd about her capture. She was lured out of her foster home by a false letter. Did you write it?"

"I can't read nor write."

"Bertran, then?"

Oswald nodded. He coughed up blood, which glistened on his lips. "He's a King's man and a good cousin of the bishop. Your brother's attack on Kilpeck enraged him. He thought to get revenge by having her taken."

"And your dealings with the wagon men gave him an opportunity?"

"Yes."

"Who are they?"

"Huck is a friend from my soldiering days. We thought to make a few pennies. What's wrong with that?"

"If you can't see that yourself, nothing I can say will make a difference. Give me their names."

Oswald shook his head. "No."

Stephen pulled out the bolt.

Oswald grunted in pain.

"The names," Stephen said.

Oswald coughed up blood again. He shook his head.

Stephen drew his utility knife and thumbed the edge.

The whites showed about Oswald's eyes. "All right."

When Stephen was done with Oswald, the monks found a board and carried him to their little hospital off the cloister.

"It looks like you're going to have to walk home," Stephen said to Gilbert.

"And I so loved that animal. I shall miss him. Would you really have gutted that man? Or was it just a threat to scare him?"

"We'll never know now."

"You are a harder man than I thought."

"It's a hard world. That's the only way to protect your family."

Everard was still standing by Dickie's body. No one had come forward to help him with it.

"Gilbert," Stephen said, "see if there is someone about who can help shroud the body, and a priest to bury him." He said to Everard, "Let's take him into the church."

Everard and Stephen carried Dickie into the church and laid him out before the altar while Gilbert hurried off on his errand.

Everard leaned against the altar and folded his arms. He looked sad.

"You've known him a long time?" Stephen asked.

"More than ten years."

"I am sorry."

"Risks of the profession."

"Speaking of that, I have a job for you."

"If it's killing Bertran you want, I'll have to decline. It's bad for business to turn around and kill a patron."

"Even if he hasn't paid you?"

"We got half before we started. It's enough."

"It's not Bertran I want dealt with anyway. I'll take care of him in due time."

"How can a penniless coroner afford my services?"

"I have come into a bit of money. I'm lord of Hafton Manor now."

"I see."

"Come down to Ludlow after your friend is taken care of and we'll talk."

Chapter 30

"What I can't understand is who set fire to the house," Harry said. He held out his cup for the girl at the Wobbly Kettle to fill. They were in the front room drinking after having had their weekly bath. The windows were open and a pleasant breeze was blowing through the house, bereft for a change of the stench of urine from the tanneries along the river.

"That would be Oswald, the porter," Stephen said. "He recognized the girl's face in your statue and didn't want it set up in the church where others could see it."

"A pity," Harry said. "He seemed like such a nice fellow."

"Was it guilt?" Gilbert asked. "Or fear that someone would recognize her that drove him to it?"

"I'd say the latter," Stephen said. "He did not seem the sort capable of guilt."

"Even in a depraved heart there is room for guilt," Gilbert said.

"Precious little room," Stephen said.

"He felt guilty at the end, and confessed. I was there, and heard it."

"Which one do you mean, to me or to the priest?"

"Both."

They got no further in probing Oswald's capacity for guilt because the door opened and Joan came in. She nodded at Stephen, who returned the nod. He drained his cup and stood up.

"That's enough," he said. "Time to go."

"Go? Damn it," Harry said, "I'm not properly drunk yet."

"It costs too much to get you drunk."

"But you're rich now. You can afford the luxury of getting your friends drunk. There is no better way to ensure a friendship."

"You're a friend? That's the first I've heard of it."

Stephen picked up Harry's board and the three of them, followed by Joan, went out into the street.

Harry expected Stephen to put the board down so he could mount it. But Stephen laid the board into a small cart that was waiting by the door.

"What!" Harry said. "Are you going to carry me again?"

"No," Stephen said. "I am done carrying you. It was unseemly before. It is more so now."

"Then how am I supposed to get back?"

Joan giggled.

"What are you laughing at?" Harry asked.

"You. You can be so thick."

"How am I thick? I'm the smartest one here."

"The cart, silly."

"What about the cart?"

"It belongs to you. His lordship had me buy it for you this afternoon."

"Lordship? What lordship? Oh, I forgot. We've one who lolls around the house. It looks like a child's cart. That's certainly a midget horse."

"Well, why are you complaining? You are a bit small for a normal horse."

"I'm not small. I'm short. Through no fault of my own."

"Only you failed to dodge the cart that ran over your legs," Stephen said.

Joan climbed on the cart and took up the reins. "Well, if you don't want it, I'll take it back."

"No, wait," Harry said. He grasped the railing and pulled himself up with ease. "Home, servant!" he commanded.

Joan gave him a look that would have turned a lesser man to jelly. When it was clear the glare had not achieved its effect, she slapped Harry across the mouth. "You will never speak to me like that again."

"Sorry," Harry said.

"I daresay!" Gilbert said, shocked and surprised. "I didn't know you even knew that word."

Joan clicked her tongue and the horse and cart moved out toward Broad Gate.

"How am I going to afford to keep a horse?" Harry said as the cart drew away.

"Work more, complain less," Joan said. "Stop moping around about Jennie. And count your blessings. Despite everything you have more than you know."

"We all have more than we know," Stephen said.

He clapped a hand on Gilbert's shoulder and they stepped out after the cart.

Epilogue

The stream of visitors to Harry's shop increased during the remainder of July. Most people came to see the statue of the Lady and to ask for her help. This would have been welcome, but Harry had stopped accepting money from people coming to see the Lady because Joan disapproved of him taking advantage of them.

"But the Church does it," Harry had protested when Joan brought up the subject for the third or fourth time. "Why can't I?"

"They give money to the Church to support its good works," Joan said. "You are not the Church and I haven't seen any good work out of you except for a few miserable bowls and spoons."

"I make a damned good spoon," Harry said.

"You can't get rich making just spoons."

So to prove he could do more, Harry made a table on speculation. It sold the first day he displayed it, and to a grocer in town who used it as a sideboard in his hall. A guest at the grocer's house liked the table and came by to order one for herself, only bigger and with carved legs.

On the last day of the month, Brother Edwin from Bromfield Priory appeared at the shop window.

"Morning, Harry," Edwin said.

"What do you want?" Harry asked, not disposed toward Edwin because of the words and hostile feeling that had passed between them.

"I was wondering if we could fulfill the terms of your agreement with Brother Bertran."

"I thought you felt my work was ugly and unseemly."

"I was angry and upset. It clouded my judgment. Can you forgive me?"

It took some time for Harry to think over this proposal, during which Brother Edwin did not move.

"I suppose," Harry said at last, letting avarice triumph over the urge to savor his grudge.

So Edwin departed with the statue, unpainted as it was, and left behind more money than Harry had ever seen in one place in his life, except for the contents of a chest that was now buried under his sleeping spot where he could watch over it for a certain lord.

Brother Edwin had the statue painted and set into the place of its predecessor in Bromfield Church's north transept. Soon She received a stream of visitors, as She had before.

A fruit seller's wife from Acton Burnell came to ask the Lady for help in finding her daughter. She cried out and fainted at the Lady's face. When she revived, Brother Edwin told her what he knew of the statue's story. The woman hurried to Ludlow, where the dead girl's identity was confirmed by the gold ring, which she reclaimed. The horde had been found by her father in an apple orchard beneath the upturned roots of a tree driven over by a storm. He kept only the ring in secret; the rest was claimed by the Wellys family who held the land. Harry told the mother the story, but not the whole news, only that the girl had somehow drowned in the river. He and Joan drove her to Wanda's grave in the pauper's yard on Upper Galdeford Road. There is a stone there now to mark the spot, small and easily overlooked amidst the tall grass and weeds, but engraved with a name, the only one of its kind, for everyone else has been forgotten.

At the end of August, Everard came to see Stephen. He brought something in a large clay pot that no one else but Ida was allowed to see.

She smiled with grim satisfaction at the object in the pot, a man's severed head, which gave off a strong stink of vinegar when Everard held it up so she could see it and to confirm that he had carried out his contract.

"Thank you, Uncle Stephen, for avenging me," she said. "I had hoped you would."

"And the others? That man Huck and those with the bear wagon?" Stephen asked Everard. "What of them?"

"Child's play," Everard said. "That one was much harder," he added referring to the head in the clay pot.

The chest was dug up and Everard was paid a handsome amount from it.

The pot was disposed of one night outside town in the pauper's yard a short distance from Wanda's grave where no one was ever likely to find it.

The bear wagon never rolled again as far as anyone knows.